COMING OUT ON TOP

NORA PHOENIX

Coming Out on Top by Nora Phoenix. Copyright ©2020 Nora Phoenix (previously published as Snow Way Out)

Cover design: Cate Ashwood

Editing and proofreading: Tanja Ongkiehong

All rights reserved. No part of this story may be used, reproduced, or transmitted in any form by any means without the written permission of the copyright holder, except in case of brief quotations and embodied within critical reviews and articles.

This is a work of fiction. Names, characters, places, and incidents either are the products of the author's imagination or are used fictitiously. Any resemblance to actual persons, living or dead, businesses, companies, events, or locales is entirely coincidental. The use of any real company and/or product names is for literary effect only. All other trademarks and copyrights are the property of their respective owners.

This book contains sexually explicit material which is suitable only for mature readers.

www.noraphoenix.com

PROLOGUE

Out of all the people in all the world to be stuck in the snow with, it had to be him. It had to be this mouthwatering, hot as fuck, push-all-his-buttons, check-all- boxes bear of a man. Strike that. Bear of a *straight* man.

Just his luck.

1

Quentin Frost anxiously awaited the verdict as Jerry, the AAA guy he'd called half an hour earlier, checked out the engine of his ancient Corolla. It had sputtered, then stalled, smoke and the distinct stench of burning oil drifting up from under the hood. He'd quickly parked the car on the shoulder of the quiet country road and had made use of his AAA membership for, like, the tenth time that year. Best. Investment. Ever. Though in hindsight, he should've maybe invested in a better car if he was gonna drive cross-country.

It had taken Jerry only twenty minutes to get there, which was awesome because Quentin was freezing his ass off. His thin jacket and jeans were no match for the arctic temperatures, but especially not for the biting wind that had free rein here out in the open.

He'd already planned on investing in some serious cold-weather gear, but maybe he should've done that *before* arriving in the northeast. A not-so-slight miscalculation on his part. He'd never been so motherfucking cold in his life. The kind of wet, icy cold that penetrated your bones, making you feel like you'd never, ever get warm again in your life.

Wait, how long did frostbite take? He looked at his hands, slightly blue-ish by now.

"I'm sorry, son, but that car is beyond saving."

Quentin refocused on Jerry's growly voice and let out a long sigh as the guy closed the hood of his car with a loud thunk. *Fuck me sideways.* He was *so* screwed right now. Jerry wiped his hands on a black-stained cloth, then adjusted his faded blue Yankees cap. Judging by the many black stains on the front of that cap, this was a habitual gesture for him.

"Now what?" Quentin asked. "I can't imagine the car can stay here."

The damn thing had broken down on the side of the road just outside of some tiny village at the foot of the Adirondack mountains. The view was breathtaking, and he'd admired it as much as he could while he drove, but fat little good that did him now.

Jerry shook his head. "Nope, it can't. I can tow it to a junkyard that will take it."

"Will they give me anything for it?"

Jerry shrugged. "Mac might. I can call him, if you want."

Quentin frowned. "Mac?"

"Mac McCain, he's our local junkyard owner. He'll take anything, and he usually pays a decent price. Want me to give him a call?"

Quentin nodded as he blew into his hands in a futile attempt to warm them up. What alternative did he have? He'd have to figure out a way to buy himself a new car, though how and with what money, he had no idea. His research grant barely covered his cost of living and did not allow for *frivolous spending*, as Professor Danson had stipulated. Would a car be considered frivolous? It would be damn hard to get around without one. What a clusterfuck.

"Mac, it's Jerry. Got a young kid with an oh-one Corolla that's toast. He wants to get rid of it. You interested?"

Young kid. He probably didn't mean it as patronizing as it came across, but at twenty-three, Quentin was sick and tired of people calling him a *kid*. Not that he could blame them. He didn't look much older than eighteen—if even that. Fuck, with his babyface, they'd probably still card him when he was forty.

Apparently, the guy on the other end was highly economical with words because seconds later, Jerry had affirmed they were on their way. Quentin watched as the man expertly hooked up his car to his tow truck, and within minutes, they were ready to go.

Jerry wiped a few hamburger wrappers off the front seat to make place for Quentin. "Where were you headed?" he asked once they were driving.

"Northern Lake."

Jerry shot him a curious sideways glance. "What the hell for? There's nothing there."

Quentin held his hands in front of the heater to warm up. "That was kind of the point."

He debated telling Jerry why he was so interested in that tiny town but decided against it. It would probably raise more questions than he was willing to answer. Plus, Northern Lake wasn't that far from here, so who knew if Jerry had been there, had friends or family there? No, he wasn't risking it, not until he'd built up a rapport with the locals. Then he could find out more about what had happened to his dad. Hopefully.

When they entered the town limits, Quentin did a

double take when he spotted a handcrafted wooden sign with the town's name. "This place is called Frostville?"

"Yup," Jerry said. "Frostville, New York. Population of 1800 and change."

What were the odds? Quentin smiled at the incredible coincidence of him landing in a town with the same name as his last name. Maybe it was destiny? Nah, there was no such thing. Facts, that was what he dealt in. Cold, hard, scientifically proven facts. Or so his professors had kept telling him. Research was all about the facts.

Frostville was a quaint little place with local stores lined up along an old-fashioned Main Street. Quentin counted a few bars and restaurants—one diner proudly claiming to serve the best burgers in the Adirondacks—and a gas station with a convenience store, and that was it. Before he could comment on it, they had left the town behind them.

"Mac's property is just outside of town," Jerry said.

"You live here?" Quentin asked.

"Yup. Born and raised. I cover a big area for my job, but I happened to be home when the call came in, since it's my day off."

"You were off today? Then why'd you respond?"

"Because my nearest coworker was fifty miles out, and I didn't want to have him drive this far at the end of his shift. It's fine. I'll be home before dinner."

Quentin let that sink in. He'd never heard of someone voluntarily working on his day off just to prevent inconveniencing a coworker. This was probably part of the small-town dynamic he was eager to study in depth. "Thank you."

"You're welcome, son. We're here."

Jerry pulled up at the entrance of a fenced-off property, and almost immediately, a big dog came running out, barking his head off. Quentin barely had time to feel properly intimidated because on the dog's heels followed his owner. Now, *that* man was a reason to be intimidated.

Quentin swallowed as he took in the man striding outside. He was a giant, wearing stained jeans, sturdy work boots, and a black jacket. But what really caught Quentin's attention was the lip and septum piercing, his dark hair, which peeked out from under his black beanie, and a dark beard as menacing as the look in his eyes.

Jerry sighed. "Like his owner, that dog barks more than it actually bites. You'll be fine."

Quentin had to take his word for it. Jerry opened the door of the tow truck and slid off the front seat. After a second's hesitation—he wanted to make sure the dog didn't attack—Quentin followed his lead.

"Mac," Jerry said, reaching for his cap again.

The guy merely nodded without even a hint of a smile. He snapped his fingers at his dog, who stopped his—her?—barking immediately.

"This here is young... Sorry, what was your name again, son?" Jerry asked.

Quentin stepped forward and stuck out his hand toward the guy who looked like he could crush his skull with one hand while throwing back a beer with the other. Manners might just prevent that from happening, though he wasn't putting his money on it. And he was *so* not giving him his last name. "Hi, I'm Quentin."

The man's eyebrows rose, but he took off his right glove and accepted Quentin's hand with a small nod. His hand was huge, enveloping Quentin's with a strong grip that almost made him wince. Quentin waited for him to speak but let go when that, apparently, wasn't on the program.

"Mac here is a man of few words," Jerry said.

Quentin expected him to slap the guy on the back in a

neighborly fashion, but Jerry kept his distance. *Interesting.* Jerry talked about Mac as if he knew him well, but the physical space between the two men did not suggest a close relationship. Moreover, Jerry's voice held a hint of hostility, with a solid dose of condescending thrown in. What was *that* about?

Respect, he would've understood, considering the guy's appearance. Fear, even. This was not a man you wanted to cross. But why that patronizing attitude?

The silence became uncomfortable. Oh, damn, Mac was waiting for Quentin to say something. He cleared his throat. "Yeah, so, Jerry said my car can't be fixed and that you might be willing to take it. For your junkyard. For a reasonable price," he quickly added before the man thought he was giving it away for free.

Jerry's phone rang, and he picked up right away. His face broke open in a big smile. "Already? Yes, honey, I'm leaving right now. I'll be there in twenty."

He ended the call and sent Quentin an apologetic look. "I gotta go. My daughter is in labor, so I gotta get to the hospital."

"But..." Quentin sputtered.

Jerry had his car unhooked in no time, Mac watching silently while Quentin cursed the AAA guy in his head. Mac hadn't named a price—and it would go down considerably now that Jerry was about to dump his car there. It wasn't like Quentin had anything to bargain with anymore. And how the fuck was he supposed to get back to town without a ride? He'd have to call a cab.

"Mac will sort you out," were Jerry's parting words, and then his truck backed out of the short driveway, leaving Quentin and his useless piece of shit car behind.

Quentin suppressed a sigh as he turned around to face

Mac, who was studying him with an unreadable expression. "Erm, yeah, my car. How much is it worth?" Quentin asked.

Mac's jaw tightened, then finally opened his mouth. "T-t-t-two hundred."

And at once, Quentin understood why the man was taciturn. Damn it, would it be cruel to try and negotiate with someone who had a speech impediment? He considered it. The alternative was treating him differently because of a perceived handicap, and would that be preferable?

"Is that the same price you would have quoted if Jerry hadn't dumped me and my car on your doorstep? It's not like I have many options here," he said, trying to look as stern as he could.

Mac's eyebrows lifted in surprise. "Ng-ng-ng-yes," he said. "N-n-no different. W-would've b-b-been the s-s-same price."

Quentin shrugged. The guy didn't look like he was fleecing him, so he'd have to trust him, even if he did look like a total badass. "Okay, then."

"Okay," Mac said, some tension in his shoulders leaving, Quentin noticed. "I'll write you a ch-ch-check."

"Is cash okay? I'm not local and don't have a bank account here."

Mac simply nodded and led the way to a small office just past the sturdy fence that gave access to a large terrain filled with cars in all shapes, colors, and states of disrepair. Along the side fence, rusty blue containers stood neatly lined up, a hand-painted metal sign signaling what the presumed contents were: batteries, mufflers, engines, and more.

On the other side of the fence stood a big wooden barn with a similar metal sign that read Shop, and at the end towered a pile of tires, some bigger than Quentin had ever seen in his life. Mac ran quite the operation here, but everything looked neat, even though it was a junkyard.

Quentin followed Mac into the office, which wasn't the mess he had expected either. The metal desk was almost empty, except for a laptop and two plastic trays labeled In and Out. Mac was an organized and systematic worker, surprisingly. Though maybe that said more about Quentin's prejudice based on Mac's appearance than about Mac himself.

Mac took off his gloves and jammed them into the pockets of his jacket, then opened a drawer and pulled out a small cash box. He handwrote Quentin a receipt for the promised two hundred dollars, then wordlessly counted them out on the desk. Quentin folded the money and put it in his wallet. "Could you maybe give me the number of the local cab company?" he asked, taking out his phone. He checked if he had any messages.

"N-n-no c-c-cab here," Mac said.

"There's no cab company? Dammit."

It did make sense in a town this size. How often would people here need a cab? Maybe, what, once a year? That didn't provide enough customers. And Uber and Lyft weren't gonna happen either. How the fuck was he getting anywhere now? It wasn't like he could hike back, what with his two suitcases in the trunk, plus his backpack.

He lifted his eyes to meet Mac's. The man had a gorgeous pair of brown puppy eyes that lowered his badass level significantly, but how many people managed to get past that intimidating first impression? There was no denying the man was hot as fuck, but Quentin's gaydar didn't even pick up the slightest buzz, so the guy had to be straight as a ruler.

"I c-c-can drive you to t-town," Mac said, the first time

he'd initiated a conversation instead of merely responding to a question.

"Would you? I'd really appreciate it," Quentin said, his insides filling with relief. "Is there, like, a motel or something? The cheapest option will do."

Mac nodded. "G-g-guesthouse."

"That'll do. Thank you, Mac."

More nodding, then Mac turned around, apparently expecting Quentin to follow him.

"I need to grab my luggage from my car," Quentin said when they were outside again. "And do I need to file something to deregister my tags?"

Mac pointed at himself. Quentin was starting to discover how much the man communicated nonverbally. "You'll do it? Thank you."

Mac hauled his two suitcases out of his car, then gestured to Quentin to check if he'd left anything else in there he needed to take out. Quentin did a quick search, but all he found were his proof of insurance, a ratty pair of sunglasses he always kept in his car, and a pack of gum. He'd already cleaned out his car before he started this crazy adventure, determined to be all adult-like. So far, that was not working out well.

Mac put the suitcases in the back of a massive pickup truck with ease, and Quentin hoisted himself inside, keeping his backpack close to him. It contained his most prized possession, his MacBook, and he was not letting it out of his sight.

They didn't speak a word during the journey—not that Quentin minded. He was usually more than happy to give his mind a break and let his thoughts wander. And it wasn't like he lacked things to look at. The gorgeous scenery around him was as pretty as a postcard.

Mac parked in front of a historic-looking building sporting a sign that read Ginny's Guesthouse. Damn, it did not look cheap at all, and Quentin cringed as he thought of the hit his credit card would take with a night in this place. Hopefully, he'd be able to find a solution tomorrow, though he didn't have a clue how and what.

Mac lifted his suitcases out of the pickup truck as if they weighed nothing. He gestured to Quentin to hold the front door for him, and he walked inside, Quentin following him.

Behind the reception desk stood a friendly-looking woman who gave Mac a curt nod, then turned to Quentin with a much friendlier expression. "Good afternoon."

"Hi. I was wondering if you have a room available."

"We sure do. Our blue room is available for one-fifty per night, including breakfast."

Hot damn, that was about twice as much as he could afford, but it wasn't like he had a choice. "Any chance we can talk about that rate?" he tried.

She sent him a sugary smile. "Our prices are fixed, hun. It's a gorgeous room, though."

Like he gave a shit about that. Besides, her definition of gorgeous was bound to be a world apart from his and would in all likelihood involve flowery patterns and quilts. Yuk. For that amount of money, it had better have fast Wi-Fi so he could spend some time with the Ballsy Boys, his favorite gay porn site, and *relax* a little. "I'll take it," he said, trying not to grumble.

"Oh, Mac, carry his luggage up, would you?" she called out, and it didn't really sound like a question.

Before Quentin could say anything, Mac strode to the narrow wooden stairs with Quentin's suitcases.

"He's a handy guy to know," the woman said. "He's a tad

on the simple side, obviously, but he can fix anything. How'd you end up with him?"

Her voice echoed through the hallway. Had Mac heard her not-so-subtle assessment of his intellectual abilities? Quentin winced at that thought. Also, Mac hadn't sounded intellectually challenged to him at all.

"My car broke down, and I had to have it towed to his place. He gave me a ride here."

Her lips pressed together. "That's right neighborly of him."

Her words said one thing but her face and tone something else entirely. Like Jerry, she had this passive-aggressive condescending attitude when she talked to or about Mac. What the hell was their problem with him? Granted, the man looked like he could kill you with one blow and not shed a tear over your corpse, but he'd been nice to Quentin so far.

Mac came back down while the woman was processing Quentin's payment. He gave Quentin a hesitant look, then rushed past him.

"Mac!" Quentin called after him. The big man turned around, surprise painted all over his face. "Thank you for your help. I really appreciate it."

The man's eyes widened, and the corners of his mouth pulled up almost imperceptibly. "You're w-w-welcome."

2

Mac hummed along to some music while stripping the kid's car down. The engine was toast, but the car still had plenty of good parts he'd be able to salvage and reuse. It looked like the kid had recently sprung for new tires. They couldn't be more than a few months old, and Mac would easily be able to resell them. If he'd noticed it yesterday, he would've upped the price to three hundred. He'd been a little preoccupied, though.

The kid—Quentin, Mac reminded himself—had acted so *normal* when he'd discovered Mac's stutter. Most people got all flustered and embarrassed, as if they wanted to apologize for him stuttering. Or they'd get frustrated when he wasn't finishing his sentences fast enough, and they filled in the words.

Most people who knew him, like everyone in town, barely spoke to him. Sure, the way his father had fucked them all over was a big reason, but they also wanted to spare themselves the embarrassment and frustration of having to listen to him murder every other word. Fact was a lot of people had simply stopped talking to him.

But Quentin hadn't. He'd never stopped asking questions and had patiently waited for Mac to get the words out, his face not showing a hint of impatience. And he'd stayed kind, even calling out to say thanks when Jody had been more than willing to ignore him. She always did—as much as she could get away with anyway. Then again, she'd lost close to fifteen thousand in the scam, so she had her reasons to be pissed at the McCains.

His phone rang. Mac took off his gloves, turned down the music, and dug his phone out of his pants. Hmm, the guesthouse. What would he have to fix this time? His money was on the heater. He'd told them a million times it was in dire need of being replaced, but Ginny didn't have the money—or so she claimed.

He took the call and grunted by way of announcing himself.

"It's Ginny. I need you to stop by as soon as possible. The heater stopped working again."

He sighed. Even if he could get the words out without choking on them, "I told you so" would not earn him any points. "On m-m-my way," he said.

He put Lucy inside the house with some dog treats to keep her happy, hung up a sign on the fence that said he was out and would be back later, and climbed into his truck to make the short drive to town. It was a bad time of year to have a broken heater, since temperatures were hovering in the low thirties. With how badly the guesthouse was insulated, it wouldn't be long before it got uncomfortably chilly inside.

Plus, they were expecting a massive snowstorm tomorrow. The forecast predicted as much as two feet of snow—

not that they'd ever gotten it right. Still, they were bound to get at least a foot, so he'd already filled up the gas tanks for the backup generator and had checked his emergency supplies, including candles and the batteries in his flashlights. Not that he ever ran out. He made sure of that. The weather was unpredictable here, and he'd been snowed in more than once. He'd come to expect it.

Ginny was waiting for him in the reception area, wearing her winter coat and a brightly colored scarf.

"You know the way," she said, not even a word of thanks first. Then again, he'd come to expect that as well. It'd been like that for years now.

He carried his toolbox down the stairs to the basement. How many times had he tinkered with her heater? This year alone at least six times, he reckoned. He systematically ran diagnostics on the heater, but after twenty minutes, he had to conclude it was beyond saving. Ginny was not gonna be happy.

With a heavy step, he made his way back upstairs, where Ginny was manning the reception desk. He shook his head when she spotted him. "It's n-n-n-not good. I c-c-can't fix it."

She let out a muttered exclamation of frustration. "Do I call the company that installed it, or do I have to buy a new one?"

"C-c-call them. B-b-but they'll p-p-probably say to replace it."

"Darn it. I have four rooms occupied. What the heck do I do now?"

Mac shrugged. That part was not his problem.

Footsteps clattered on the wooden stairs. "Excuse me," a familiar voice called out. Quentin hurried up to the reception but came to a sudden stop when he noticed Mac.

"Hi," he said, sending Mac a hesitant smile.

Mac raised his hand, then forced himself to speak. "H-h-hi."

"Erm, ma'am, I have no hot water, and the heating doesn't seem to work either."

Ginny sighed. "Yes. I'm sorry to report our heater broke down early this morning. Unfortunately, our repairman just told us he can't fix it, so I don't know when we'll have it back on."

Quentin's face fell. "What does that mean? Is it gonna be off all day?"

Ginny looked at Mac as if she expected him to come up with a solution. "C-c-could take d-days," he told her. "Especially w-w-with the snows-s-storm."

"Snowstorm?" Quentin's eyes had grown big.

Mac pulled out his phone and brought his weather app up, then held it out so Quentin could see.

"Two feet of snow? Are you fucking kidding me?"

Mac would've laughed at his tone, as if this storm was a personal insult to him, if he hadn't realized the predicament the kid was in. He had no car and was now trapped in a place that had no heating and warm water.

Ginny cringed slightly, then plastered a professional smile on her face. "Obviously, we will discount you for your stay, and I will try to find you alternative lodging."

Quentin's eyes narrowed. "*Discount*? I think you mean I'm staying for free. It's crystal clear I'm not paying for a place that has no warm water and heating."

Mac suppressed another laugh. Damn, the kid had balls, negotiating in a situation like that. Then again, Mac couldn't blame him. It was obvious he wasn't rolling in dough, so any chance to get back the money he'd paid for his room he would grab with both hands.

"You did use the room, hun, so I think it's reasonable you pay for that," Ginny protested.

"I can't even take a fucking shower! And what do you mean by alternative lodging?"

Ginny's mouth drew into a straight line, no doubt caused by Quentin's cursing, something the woman had little tolerance for. "I'll contact other hotels and inns in the region to see if they have rooms available for my guests, at no extra charge."

"Fat lotta good that's gonna do me," Quentin muttered, "as I have no car."

"Well, your lack of transportation is, unfortunately, not something I can help you with," Ginny said, a spark of glee in her tone. "I can only provide another room. How you get there is up to you."

Quentin's face fell.

"N-n-no new c-car?" Mac asked him. Ginny's head jerked to him in surprise, as if she had forgotten he was even there.

Quentin dragged a hand through his hair. "No. I called a few dealers in the area, but no one has anything in my price range."

If Mac had to take a guess, he'd estimate the kid's price range was dirt cheap. And he'd have to travel farther out of the area to find anything like that. Or maybe buy from a private owner. He felt for him, this sun-tanned kid who clearly wasn't prepared for what he'd encountered here, including the weather. His thin long-sleeve and jeans with the Converse underneath were no match for the cold here. *Converse*, for fuck's sake. He'd get frostbite within minutes if those got wet.

"You c-c-can stay with m-m-me," he heard himself say. "After the s-s-storm, I can help you f-f-find another c-car."

Quentin's mouth broke into a smile, and Mac's insides did a funny, swirly thing. "Are you serious?"

Mac nodded without hesitation. Was the kid really gonna take him up on the offer? Damn, he was fearless. He had no way of knowing Mac's reputation in town, but even then, Mac didn't exactly radiate warmth and safety, and still the kid jumped at the offer. Mac was grateful. At least, that was what that warm feeling inside him had to be. Gratitude at being treated like a decent human being for once.

"Thank you! I won't be a bother, I promise. I'll go pack right now." Quentin was halfway to the stairs when he turned around and shot an icy glare at Ginny. "And I'm expecting a full refund on my credit card charges."

3

Quentin was still shocked as hell about Mac's offer. He certainly hadn't seen that one coming, even if he no longer believed the man to be quite as scary as his outward appearance. The guy might look intimidating, but Quentin was starting to suspect he was a softie at heart. Something about him radiated vulnerability, and it tugged at Quentin's heartstrings. What was he hiding behind that tough exterior?

Quentin hadn't hesitated for a second in accepting Mac's hospitality. He'd instantly realized his predicament, caught between no heating, no car, and no alternatives. For some weird reason, his gut told him he could trust Mac. Plus, he damn well knew how to defend himself if need be. It would be one hell of a challenge, going up against a guy that size, but he could do it if he fought a little dirty. Probably.

"Are these snowstorms normal?" he asked once they were in the truck.

Mac looked sideways, then turned his attention back to the road. "Yes. We g-g-get a few m-most years."

"Huh. How do you deal with them?"

Another quick look as if Mac had trouble believing Quentin was actually talking to him. "You m-make s-sure you have enough f-food and sup-p-plies. Then you r-ride it out. S-s-stay inside."

"Do you lose power?"

Mac nodded. "S-sometimes. B-but I have a b-backup gener-r-rator."

"How long does it takes for the roads to be cleared?"

"It de-p-pends on the am-mount of s-snow. Usually, t-t-twenty-four hours, b-but I do the road t-to my prop-p-perty myself."

"Why?"

"F-f-faster. It's not a p-priority for the t-t-town."

"Oh, okay. So, do you have enough supplies for both of us?"

"Always. I'm p-p-pretty s-s-s-self-supportive."

Somehow, that didn't surprise Quentin. Mac was quiet for a minute, but as they neared his property, he asked, "Why d-d-do you ask m-me so m-m-many questions? Doesn't it b-b-bother you?"

He could only be referring to one thing, and why the hell would he think it would bother Quentin? His heart broke a little for this man who'd clearly been hurt by others. "No, your stutter doesn't bother me at all. And I'm curious, always have been, and that manifests itself in tons of questions. Does it bother you that I ask questions?"

Mac pushed a button on the visor, and the gate slowly swung open. He waited with answering until the truck was parked and the engine turned off. "N-no," he said without looking at Quentin. "I l-l-like it."

How sweet was that? Quentin smiled. "Good."

They got out of the car, and Mac hauled his suitcases out

the back of the truck. When he opened the back door—which was locked with two locks, Quentin noted—excited barks could be heard from inside. "What's your dog's name?" Quentin asked.

"Lucy." Mac let out a sharp whistle, and Lucy stopped barking right away. As soon as Mac had opened the door, she came to his side, her tail wagging like crazy. "I can't s-s-scratch your head, s-silly. I have my hands f-full," Mac said, his voice changing in tone. It was lower, much sweeter. Lucy licked the back of his hand, then came trotting over to Quentin.

"Lucy, f-f-friend," Mac said. As if the dog understood him, she nuzzled Quentin's hand with her wet nose, then licked it.

"Hi, Lucy," Quentin said, rewarding her with a pat on her head. "Oh, aren't you a good dog?" He scratched her head some more when it was clear how much she liked it. "What kind of dog is she?"

"German s-s-shepherd mix. She's really s-smart."

"You can tell. She looks at us like she understands every word we say."

Mac nodded, a hint of a smile on his lips. He gestured Quentin to follow him, and they stepped into a tidy living room with a comfortable couch with a variety of colorful pillows and a coffee table that appeared to be handmade. One wall was covered with bookcases, stuffed with books from literature and thrillers to self-help, popular psychology, politics, and history. *Wow, he is a big reader*. Damn, that was definitely an unexpected side from Mac.

Mac kept on walking and led him into a hallway with several doors. He opened one of them and flicked on the light in what had to be a guest room. He put Quentin's suitcases down.

A four-poster queen bed was the centerpiece in the room, with a matching dresser and makeup table against the wall. The pink rose-patterned comforter looked comfortable but distinctly feminine. Quentin had assumed Mac was single, but he hadn't even bothered to ask. This room somehow felt like a woman's room, however, so maybe Mac had been married at some point? Was he divorced?

"The b-b-bathroom is across the hallway," Mac said. "I will p-p-put out clean towels s-s-so you can take a s-shower."

If the guy was indeed single, he was remarkably polite and hospitable. He'd paid attention before, when Quentin had complained at the guesthouse he'd wanted to take a shower when he'd discovered they had no hot water.

"Thank you," Quentin said.

"You're w-welcome. I will f-f-fix lunch. Is there anything you d-d-d-don't eat?"

Quentin shook his head. "Nope. No allergies and I eat everything. And I should've maybe mentioned before you offered so kindly to take me in, but I eat a lot."

Mac shot him an incredulous look. It was such an honest reaction that Quentin giggled. "I'm serious," he said. "I probably eat more than you do."

Mac softly shook his head. "Imp-p-possible," he said with a half smile. "But we'll s-see."

Quentin watched him walk out, doing some heavy internal drooling. Out of all the people in the entire world to be stuck in the snow with, it had to be him. It had to be this mouthwatering, hot-as-fuck, push-all-his-buttons, check-all-boxes bear of a man. Strike that. Bear of a *straight* man. Just his luck.

He took a quick shower, not sure what Mac's water supply was and if the hot water could run out. He hung the thick, white towel on the towel rack and made sure he left everything behind as neat as possible. Mac was a bit of a neat freak it seemed from how well organized his junkyard and office had been, and his house was tidy as a pin as well. Quentin could appreciate that.

As he opened the bathroom door, a chilly draft hit him. Goose bumps broke out over his body, and he shivered in his tight, white boxers. "Damn."

He shuddered as he stepped on the cold floor. A sharp intake of breath sounded next to him. He jerked his head around. Mac stood a few feet away, his eyes wide and his mouth slightly open as he stared at Quentin.

Quentin always thought of himself as a too-skinny guy, a teen who hadn't fully grown into those awkward arms and legs. Plus, he had freckles all over his freaking body, which was not something he was happy with. His face was kind of okay with his messy hair and green eyes, though he always found it was a little too angular.

But right now, Mac looked at him as if he was seeing something else entirely, something that fascinated him, and his gaze slowly traveled down. The man's Adam's apple bobbed as he swallowed. His eyes never left Quentin's body. Oh, Mac's eyes *wanted*. Despite Quentin's earlier assessment, it was crystal clear that Mac was anything but straight. The wonder and hunger in his expression spoke volumes.

Quentin turned toward him, strangely compelled to stand there and let him take his fill. His perusal held such a vulnerable honesty, as if Mac had never had the chance to look at another man. Finally, Mac blinked, and his eyes found Quentin's. A soft smile curled Quentin's lips. No judgment whatsoever, not for something that felt this precious to him.

"I'm s-s-s-s-sorry," Mac said. His cheeks flushed under

his beard, and he jammed his hands into his pockets. "I d-d-didn't m-m-mean t-to b-be rude."

If Quentin had to take a guess, he'd say that stress made Mac's stutter worse. The man had stumbled over almost every word in that sentence. "It's okay, Mac. No harm done."

Mac hunched his shoulders and swiveled around. "L-l-lunch is r-r-ready," he said with his back toward Quentin.

"Thank you. I'll be out in a minute."

Mac strode toward the kitchen without looking back.

Quentin walked into the guest room and softly closed the door behind him. So, Mac was gay. Or bi. But after seeing the expression on his face as he took Quentin in, it was obvious that he was not straight. He'd looked like Quentin was his favorite snack in the world...and he couldn't wait to dig in. Well, that complicated things, didn't it?

The prospect of sharing a house with Mac had certainly become a lot more attractive now. Hot damn, he wouldn't mind fooling around with that gorgeous man—even if it did mean playing the role that was expected of him. It was better than nothing, right? It had been *months* since his last hookup as he'd been too busy finishing his degree to make the time. He was dying for a round of hard, sweaty sex, even if he'd have to compromise. Story of his life.

He got dressed quickly, rubbed a bit of gel in his hair to achieve his standard messy look, and made his way to the living room. Mac had set the table in the kitchen, and on a white serving plate were the biggest, most mouthwatering egg salad sandwiches Quentin had ever seen, with thick slices of bread, lettuce, and bacon.

"Oh damn, those look amazing," he said to Mac, who had his back turned toward him, stirring in a pan. "And what's that delicious smell?"

"S-s-soup," Mac said, his voice and posture stiff.

Hmm, he was uncomfortable after what had passed earlier. Maybe Mac wasn't out? That made sense in a small town like this. Or his gaydar sucked, and he wasn't sure if Quentin had appreciated his slow perusal or not. Quentin figured the best way to get past it was to pretend nothing had happened. He walked up to Mac, who poured the soup into two mugs. "What kind of soup?"

"T-tomato. From my homegrown t-t-tomatoes. I m-m-made it in Aug-g-gust and f-f-f-roze it."

"You grow your own tomatoes? I would've thought the climate is too hard here, isn't it?"

Mac put the ladle back in the pan, grabbed the two mugs, and placed them on the table. "N-n-normally, yes, but I b-b-built a sheltered area in m-my vegetable g-g-garden. K-k-kinda like a g-g-greenhouse."

Quentin sat down at the table, inhaling the fragrance of the soup. "That's awesome. What vegetables do you grow?"

Mac joined him, still avoiding Quentin's eyes. "Everything. As m-m-much as I can. I also have f-f-fruit trees and ch-chickens."

"You have chickens? So we're eating egg salad from your own eggs?"

Mac finally looked up and nodded.

Quentin took a bite from his sandwich, moaning when the combination of the crispy bacon and the rich egg salad hit his mouth. "Damn, this is *good*. How did you get that egg salad so creamy? And holy fuck, what bread is this? That's the best I ever tasted."

"I m-m-make my own m-mayonnaise. That's in the egg s-s-salad. And I b-b-bake my own b-bread."

Quentin hummed in pleasure with his mouth full of perfect sandwich. Mac baked his own bread? What kind of wonder guy was he? He résuméd chewing to quickly empty his mouth. "If you keep feeding me delicious shit like this, I may never leave."

Mac's face broke open in a smile, and Quentin's belly did a little flip. The guy was intimidating with his piercings and dark look, but all that disappeared when he smiled. When he did that, he was beautiful. Stunning.

To distract himself, Quentin took a careful sip of the soup, then moaned all over again as the rich, full tomato flavor invaded his mouth. "Fuck, this is so good! Where did you learn to cook like this?"

Mac's smile disappeared, and his face tightened. "I'm n-n-n-not s-s-s-stupid."

Wow, he'd hit a nerve there. Quentin put his spoon down. "I never said you were." The pain in Mac's eyes was heartbreaking. "You heard what that lady behind the reception said about you," Quentin said.

God, Mac's face was so full of hurt. It was hard to witness. "She's n-n-not the f-f-first to say that. They all th-think it."

"You were born and raised here, in this town, right?" Quentin asked.

Mac nodded.

"So why do they think you're slow? Because of your stutter?"

Another nod.

"Well, I'd say that makes *them* stupid, not you. Having a speech impediment has nothing to do with intelligence. I wasn't asking where you learned to cook because I was surprised you were good at it or because I thought you were stupid. I *know* you're smart. I was asking because I was genuinely curious if someone taught you or if you taught yourself."

"You think I'm s-s-s-smart?"

Disbelief was dripping from Mac's voice, and it caused another crack in Quentin's heart. "Mac, you run a successful business, from what I hear you can fix anything, your house looks like a dream, you can cook like it's nobody's business... and I saw your books. They're not here for decoration as most of them look well read."

Mac stared at him, and Quentin let him because it was obvious the man had a lot to process. He finished his sandwich, then dug back into his soup. All that time, Mac was staring, but it didn't bother Quentin. He'd lost most of the tension in his face, though a small frown on his forehead remained.

"I t-t-taught myself," Mac finally said. "F-f-from cookbooks and YouT-t-tube."

"That's amazing. Can I have some more soup, please?"

"You really eat a l-lot," Mac said with wonder in his voice. "How c-come?"

Quentin chuckled. He loved that Mac was starting to feel comfortable enough with him to ask questions back. "I grew up poor. My dad wasn't part of my life, so it was just my mom and me, and we lived in a trailer park. We never had enough to eat, and I basically grew up always hungry. Now I can afford food, but that hunger is still there. Plus, your sandwiches and soup are the best I've ever tasted."

Mac's smile was careful. "I c-c-can teach you."

"To cook?" How sweet that he offered...and that he counted on Quentin being there long enough to learn. "I have two left hands. Honestly, I can't even boil an egg."

Mac's face displayed pure horror. "What d-do you eat?"

"Microwave dinners. Ready-to-eat shit from the freezer. Lots of bread and pasta. I make a mean peanut butter and jelly sandwich."

"That's n-n-not food, only empty c-calories."

"I know, but I can't cook, and there's no one else to cook for me."

Mac's expression sobered. "N-n-no family?"

"My mom is still in California, in the same park I grew up in. That's it, no other family."

"Why are you h-h-here?"

"In the area, you mean? I was on my way to Northern Lake to do research on small-town dynamics. I have a master's degree in sociology, and I'm hoping to get accepted into a PhD position at the university after I finish this project."

Something flashed in Mac's eyes that looked a lot like longing. "You're r-r-really s-smart, then," he said.

"Yeah. That, and I worked my ass off to get scholarships so I could afford college."

Quentin had never understood why people felt the need to downplay their own intelligence or accomplishments. He was smart, and why should he hide that? He never failed to stress he'd worked incredibly hard to get where he was, so it wasn't like he was bragging. He'd be paying off student loans till he was forty, but at least he'd kept his debt reasonable, considering his earning potential. It still made him sick, knowing how much he owed, but there had been no other way.

"Why N-n-northern Lake?" Mac asked.

Quentin slowly put down his spoon and let out a deep sigh. He hadn't told anyone, not his friends, his professor, or even his mom. Sitting here in this homey kitchen with this fascinating guy across from him, Quentin felt compelled to share, however. "It's where my dad was from."

4

Quentin's answer felt loaded to Mac, as if he was saying a hell of a lot more than just a simple statement about his father. It had to be because he'd said his dad hadn't been in his life, so why would he be interested in finding him?

Just when he wanted to ask something, Lucy started barking, and Mac went on full alert. He got up from the table, pulling his gun from his waistband, where it had been hidden from Quentin.

The kid's eyes went big, and he shoved his chair back with force. "What the fuck? Put the fucking gun down."

Someone knocked at the front door, audible between Lucy's barking. Mac snapped his fingers at Lucy to quiet down, and she obeyed instantly. "S-s-sorry," Mac said to Quentin. "D-d-didn't mean to s-s-scare you. S-s-stay here."

He checked through the safety glass who it was. Lewis Paige. Mac sighed. He opened the door with his left hand, keeping the gun out of sight in his right. He didn't even bother greeting the other man, a balding, fiftysomething guy whose hard life showed in every line on his tired face.

"How m-m-much?"

"Five hundred."

Mac nodded. That, he could spare right now. "Wait," he told Lewis. He closed the door again. Fuck, he was so tired of this, so tired of them all. Most of all, he was tired of carrying the burden of his name.

He rolled his shoulders as he walked over to the small vault in his bedroom and opened it to get Lewis's money out. Two more years, and he was done, forever. Two more years and he'd be free.

Freedom had never beckoned more as it did now, after meeting Quentin. Fuck, what Mac wouldn't give for a chance at getting to know him better, at building a friendship...and so much more. Right now, he had nothing to give but captivity, but in two years, he'd finally be a free man. Free to leave, free to live, and dammit, free to love.

Without a word, he handed the money over to Lewis, the man only acknowledging the gift with the barest of nods. He made him sign the receipt, then locked the door behind him, and noted the entry in his ledger. Five hundred dollars to Lewis Paige. Remainder: three thousand bucks, give or take a few. He was so fucking close he could taste it.

He walked back to the kitchen and almost bumped into Quentin. He'd forgotten about him. The kid was staring at him, his face tight with worry. "What the hell was *that*?" he asked.

"N-n-not your c-c-concern," Mac said, suppressing a smile that the kid had the balls to even ask about that.

"When you start waving a fucking gun around, it *is* my concern," Quentin said, a stubborn look on his face.

"Just a p-p-precaution," Mac said.

"Yeah, I don't do guns. They're fucking dangerous. So if

you can't tell me what the hell that was, I'd like a ride back into town, please. I'll find some other place to stay."

Mac frowned. Was he serious, or was this some lame attempt to twist Mac's arm? "There is n-n-nothing else. And it w-w-will start snowing in a f-f-few hours."

Quentin let out a colorful curse. "Not your fucking problem, now is it? I told you, I don't do guns."

"Everyone has g-g-guns here," Mac said. "This is the b-b-backcountry. We have b-b-bears, and we hunt."

Quentin's eyes narrowed. "You're carrying a .45 because you wanna shoot bears and wildlife? I don't think so."

Huh, how about that? Quentin claimed to hate guns, but he knew enough to recognize the type of gun Mac was carrying. "N-n-no," Mac admitted. "I have other r-r-reasons, but I c-c-can't tell you."

Quentin scoffed. "You mean you won't. Big difference."

"You're right. I w-w-w-won't. B-b-but you're safe. I w-w-would never hurt you."

"Well, it's not like there's anything I can do about it, is there? I mean, I have no car, there's a storm coming, and you have the gun. I'd say that leaves me without options."

Mac's heart filled with sadness. He didn't want Quentin to be afraid of him, but he couldn't fault him for it. Anyone in his circumstances would be. He walked over to the small vault in the living room, quickly punched in the code, and grabbed the nine millimeter he had in there. He took the chamber out, checked it had bullets, then handed it to Quentin. "H-h-here. N-n-now you have a g-g-gun too."

Quentin hesitated for a second, then took it. Mac watched as he expertly checked the gun, then put the chamber back in and flipped the safety on. With that fluid move, he'd assured Mac he knew what he was doing. How had he learned to handle firearms that well if he hated them? Not something he could ask right now, not after he'd refused to share his own secrets. It seemed like they both had things to hide.

"I'm g-g-gonna work outs-s-side," he said.

Quentin studied him for a second, then nodded. "I'll come with you."

"N-not dressed like that. You'll f-f-freeze."

"I'll put on a sweater, and I'm sure you have an extra pair of gloves. I'll go stir-crazy if I have to stay inside all the time."

Mac eyed him, gauging his size. "I have a w-w-winter jacket that sh-sh-should fit."

"Not yours, then," Quentin said, curiosity dripping from his voice.

Mac walked into the guest room where Quentin was staying and opened the walk-in closet. He'd gotten rid of most of his mom's stuff, but he'd kept some items that reminded him of her. She'd been a strong woman mentally, but her body had been frail.

He took her winter jacket off the hanger, breathing in deeply. Her smell was long gone after ten years, but he could still imagine it. Lavender, from the little handmade sachets of dried flowers she always put between fresh laundry, and lemon because she'd cleaned everything with lemon-scented cleaner. Mac still did.

Her simple black winter jacket had been expensive—one of the few items of clothing they'd spent good money on. They had little choice in this climate, especially since she'd been wheelchair bound already and had been sitting still a lot. Mac had bought her a man's coat, a sturdy, three-layered ski jacket that had kept her warm, even if it had been too big on her near the end.

"It was my m-m-mom's," he said as he handed Quentin

the jacket. He also found her hat and gloves, made from the same sturdy material. Pretty wasn't a concern in the junkyard. Rugged, warm, and black so stains wouldn't show, that was his motto.

"Thank you," Quentin said.

He put on the jacket. It was a little on the short side, but it would do. Mac eyed his Converse critically. They looked like they wouldn't last a day outside, and they were too cold. "W-w-what's your sh-sh-shoe size?"

"Size ten and a half."

"R-r-really? You have b-b-big feet for your s-s-size," Mac said. Damn, the kid only wore half a size down from his own. Granted, his feet were on the small side, considering his height, but still.

"You know what they say about men with large feet..." Quentin said. Mac met his laughing eyes. "Large feet, large...shoes."

Mac grinned. "You're a th-thief. That's f-f-from N-notting Hill."

Quentin shrugged, smiling. "I was hoping you hadn't seen it so I could take credit."

Two minutes later, they were outside, Quentin wearing a pair of Mac's thick ski socks and his old boots.

"What are we doing?" he asked.

"S-s-stripping down your c-car."

"Oh, okay. Cool."

They worked side by side, Quentin asking a thousand questions and Mac answering them all. He'd never talked so much in his life, at least not since his mom had passed away. She'd been the only one who'd never gotten impatient of his stutter. When the first snowflakes started falling, Mac said, "It's t-time to head inside."

It stayed silent, and Mack turned around. Quentin stared

at the sky in wonder, his face raised. His cheeks had grown red from the cold, and he looked beautiful to Mac. A deep longing settled in his belly, then traveled straight down to his cock. Meeting Quentin had answered every question Mac had ever had about himself. Well, about his lack of sex drive anyway. He'd fucked women, but it had never grown beyond pleasant.

All these movies and series he'd watched, every book he'd read had all shown love as this grand feeling, this overwhelming emotion. Even sex had always been portrayed as intense, a primal urge—something Mac had never, ever felt, not until he'd encountered Quentin in the hallway, his slender body shivering from the cold. He'd been so gorgeous, so perfect, so...

Mac struggled to find words, even in his head. Quentin had been everything Mac had been missing, everything he wanted—and he'd never realized it.

The snow was coming down for real now, and Quentin let out an excited laugh. "It's beautiful!" he exclaimed, twirling around till Mac got dizzy from watching him.

"It's just s-s-snow," he said, but he couldn't help but join Quentin in laughing, since his joy was damn infectious.

Quentin slowly brought his head down and looked at Mac. "I've never seen snow. Well, from a distance on the mountains when I drove here, but I've never been in a snowstorm. I didn't expect it to be this pretty."

Mac opened his mouth to tell him that he'd be singing a different tune once he had to shovel a foot of snow but then decided against it. Let the kid enjoy it while it lasted. And he'd better keep thinking of Quentin as a *kid* because he was way too young for him. Too pretty.

"I n-need to lock up, and then we'll g-g-go inside," he said.

He did his usual round around his property, a happy Quentin on his heels, studying his every move, it seemed. Mac made sure to lock the gate with the thick chains, and he checked the individual locks on each of his containers and sheds, especially the one on his shop. He didn't expect anyone to pull a stunt during a snowstorm, but in this town, you never knew.

"What's in there?" Quentin asked.

"P-p-personal p-projects."

"That's pretty vague, isn't it? What kind of projects?"

"D-d-don't you think if I w-w-wanted you t-to know, I would've elab-b-borated?"

"Could be a force of habit to keep it vague," Quentin said, his laughing eyes growing serious. "After all, you're not used to someone being interested in you, are you?"

Mac swallowed. "N-no. Are you?"

Quentin took a step toward Mac. "Interested in you? Yes."

Mac was used to struggling to speak, but this was on a whole other level. His coat felt too tight around his throat, and sweat broke out on his back. It was utterly ridiculous. He was a grown man, thirty-eight years old, strong as fuck, and by most standards pretty damn intimidating. So how could this mere *boy* scare the fuck out of him?

"Why?" he finally managed.

Quentin closed the distance between them, standing only a few inches away, their breaths mingling between the snowflakes. Little specks of snow clung to his long lashes, and Mac's belly went all weak again. He was so damn beautiful, like something precious and fragile he wanted to cherish for the rest of his life.

The thought sobered him. It wouldn't be him cherishing

Quentin. It couldn't be. Once he knew the truth, Quentin would run as fast as the others.

"It's okay, Mac," Quentin said softly. "Whatever you're feeling is okay."

Mac sighed, stepping back. "That's w-w-where you're wrong. I haven't b-been okay in a long time."

5

Despite Mac's cryptic remark outside, the atmosphere between them wasn't tense, Quentin concluded—much to his relief. He would have hated to see Mac get stressed over something he'd said without thinking.

Mac was making dinner, and the house filled with a delicious smell that made Quentin's stomach rumble loudly. He peeked into the Dutch oven Mac was stirring, but couldn't determine what he was making.

"What's for dinner?"

Mac smiled. "You c-c-can't be hungry again. You just ate h-h-half a bag of c-c-cashews."

"I told you I'm always hungry. My mom always calls me a garbage can."

"It's s-stew. I often m-m-make it in the w-winter because it's n-nice and warm in your b-belly. But this one is f-f-from the freezer. I m-made it last week."

"It smells like heaven," Quentin said, taking another deep sniff.

"It's got herbs and b-b-beer in it," Mac said.

"Beer? In stew?"

Mac nodded. "D-dark beer. And I a-a-always add a l-little vinegar. It s-softens up the m-meat."

Was it Quentin's imagination, or was Mac starting to talk more to him, making longer sentences? He loved pulling this man out of his protective shell, seeing the tender heart behind the badass exterior.

"Huh. It sounds delicious. When is it ready?"

Mac laughed, a belly laugh that echoed through the room, and made Quentin breathe in deeply to push down the weird flutters in his belly. What a rich sound it was.

"T-t-ten more minutes. I'm m-making mashed p-p-potatoes and c-carrots to go w-with it."

"I'm usually patient but not when it comes to food," Quentin admitted with a laugh.

"I w-w-would have n-never guessed," Mac deadpanned.

Quentin shrugged. "Hey, I warned you I eat a lot."

He made his way over to the bookcases. The books were neatly organized by genre, thrillers separated from general literature, and authors grouped together. Mac liked John Grisham and David Baldacci, it seemed. He also had a surprisingly big category of young adult fiction.

The nonfiction was shelved by topic. The man had a broad range of interests. Self-help took a few shelves, with a bunch of popular psychology books thrown in as well. He had a whole section on architecture and engineering.

Quentin picked up a book on building sheds, flipped through it, and put it back between the other books on wood crafts. Then there were many books on historical subjects. He followed the spines with his finger. "US presidents, Civil War, Second World War, Vietnam war. You have quite a collection." Even more than Quentin, and he loved to read pretty much everything he could get his hands on.

"N-not m-much else to d-d-do but read and w-w-watch TV."

Didn't he have friends? Other family? A girlfriend?

Quentin trailed back to the kitchen, where he found a spot at the sturdy kitchen table. It was no hardship to watch Mac cook. The guy had a grace to his movements despite his size. And damn, his ass was...perfect. Mac had big muscles, sculpted by doing years of hard manual work, but his ass was wonderfully plump and round. It would bounce and jiggle deliciously when someone fucked him...Quentin got hard even thinking about it.

He could picture it, his long cock sliding in and out of that gorgeous, full ass. He'd put Mac on his stomach first so he could enjoy that ass, watch it ripple as he took him. Then he'd turn him onto his back because he'd want to watch every emotion on the man's face as he brought him to a climax. Mac's cock would be rock hard in his hand, straining against his touch, begging for more.

And of course he'd torment him a little. Maybe put some nipple clamps on him or tie his hands to the bed. God, that would be a sight, a man like him writhing underneath him, begging him for mercy...

"Q-q-quentin?"

Quentin's head shot up.

"A-a-are you okay?"

He swallowed. "Yeah, I'm fine. Why?"

Mac studied him for a second. "You w-were g-groaning. Like you had p-p-pain."

Oh, god. He'd been doing it again, allowing himself to be sucked into a daydream. "I was thinking of something and must have made a sound. I'm fine, I swear."

He fought back the urge to cover his crotch, where Mac would be able to spot his hard-on easily. If he didn't draw attention to it, maybe Mac wouldn't notice. To his relief, Mac kept his eyes trained on his face before he turned around to the stove again.

Quentin let out an inaudible sigh. Dammit, he needed to stop daydreaming about something that would never, ever happen. As if a man like Mac would ever bottom for a guy like Quentin. Fat chance. He still wasn't even sure if Mac *liked* him, since his signals were so mixed. The guy was definitely not straight, considering his reaction when he'd spotted Quentin in his underwear, but he'd also hinted at not being interested in Quentin.

Quentin suspected Mac's reasons had nothing to do with him and everything with something from his past, but it didn't matter. Fact was that the man didn't want him, and even if he did, he would not want him to top. No one ever did. And the thought of him dominating Mac was even more insane.

They chatted throughout dinner, Quentin noticing once again that Mac was getting freer with his speech.

"D-do you w-want to play a game? A b-b-board game?"

"Yes! Oh god, that's perfect with the storm outside."

Mac had started a fire in the open fireplace, the warmth enveloping Quentin. He breathed in deeply, the scent of the crackling wood completely new to him. It smelled like...like home, somehow.

"What g-game do you w-w-want to play?"

Mac opened a wooden cabinet, revealing dozens of board games. "Holy moly, that's a lot."

Mac's face filled with sadness. "M-m-my mom loved t-to play them. She was s-s-sick and c-couldn't walk well anymore, so we p-p-played lots of g-games."

"What did she have?"

"MS. B-b-but the p-progressive kind. She p-passed away t-t-ten years ago."

Quentin put his hand on Mac's arm, the strong muscles tensing under his touch. He waited a beat, but when Mac relaxed, he left it there. "I'm so sorry, Mac. You guys were close, huh?"

"Yeah." For a second it seemed as if he wanted to say more, but then he closed his mouth again. Quentin wasn't gonna ask him about his dad. If he'd been in the picture, Mac would have mentioned him, so it seemed better to leave that topic rest.

He gave Mac's arm another squeeze. "What's your favorite board game?"

"I l-l-like them all."

He'd have to pick, then. "Let's play Ticket to Ride. I haven't played that in, like, forever."

Mac made hot chocolate with whipped cream, and they played until suddenly the lights went out. Lucy let out a frightened bark, but Mac shushed her with a single whistle.

Quentin sat frozen in his seat, his heart beating wildly. When Mac had warned him about the possibility of losing power, Quentin had conveniently forgotten how much he hated the dark. The faint light from the fireplace was their only light, and god, he despised it.

"I'll s-start up the g-g-generator. Give me a few m-m-minutes," Mac said. He got up from his chair and grabbed the flashlight from the kitchen counter.

"L-lucy, stay," he told the dog and disappeared into the hallway. Quentin heard rustling as Mac got dressed. Then the front door opened and closed.

The wind was howling around the house. It had grown pitch-dark, nothing of the snow visible, but the radar

Quentin had checked on his weather app not a half hour ago had shown it wouldn't stop snowing for hours yet. It was so fucking *dark*, and what if the backup generator didn't work?

In the distance, a loud snap broke through the silence. What the hell was that? What if a tree came down under the force of the wind and the snow and fell on the house? Where the hell was Mac, and why hadn't that stupid generator kicked in yet? Quentin tried to breathe, tried to stay calm, but his heart beat faster and faster. He shouldn't be scared of something so stupid as the dark. He wasn't a *child*, for fuck's sake.

It wasn't even completely dark, since he still had the light from the fireplace, and he wasn't alone because Lucy was right there. She trotted toward Quentin and nuzzled his hand. Was she sensing his distress?

He slid his fingers through her fur, then scratched her ears. "You're a sweet dog, aren't you? You look mean, but you're a softie on the inside, just like Mac."

Lucy answered by licking his hand, and it made him painfully aware of the level of his fears. He was such a wuss when it came to shit like this.

A loud rumble signaled the generator had started, but no lights came on yet. Shivering despite the heat from the fireplace, Quentin sat, his hand holding on to Lucy as if she was the one thing keeping him from going into a full-blown panic attack. She probably was, he thought wryly. How could he ever expect his sexual partners to take him seriously, let alone be in charge, when he was still afraid of the dark? When he couldn't even cook and properly take care of himself like an adult?

"A-a-are you okay?"

Mac's voice yanked him out of his disoriented, jumbled

thoughts. He hadn't even noticed Mac coming back in, too focused on not falling apart.

"I'm... Dammit...the dark, I don't like the dark," he managed.

Mac wordlessly brought over a couple of large candles and placed them on the table, lighting them quickly. "B-better?"

Quentin nodded, the band around his chest still too tight to breathe comfortably. Mac's worried eyes studied him, and Quentin felt like the biggest loser ever. Any shot he'd had with Mac was certainly blown to hell now.

"D-d-do you w-w-want to b-b-be held?"

Mac's stress showed in how much he wrestled with his words, but the meaning registered loud and clear with Quentin. "God, please, Mac. Tight."

Mac sat down on the couch and gestured, and Quentin didn't even hesitate. He all but dropped his dead weight on Mac's lap, tears forming in his eyes when those strong arms came around him and pulled him close. He leaned his head against Mac's chest, wrapped his arms around the man's waist, and held on.

6

Mac held Quentin tight, feeling his tense body struggling to breathe normally. How the hell had he missed this when he went outside to start the generator? Quentin hadn't said a word, but maybe he hadn't been able to.

Mac knew all about fear, the crippling panic that could wreck your body and make it unable to do anything. He'd experienced it plenty of times when being forced to give a presentation in school, to say anything in public. One experience had been so bad he'd almost peed his pants. Literally.

Quentin's breathing slowed down, but his body was still tense. Mac found his head with his left hand while keeping him close with his right and gently stroked his hair. Quentin had such beautiful hair, all wild and messy and so *different*, outside the norm—like Quentin himself. Not many men here wore a haircut like that, and Mac fucking loved it.

Lucy had been trotting back and forth, on high alert, sensing Quentin's stress, probably. Now she settled at Mac's feet, her body warming his cold feet. The rest of him was scorching hot, reacting to the sensation of having a man in his arms.

Holding Quentin was everything he had imagined—and then some. His cock had grown hard in seconds, but he made no effort to hide it. Apparently, he was gay or maybe bi. Either that, or he belonged somewhere on a spectrum of people who simply fell in love, regardless of gender. He'd read books, seen documentaries about things like this. But he'd never recognized himself in the descriptions until Quentin had walked into his life.

And he was fine with it. His life sucked in many, many ways, but this feeling, this overwhelming sensation of wanting to disappear into someone else, this was the best thing that had ever happened to him. His closet was already jam-packed with secrets and guilt. It did not have room to shove himself in.

And so he held Quentin, and he started humming until he felt his slender body respond by relaxing. Quentin rubbed his cheek against Mac's chest—well, technically, against the thick hoodie he was wearing. Mac kept stroking his hair as he hummed, one mindless tune after another.

He knew exactly when Quentin became aware of the very hard cock under his ass. He shifted slightly, rubbing against Mac. Quentin's breath caught, and then he moved again, more subtle but unmistakably putting pressure on a very specific spot.

Mac couldn't see his face, since it was still pressed against his chest, so he felt safe enough to smile a little. That smile turned into biting his lip to keep himself from groaning when Quentin repeated his move. If he kept doing that, Mac's cock wouldn't stay hard long. It would fucking explode.

"Q-q-quentin," he said, as much a plea as a warning.

Quentin's head came up, and their eyes met. His face looked even more angelic with the soft light of the candle dancing over his perfect skin. He looked so young, so innocent. Then he ground his ass against Mac's cock again, and Mac let out the moan he'd held back before. This little tease wasn't nearly as innocent as he looked.

"What are you d-d-doing?" he tried again.

With a lightning-fast move, Quentin switched position and straddled Mac. Mac automatically held on to him, and Quentin's hands came to rest on his forearms, then traveled to his biceps, squeezing slightly.

"I'm showing you just how interested I am in you," Quentin said softly. "Is it coming across?"

"I r-r-read you l-loud and c-clear..." Mac's eyes rolled back in his head as Quentin ground down again. "D-dammit, you're k-killing me."

A devious smile played on Quentin's lips. "Then I must be doing it right. I'm gonna kiss you now, okay?"

Mac could only stare at him, breathless, his heart racing.

"Mac, now's the time to say no if you don't want this," Quentin said.

Say something? God, he couldn't even form a coherent thought, let alone make actual words. The things Quentin was doing to him...and he had barely gotten started by the looks of it.

"N-n-no," he finally managed.

Quentin reeled back, as if Mac had hit him. "You don't want this?"

Mac's eyes grew big. Oh, fuck it all to hell, he was fucking this up. "N-n-n-n-o, p-p-please..."

He cursed his stupid brain or whatever the fuck was preventing him from forming actual words like a normal person. Quentin's face fell, and he let go of Mac's arms and moved backward.

Dammit, Mac had inadvertently said no again, hadn't he? He grabbed Quentin's hands. "S-s-s-stop. W-w-wait."

Quentin must have seen something on his face because he did stop. "Did I misunderstand?"

Mac nodded quickly, then took a deep breath. Stress exacerbated his stutter and made it ten times worse as he'd experienced too many times to count. He had to try and stay calm, and so he fought to swallow back the stress and ignore his racing heart and his clammy hands.

Quentin put his hands back on Mac's biceps and squeezed gently. "It's okay, Mac. I'll wait until you're ready, okay? I'll listen."

Had anyone ever shown him this level of kindness and understanding, aside from his mom? Not that Mac could remember, and that realization only added to his inability to speak. So he did the only thing he could manage right now, and he laid his fingers on Quentin's soft lips, then on his own.

"You want me to kiss you, Mac?" Quentin whispered.

He nodded. Then to make it even clearer, he put his hands on Quentin's ass and pulled him closer again, to his original position.

Quentin brought his right hand from his biceps up to Mac's face. He trailed his beard with one finger, then traced his lips. "Have you ever kissed a man before?"

Mac shook his head.

"I love that I get to be your first."

Mac's muscles trembled with nerves, but thank fuck, Quentin took pity on him and slowly brought his mouth closer and closer and...

Warm, velvet lips touched his in the sweetest kiss he'd

ever received, and yet, it felt different than any kiss Mac had ever shared with a woman. Maybe it was the body pressing into his that was unmistakably male. Maybe it was the tiniest fuzz on Quentin's chin. Maybe it was his strong hands, those elegant fingers now grabbing his beard. And maybe it was because he knew that after this, nothing would ever be the same.

Quentin increased the pressure, and then his tongue darted out and licked his lip piercing. Mac groaned against his mouth, opening immediately. That sweet tongue entered his mouth, and all Mac could do was hang on to Quentin, hold on to him with both hands while his mouth was being thoroughly explored.

He closed his eyes, too overcome by all the sensations in his body to handle the sensory input, and he let Quentin kiss him until he was one hot mess of a man. His hands dug into Quentin's ass, and his cock was rock hard, dying to break free from the confines of his underwear and jeans. Then Quentin ground against him, rolling his hips in slow, deliberate circles against Mac's crotch.

Mac's eyes flew open. Oh, fuck, if he kept that up, Mac would... "Q-q-quentin..." Mac moaned against his mouth. "P-p-please..."

Quentin gently bit Mac's lower lip, sending another wave of want through him. "I like hearing you beg..."

Mac was helpless against the onslaught of sensations. His body was on fire, not just his mouth but everywhere. He didn't even recognize himself, moaning under the ministrations of this guy half his size. What was Quentin *doing* to him?

"I love the sensation of that hard cock of yours against my ass," Quentin mumbled against Mac's lips. "And you feel big, Mac. How big are you?"

He was supposed to *talk* now? How the fuck did Quentin think he could manage that when he needed all his brainpower to keep himself from coming?

"God, look at you," Quentin said with awe. "I love watching you unravel...this big, strong man, completely at my mercy..."

Then he put his teeth into Mac's bottom lip again, and it hurt, but that sharp sting also fueled his want. It was so confusing. Quentin brought his hips down, and Mac was toast. His hips undulated, rutting to create that perfect friction, once, twice, and then his balls exploded. He came and came and came, jerking and twitching, moaning low and deep into Quentin's mouth.

Before Mac could say a word—not that he would have been able to—Quentin kissed him again. Not a sweet kiss this time, but a hot invasion of his mouth, a sexy-as-fuck seduction that left Mac's head reeling. All he could do was surrender and let Quentin take whatever he wanted.

Quentin grabbed Mac's hand, wriggled it between them, and pushed it against his own dick. Mac quickly got the hint. He folded it around Quentin's cock and squeezed gently. Quentin hummed a low moan of approval and started rutting against his hand, still kissing the shit out of Mac.

"Fuck, you taste so good," Quentin murmured. "And I love the sensation of your beard against my skin. I could kiss you for hours."

"N-n-no obj-j-jection," Mac whispered.

"And that big hand of yours on my cock... Won't take long now."

He threw his head back, and his face pulled tight in concentration as his hips pistoned faster. He'd been beautiful from the second Mac had laid eyes on him, but now he was mesmerizing…and hot as fuck. Mac pushed back against Quentin's cock, squeezing again.

"Oooohh!" Quentin spasmed, and pure bliss bloomed on his face. "Oh, fuck, that was a good one…"

He slowly bent his head and met Mac's eyes. Mac couldn't take his eyes off that angelic face with his swollen lips, his flushed cheeks, and the red beard burns on his chin. "You're b-b-beautiful."

Quentin's mouth curved up in a sweet smile. "Oh, Mac, what am I gonna do with you?"

"F-f-fuck me?"

7

No way had Mac meant that literally, right? No, he'd probably meant it as an expression, as a quicker way of saying "I really love your ass, so can I fuck you, please?"

Story of his life.

Quentin slowly climbed off Mac's lap, careful not to step on Lucy. Mac grabbed his hand. "D-d-did I s-say something w-w-wrong?"

Quentin's heart clenched painfully. He was vulnerable, this big, strong man. So damn fragile. His protective instinct kicked in with full force, even more when he caught Mac's eyes, filled with insecurity.

"No, baby, you were perfect. You *are* perfect. It's...don't you need time to process?"

Mac slowly let go of his hand. "P-p-process what?"

Quentin took position between Mac's legs, cupping his face in both of his hands. "That you're attracted to men."

Much to his surprise, Mac scoffed. "W-w-why would I n-need time t-to process that?"

Quentin frowned. "I thought it was news to you, that you'd only been with women before."

"F-four. F-f-four women. And I'm thirty-eight, s-s-so you d-do the math."

Quentin dropped his hands from Mac's face, looking at him in utter surprise. "You slept with only four women in all those years? Were you in a relationship with them?"

Mac shook his head. "Onetime s-sex. I d-d-didn't m-miss it. The s-sex. N-n-not until..."

Quentin could have sworn he blushed, but the faint candlelight made it hard to see. He laid his thumb on Mac's full bottom lip. "Did you like kissing me?" he whispered.

"I d-d-didn't kiss you. You k-kissed me."

Fuck, Quentin loved feeling Mac's lip tremble as he spoke. What a rush to make this man quiver for him. "I didn't hear you protest."

"N-n-no, I l-loved it. You c-can kiss me anyt-t-time."

He pushed his thumb against Mac's mouth, and he sucked it in, wrapping his soft lips around it, then lapped it with his tongue. The sensation shot straight to Quentin's balls. His very *sloppy* balls, where cum was now drying up in a most uncomfortable fashion.

The knowledge that Mac was putty in his hands fired up all the bossy instincts Quentin tried so hard to suppress when he was with another man. None of them had ever appreciated these, so he'd tried to curtail them as best he could. But lord, the things he wanted to *do* to this man... He would be stunning when Quentin made him suffer for him. Just enough to drive Mac mad with need and to satisfy this yearning inside himself to see someone kneel for him.

"Hmm, that feels so good, Mac. Your wet mouth around my thumb..." He lowered his voice, fighting to keep his breathing calm when Mac moaned around his digit. "You like doing that, baby? You like having something in your mouth?"

He slowly pulled his thumb out, then pushed it back in again, while Mac nodded earnestly. God, what a rush to see this man come undone at his hands. He kept fucking his mouth with his finger, never taking his eyes off Mac, who seemed remarkably content to let Quentin take the lead. Could he...?

Visions of him fucking Mac flashed through his mind again, but he pushed them down. He couldn't, not with this man. If he was the dominant one here, he had the responsibility to set the right pace. All this was new to Mac. Hell, the guy had never even been *kissed* by a man. Quentin couldn't steamroll him with anything more.

He reluctantly pulled out his thumb, which had softened under Mac's thorough sucking. Mac's brown eyes flashed with uncertainty, and Quentin bent down to press another kiss on those perfect lips.

"Let's get cleaned up, and then you get to pick what we'll do."

"W-w-will you read t-to me?" Mac asked after a brief hesitation.

"A book?"

Mac nodded, and Quentin smiled. He'd never done that before. Hell, he couldn't even remember anyone ever reading to him. His mom, probably, but since he'd learned how to read at four, that was a long time ago.

"I'd love to."

Mac handed him a flashlight, and they both stepped into their bedrooms. Mac's room had a master bathroom, apparently, because Quentin heard water running there while he quickly cleaned up in his bathroom and put on clean underwear. Damn, it had been a long time since he'd come in his pants like that. What an amazing experience it had been to see Mac come.

"What book do you want me to read?" he asked Mac when they were both back in the living room, Mac having exchanged his work jeans for far more comfortable sweat pants. Quentin still shivered from walking through the dark with only his flashlight. It was much better here with the candles and the light from the fire—and also a hell of a lot warmer. His bedroom had been freezing cold.

"D-d-do you w-want me to turn the l-lights on? I can hook them up on the g-g-generator."

Quentin put his hand on Mac's arm. "Thank you, but I'm okay as long as I stay here. The fire and the candles help."

Mac nodded, then handed him a book. The first Harry Potter book, one of Quentin's favorites. "Oh, I love that one!"

He plopped down onto the couch and grabbed a fleece blanket to huddle under. Mac sat down beside him and, after a quick look sideways, moved in closer. "Is this o-o-kay?" he asked.

God, he was so fucking adorable. "Wanna cuddle?" Quentin asked him, his voice soft.

Mac dipped his head eagerly, and before Quentin realized what was happening, the big man was comfortably leaning against him, his head on Quentin's lap.

Quentin did a mental calculation. Mac's mom had passed away ten years earlier. He'd only fucked four women since, all one-night stands from what Quentin understood. For some reason, he wasn't very popular in town—and why people would just show up at his door and demand money was a whole other story. Clearly, Mac was not just alone but *lonely*...and he was starving for touch.

Quentin couldn't deny he loved the way Mac gravitated

toward him, almost...submitting to him. It didn't make sense that he'd be happy bowing to another man, but he truly seemed to be. At the same time, it made Quentin deeply aware he had to tread carefully here. Mac was vulnerable, and he had to respect and honor that.

"Do you like it when I touch you?" he asked.

"I l-l-love it."

That was the other thing. As shy and hesitant as Mac seemed, he didn't appear to be ashamed of how he felt or reluctant to express what he liked and wanted. It was the strangest dichotomy, and Quentin found him all the more interesting.

Quentin ran one hand through Mac's hair, held his book with the other. "That's good because I really like touching you," he said.

With a smile on his face, he started reading, transporting them both to a different world with wizards and muggles and a boy who lived under the staircase. Mac listened to him, softly responding every now and then with chuckles and sighs and little sounds of distress. Quentin kept gently stroking his head while reading. After an hour, he was parched, and his voice was turning croaked.

"C-c-can I m-make you some t-tea?" Mac asked.

"Yes, please. And something to snack would be good." Quentin said in a hopeful tone.

Mac laughed, raising his head from his position on Quentin's lap. "I s-s-should have known."

He got up from the couch, stretching and yawning as he stood, his muscles flexing and showing off in a way that made Quentin's insides go a little weak. Mac bent over and kissed Quentin on his cheek. "Thank you f-for reading t-to me. You have s-such a l-l-lovely voice, and you r-r-r-read really well."

"You're welcome," Quentin said. How special it was that he could bring this man pleasure by doing something that was so basic to him, so natural. He'd never take speaking for granted again after meeting Mac, that much he knew.

He extended his hand and let Mac pull him up, deliberately letting himself fall against Mac's body. His arms came around him, and Quentin hugged him back, resting his head on the bigger man's shoulder. It was strange how he wanted to dominate the shit out of Mac yet loved being held by that strong body at the same time. Fuck if he knew how that could possibly work.

He nuzzled Mac's neck, smiling when Mac's warm hands dipped under his hoodie and caressed his bare back. His calloused fingers felt wonderfully rough on his skin, slightly scratching and yet delightfully sweet.

"Is this o-o-okay?" Mac asked softly.

"Yeah." Quentin sighed. "God, your hands feel good on me."

"N-n-not too r-rough?"

Quentin spoke without thinking. "I like it rough."

He froze instantly. Oh, dammit. Mac had better not interpret that the wrong way. He'd been in that situation before, with some biker dude, and fucking hell, he'd almost literally had to fight him off to prove that *rough* didn't mean "oh, please, fuck me right now and ignore me when I protest."

But Mac simply continued his tantalizing exploration of Quentin's back, not missing even an inch of skin. "Y-y-your skin is s-so soft…"

For minutes they stood there, Mac exploring and Quentin taking the assault on his system, forcing himself to resist the urge to push Mac against a wall and kiss him senseless, before ripping off both their clothes and…

Yeah, not helpful.

His cock disagreed with his intentions and protested rather vigorously, but he ignored that too until Mac had taken his fill.

He let out a contented sigh, then dropped Quentin's shirt and stepped out of the embrace. "I'll m-make you s-some tea."

While Mac got busy in the kitchen, Quentin fought to get his body back under control. Dammit, he *wanted* this man.

Armed with a huge mug of steaming hot tea and a small plate of chocolate chip cookies—Mac actually apologized they were store bought—Quentin took position up on the couch again. Mac didn't even ask but snuggled up again in his previous spot. He'd thrown a few more logs on the fire, and the room was wonderfully warm and cozy, vague sounds of the storm outside rising above the crackling fire only occasionally. With Mac plastered against him, Quentin didn't experience even a trace of fear for the dark. And so Quentin read, sipping his tea and nibbling on the cookies until Mac's deepening breaths alerted him the man had fallen asleep on his lap.

"Oh, Mac," he whispered. "You beautiful, kind man... How the fuck am I supposed to resist you?"

He finished his tea, devoured the last two cookies, then gently lifted Mac's head off his lap and laid it on a pillow. He debated going to his bedroom, then realized the monumental stupidity of that plan. His bedroom was dark, cold, and fucking lonely. Why the hell would he choose that over the warm, comfy spot he was in right now?

Instead, he stretched out next to Mac on the—thankfully rather deep—couch. Mac gathered him close in his sleep, snuggling as tight against Quentin's body as he possibly could. Quentin spread the blanket on top of both of them and settled his head on Mac's shoulders. Lucy jumped onto the couch too, laying herself down at their feet, and Quentin smiled. He closed his eyes and drifted off to sleep.

8

When Mac awoke, it took him a few seconds to figure out where he was...and why he was so warm and toasty, even though the fire had almost gone out. Quentin was sleeping in his arms, his face pressed against Mac's chest, his head resting on Mac's shoulder. His slender body was draped half over Mac, touching him wherever possible.

Mac smiled. Who would have known Quentin was as much of a snuggler as he himself was? The fact that he appreciated the intimacy afterward far more than the actual sex was one of the things that had made those hookups with women awkward. One woman had all but called him a pervert, saying she wasn't into weird shit like that. Now that he'd met Quentin and had discovered feelings and desires he'd never known he was capable of, it all made a hell of a lot more sense.

And yes, he did love cuddling. Whatever. Lounging on the couch with Quentin, listening to his crisp voice reading Harry Potter while his hand kept caressing Mac's hair had been one of the best experiences of his life.

Maybe even the best yet. Not that it had much competition.

His mom had loved him with everything she had, and she'd tried her damnedest to compensate for the cruelty he'd encountered from the locals. She'd been a hugger too, and he hadn't realized how much he needed that human connection until she'd passed away, leaving him by himself.

Touching Quentin was like giving water to a man who'd been walking around in the desert for weeks. He couldn't get enough of it, of him, and Quentin didn't seem to mind—thank fuck. Though if he was honest, he wanted to do a whole lot more than *hug* Quentin. He couldn't believe he'd come right out and said it.

Fuck me, he'd said. What the hell had he been thinking? Not that he'd been lying, because holy hell, he'd been putty in the boy's hands, but seriously, he couldn't afford to be impulsive like that. Quentin deserved to know the truth about Mac before they went any further. If they got involved, or whatever it was called, even if it was for a brief time—his heart contracted painfully at the thought of Quentin leaving again—he couldn't keep this from him. If Quentin found out afterward, he'd feel so betrayed he'd never speak to Mac again.

That thought resulted in another painful protest from his heart, and Mac sighed. What the hell had happened to him that Quentin had gotten into his system so fast, so deep? He had to be careful here, or he'd scare him away by wanting too much, too soon.

"It's way too dark to be thinking that hard," Quentin murmured, jolting Mac out of his musings. He was looking at Mac through half-lidded eyes, which, of course, made him even more gorgeous and sexy than he already was.

"S-s-sorry," Mac whispered.

Quentin's mouth curved into a smile that sent tingles down Mac's spine. "God, you're so fucking adorable with your bed hair and your crumpled face. Come here." He pushed himself up, pulled Mac's face down, and pressed their mouths together.

Mac's brain stopped working, and he lost all coherent thought and could only feel. Quentin's soft, warm lips on his, that devious tongue sneaking its way into his mouth, the swirls in his stomach as Quentin devoured him. Mac dragged Quentin's body on top of his, needing to *feel* him, wanting to be even closer to him.

When Quentin started grinding into him, he brought his hands to that perfect ass to touch and knead, and fucking hell, his body was on fire. He drove his hard cock into Quentin's body, seeking more friction, and Quentin managed to wriggle his right hand between them and grab Mac through his sweat pants.

"Ohhh," Mac moaned, lifting his hips to push into that hand. "P-p-p-please..."

Quentin scratched his lower lips with his teeth, just rough enough to get Mac's attention. How could that bit of pain feel so good?

"You like that, huh? Look at you, rutting against me."

"M-m-more," Mac begged. Pride be damned, he needed Quentin's hand on his bare... "Ungh!"

Another squeeze of his cock had his head reeling. Dammit, he was ready to *beg* for more.

A massive crack from outside broke through his sex-hazed brain. What the fuck? He froze, and so did Quentin. Another ear-splitting *thwack* reverberated through the house, causing the glassware in the cupboard to rattle.

"What the hell was that?" Quentin asked.

Mac's stomach sank. "It s-s-sounded like a l-large branch

off a t-tree has fallen off, m-maybe a whole t-t-tree. I n-need to check it out."

"I'll come with you," Quentin said.

Mac wanted to refuse the offer, but one look at Quentin's face made him reconsider. He wasn't offering Mac to help; he was *telling* him that he was coming with him. He kissed him one last time, all thoughts of sex forgotten now. "Th-th-thank you."

They bundled up, and Mac grabbed the snow shovel from the garage before they stepped outside. It was still dark as fuck at six in the morning, the heavy snow almost blinding in the broad beam from his flashlight. Damn, there had to be a foot of snow on the ground already, and it was still coming down hard. The weather channel's estimates were solid for once. Go figure. He'd plow the driveway and road later with his truck, which had a snowplow on the front, but for now, he needed to make a path to whatever the hell had crashed down.

"H-h-hold this," he told Quentin.

Quentin took the flashlight and lit the way. A sweat broke out on Mac's back as he silently cleared the walkway to the fence that separated his house from his junkyard. There was little sense in doing the junkyard itself, not while it was still snowing anyway, so they'd have to trudge through it to get to wherever the problem was. But if he waited with shoveling the path to his house, it would be too much snow to clear by hand. He had a snowblower, of course, but it was a hassle on the small path, and he preferred doing it by hand.

"Holy fuck, that's a *lot* of snow," Quentin commented.

Mac nodded as he put the snow shovel against the fence, then opened it with the key on his keychain. He couldn't see far, but he had an idea of where the noise had come from.

He took the flashlight from Quentin and waded through the snow, Quentin on his heels in the path he'd created.

As soon as he saw, he had to swallow back bile. Out of everything that could have gotten damaged, why did it have to be his shop? Even through the heavy snow that was still coming down, the massive tree branch that had crushed the roof of his shop was clearly visible.

"Oh, damn," Quentin said with a sort of awe in his voice.

The oak tree on the edge of his property had lost one of its lower limbs—a huge branch that had collapsed under the weight of the snow. Dammit, he should've cut that tree down in the fall. He'd seen it getting old, knowing it was a matter of time before it would come down, but he hadn't wanted to deal with it on top of everything else he had going on. He'd figured it would hold for one more season. Well, he'd figured wrong. Damn it all to hell.

When they got closer, Mac inspected the damage. The roof had partly been shattered, but the branch was still resting on top of it, not on the ground. That meant it was unstable, making it dangerous to go anywhere near it. Still, he had to try and salvage what he could.

"Can we drag it off?" Quentin asked.

Mac loved that he tried to help, tried to come up with a solution. "N-n-no. T-too heavy. I n-need my truck, b-but I can't drive here until the s-s-snow has been c-cleared. W-we n-need to wait f-for daylight."

"Is there anything inside we should protect from the snow?"

He sighed. There was no use in trying to keep it a secret now. Quentin would find out anyway. "M-m-my projects."

"Projects? What kind of projects?"

"I m-m-make things. F-from junk."

"Things... You mean like art? Sculptures?"

Mac hesitated. He'd never labeled it as anything else but projects. No one had ever seen them. Not even his mom, since he'd started on them after she passed as a desperate attempt to do something with the pain and grief and rage inside him. Was it worthy enough of being called art?

"I g-g-guess," he said slowly.

Quentin stepped closer and tilted Mac's chin up with his gloved finger. "Will you show it to me when it gets light?"

Mac nodded.

"Do we need to protect them?" Quentin asked again.

Hmm, that wasn't a bad idea, actually. He had some tarp to cover them up as best he could. And if he propped up the roof with some beams, maybe he could prevent the whole shed from tumbling down when he pulled off that tree branch.

"W-w-will you help m-me?" he asked Quentin.

He was rewarded with a quick kiss. "Tell me what to do."

Together they managed to secure most of his sculptures under the thick tarp, though Mac refused to remove the ones that were directly underneath the branch. He was too afraid the entire roof would cave in, crushing whoever was underneath it. If those projects were a total loss, well, so be it. He was already relieved he hadn't lost all of them. Some he had worked on for months.

Quentin proved to be a great help. What he lacked in physical strength, he made up in following instructions to the letter and being stubborn as hell until he'd finished what needed to be done. By the time they had the tarp in place and Mac had raised three sturdy beams that would hopefully provide enough support for the roof, they were exhausted.

"I'm hot and cold at the same time," Quentin said as they plowed through the snow, back to the house. "My upper body is sweating like crazy, but my legs and feet are freezing. I would kill for a big breakfast and a hot bath."

"W-w-which would you l-like first?"

Quentin's delighted smile radiated in the early morning light. "We can take a *bath*? Seriously?"

Mac nodded, his insides doing a happy roll at the word "we." Would Quentin really want to take a bath together? The bathtub was certainly big enough. He'd installed it when his mom was diagnosed, so he'd have enough space to help her get in and out when she'd need help. "The h-hot water is on the b-b-backup generator. S-so is the s-s-stove."

"Best news ever," Quentin declared. "First food, then a bath."

"Y-y-you can c-cook breakfast while I t-t-take a b-bath first."

Quentin spun around to search Mac's face, then broke out into a happy laugh. "You're teasing me! Fucking hell, Mac, you keep surprising me."

Mac smiled as he opened the door for Quentin and let him enter the house first. Lucy barked a happy greeting, then ran outside to do her business.

Quentin took off his gloves, then pulled Mac's head down for a quick kiss. "I love seeing you smile, baby," he said softly, cupping Mac's cheeks with his hands. "You're so stunning when you do."

"N-n-not as b-beautiful as you," Mac whispered.

"You think I'm beautiful?"

"You t-t-take my br-br-breath away."

"On second thought, breakfast can wait," Quentin said, then dragged his mouth down to claim it.

9

Within seconds, he'd stripped himself out of his jacket and boots, noticing with satisfaction as Mac did the same. God, the man had such an amazing body, those big muscles flexing and rippling. The way he'd worked outside, hauling those heavy beams without breaking a sweat... It would've been pure muscle porn had he been shirtless. Quentin could've watched him for hours.

Right now, he had far less patience, desperate as he was to get his hands on him again and to feel those rough hands on his body. He stepped in, put his hands on Mac's chest, and pushed, delighted when Mac let himself be forced with his back against the wall. He had to stand on his toes to kiss him properly. Mac had a couple of inches on him—and he was twice Quentin's size in mass.

Those big hands found Quentin's favorite spot—his ass — cupping both his cheeks and pushing their groins together. What was it about this man that was so damn addictive? Maybe it was because he was so *hungry*, letting Quentin kiss him and kissing back as if he was starving. And the rougher and more dominant Quentin got, the more Mac responded with these intoxicating little whimpers and sighs and those low grunts and groans that shot straight to Quentin's balls. God, he wanted him in the worst way.

He managed to get his hands under Mac's thick hoodie, running them over his chest and back, reveling in the powerful muscles that quivered under his touch. "Fuck, baby, I want you. I want to..."

Just then, his stomach let out a loud growl, and Mac's mouth split into a grin against his. "You w-w-were s-saying?"

Quentin blew out a frustrated sigh. "Dammit."

Mac kissed him one last time, then released him. "B-b-breakfast first, then. P-p-pancakes or french t-toast?"

Quentin's mouth watered, his sexual frustration forgotten. "You make french toast with your homemade bread?" he asked hopefully.

Mac's smile widened as he nodded.

"With scrambled eggs, maybe?"

"Y-y-you really have a b-b-bottomless s-stomach..."

Quentin stepped up and nuzzled Mac's neck, hugging him once more. "Thank you for cooking for me. It makes me feel special."

Mac kissed the top of his head. "Y-y-you're welcome. I l-l-love cooking for you. Makes m-me feel ap-p-preciated."

Huh, how about that? Maybe cooking for him meant as much to Mac as it did to Quentin. He'd never looked at it that way.

Quentin stepped back and, when Mac half turned, slapped him on his ass. "Get to work then, baby. Take care of your man."

He said it spontaneously, but his words suddenly hung heavy in the air. *Your man.* It was a bit much, considering they'd only known each other for, what, two days?

Mac's smile disappeared, and he let out a deep sigh. "W-w-we need t-t-to talk."

Yeah, big surprise there. Holy crap, when would he ever learn not to jump into shit with both feet? He had such a great brain—or so everyone kept telling him—so why couldn't he control his damn impulsivity?

He jammed his hands into the pockets of his jeans. "Yeah, whatever. Save it. I get the message, okay?"

Mac's eyes widened. "N-n-no, y-y-you don't... This is ab-b-bout me, n-not you."

"Right, so it's a variation on 'it's not you, it's me'? Yeah, trust me, I'm familiar with it."

"Oh, Q-quentin..." Mac sighed, and he sounded infinitely sad. "Who h-h-hurt you?"

Asshole, thy name is Justin. But how did he explain that one to Mac without giving it all away? Not that things were looking too peachy now, but he'd hoped for at least a few more days before Mac, too, got tired of him.

"You don't need to explain anything," he told Mac. "I get it, okay?"

When he wanted to walk away, Mac grabbed both his shoulders and made Quentin face him. He did, resentment probably painted all over his face. Mac's tone was kind but firm when he spoke. "S-s-stop. Y-y-you don't unders-s-stand s-shit. I l-l-like you, and I w-want to b-be with you, but I n-need to t-t-tell you something first. N-n-now sit d-down, and I'll m-make breakfast. You're p-p-probably also c-cranky from the h-h-hunger."

He was, but how had Mac figured that out so quickly? He tended to get short-fused when he was running low on fuel, and after working outside for almost two hours to secure Mac's shop, he most certainly was depleted. "I'm sorry," he said.

"'S okay. S-s-sit."

He was gently pushed into a chair, and within a minute, Mac handed him a glass of freshly made orange juice. "D-d-drink. It w-will help your s-sugar level g-g-go up."

He drank, suddenly exhausted. For some weird reason, tears were burning in his eyes. "Thank you."

Mac nodded as he grabbed all kinds of stuff from the fridge and cupboards. Bread was sliced into thick pieces, then coated with a mixture of milk and egg and—Quentin breathed in deeply—cinnamon. Mac heated butter in two pans, then quickly whisked a few eggs, mixing them with herbs and a dollop of cream. Minutes later, the kitchen was filling with delicious aromas, and Quentin's stomach rumbled again, even louder this time. It earned him another smile from Mac, who'd apparently been able to hear it even over the sizzling french toast.

When Mac put the plate of steaming food in front of him, Quentin almost moaned. God, it smelled so good. Mac put sugar and maple syrup on the table, as well as salt and pepper before he, too, sat down.

The first bite of french toast was a taste explosion in Quentin's mouth. "So fucking delicious," he groaned with his mouth full.

They barely spoke, Quentin too focused on shoveling the food into his mouth and Mac apparently content with watching him while enjoying his own breakfast.

"B-b-better?" Mac asked when Quentin had cleared his plate and shoved it back with a contented sigh.

"Yeah. Sorry for being grumpy," Quentin said sheepishly. He did feel rather stupid now that he had food in his stomach. He'd been overreacting a bit, hadn't he? He always forgot what being hangry did to him.

"D-d-do you w-want to take a b-bath now?" Mac asked.

He was so fucking sweet. "Only if we take one together."

"Why d-d-do you t-trust me?"

Quentin had no trouble sensing the emotions behind that loaded question. "I don't know what's going on in your life, Mac, that has made you guarded and gruff, and what has happened to make you need to carry a gun, but I do know this. You're sweet and kind, and you wouldn't hurt me."

Mac stared at him for the longest time, emotions flashing across his face. Disbelief. Confusion. And then hope? "Q-q-quentin, w-w-will you hold m-me? P-p-please?"

He rushed over to where Mac was sitting and pulled the man's head against his chest. Mac's arms came around his waist, and he leaned in, closing his eyes. A rush of warmth filled Quentin's insides. Mac *needed* him. For the first time in his life, someone needed him.

He kissed Mac's head, then laced his fingers through his hair and scratched his scalp. His other hand gripped the man's neck, holding him with enough pressure so he'd feel it.

Mac didn't speak for a long time, and when he did, his voice was muffled from his face still hiding against Quentin. "I've n-never felt accepted b-b-by anyone b-but my m-mom. I...it's..."

Quentin waited with speaking to make sure he wasn't interrupting. "It's okay, baby. I've got you."

"I d-d-don't unders-s-stand," Mac said finally.

Quentin smiled. "That makes two of us. But we'll figure it out, okay? We'll talk, and I promise I won't overreact again."

Mac leaned his head back and looked up at Quentin. "S-s-sure you will. Y-y-you're imp-pulsive. But it's okay."

Quentin's smile widened. "You got me pegged already,

don't you? You're right. I shouldn't make promises I can't keep. Just call me out on it, okay?"

Mac nodded.

"Now, how about that bath? You ready to take that plunge with me?"

MAC WASN'T SCARED of a whole lot of things in life. Crawlers and snakes were not an issue for him, and while he'd never flown on an airplane, he figured he'd be okay with it. Pain didn't faze him, and neither did death—not after he'd watched his mom die peacefully, a smile on her face. He was scared to hell of public speaking, but since that was relatively easy to avoid, it wasn't something he had to face often anymore.

But right now, watching Quentin take off his hoodie, then start on the buttons of his jeans, he was fucking *terrified*. What if he fucked up and did something wrong or accidentally hurt Quentin with his strength? What if Quentin wanted more and Mac would suck at it? Well, maybe sucking wasn't the right expression here, as that would certainly be involved, but in a good way, hopefully.

Come to think of it, what if he couldn't bring him pleasure? The women he'd slept with hadn't been exactly overwhelmed with his...*skills*. No wonder, since he'd had no idea what to do, except emulating the porn he'd seen. But he'd never viewed gay porn. He was pretty sure of the anatomy involved, but what if he was bad at it? And didn't you need to prepare for anal sex?

"Mac, where did you go in your head?"

Mac looked up, shocked to find Quentin standing in front of him, dressed in only boxers. He swallowed at the sight of Quentin's beautiful body, shivering in the cold, his nipples hard—and his cock as well.

"I'm s-s-so f-fucking s-s-s-scared."

Quentin stepped in, cupped his cheeks. "Oh, baby, what are you scared of? Nothing's gonna happen unless you want it to."

"I w-w-want it s-s-so much. B-b-but what if I s-s-suck at it?"

Quentin's eyes lit up, his mind undoubtedly jumping to the same lame association Mac himself had earlier, but he composed himself again.

Mac sighed. "G-go ahead. M-m-make the joke."

"I was gonna refrain," Quentin protested. With a smile, he raised his lips and kissed Mac. "But seriously, baby, try not to fret, okay? We'll figure this out, whatever this is."

Mac closed his eyes for a second, inhaled deeply. "P-p-promise me that w-w-whatever we do, w-w-we'll make it g-g-g-good for you."

Quentin seemed to hesitate, then kissed him again, a sweet, lingering kiss. "I promise." He released Mac's face. "Now, can we please get a move on before I turn into a fucking popsicle?"

Mac quickly got rid of his clothes, folding them neatly and putting them on the chair in the corner of the spacious bathroom.

"You're not shy about your body," Quentin remarked, ogling him without any effort to conceal it. "Not that there's any reason to, because hot damn, you're hot as fuck. Look at you..." Hungry eyes perused Mac's body, and he took it gladly, his cock growing rock hard. "God, you're fucking perfect. One day, I hope you'll tell me why you decided to take the piercings and the tattoos, but for now, I just wanna get wet with you."

He got into the tub first, smiling when Quentin was unashamedly checking out his body all over again, then watched with similar interest as Quentin lowered himself between his legs and leaned back. Mac wrapped his arms and legs around him, wanting to feel and touch him everywhere. He'd never felt so close to another person in his life, and it was exhilarating.

They sank into the water, only their heads sticking out. Mac's body and brain were going into overdrive, trying to process all the experiences. Quentin's smooth body was grazing against his much harder and rougher one in the best way. His legs were wrapped around Quentin, whose hands rested on Mac's thighs. Mac rubbed circles on that flat stomach with the soft skin. Quentin didn't have a hair on his body, except for some light pubic hair. It made the contrast between them even bigger, and fuck if Mac didn't love it.

"This is serious the best tub I've ever seen," Quentin said with a sigh.

"I o-o-ordered it for my m-mom when s-she got ill. It h-h-helped her with the pain."

"Did you grow up in this house?"

"Yeah. It w-w-was my m-mom's. Her d-dad owned the j-junkyard."

"Mmm. What was your mom like?"

Mac couldn't help but snicker. "W-w-we're naked in a t-tub, and y-you wanna t-talk about my m-m-mom? B-b-buzzk-killer."

Quentin half turned his head and sent him a cheeky smile. "I thought it might help you relax."

"If b-by relax, you m-mean s-s-soft, that's n-not gonna happen. N-n-not even the m-mention of m-my mom could m-m-make me l-lose my h-hard-on."

"You're such an enigma, Mac, you know that? You're shy

and insecure one minute, and then you go and say something like that. Not that I blame you, for the sentiment or the hard-on." Quentin took Mac's hand and put it on his own cock, which was also still as hard as Mac had seen it before. "As you can feel, I have a similar problem."

Mac's breath caught with a sharp inhale. "C-c-can I t-t-touch?"

Quentin dragged his head down for a quick kiss. "Would I put your hand there if you couldn't? Do anything you want, baby. I'm your willing victim."

Mac's left hand wrapped around Quentin's cock. It was firm and thick in his hands, his size bigger than Mac would have expected, considering his slim build. He gave it a squeeze, delighted when Quentin shuddered in his arms.

"Fuck, your hand feels good around my cock, so rough and strong."

Emboldened, Mac let his right hand explore Quentin's chest farther. Judging by the little moan he let out when Mac flicked his nipples, that was a sensitive area. He also seemed to like it when Mac used his beard to scratch his neck. Meanwhile, his left hand kept pressure on Quentin's cock, making slow, deliberate strokes.

He longed to caress that perfect round ass or see what his balls felt like, but he couldn't—not in his current position, at least. Instead, he circled Quentin's slit with this thumb, alternating with pressure, soft caresses, and little scratches with his nail. The little whimper falling from Quentin's lips had him smile with satisfaction.

"You like touching me, baby?"

"G-g-god, yes."

"What else would you like to do to me?"

"C-c-can I m-make you c-c-come?"

Quentin moaned when Mac squeezed his cock again,

down and up and down again, keeping perfect pressure on it. "Fuck, yes. Make me come, baby. Make me come so fucking hard."

He didn't need any more motivation but ramped up his strokes. Quentin bucked against him. He was fucking into Mac's hand now, lifting his hips and seeking more friction.

"Oh, fuck...harder, Mac, please..."

He liked it *rough*, Mac remembered. So he found Quentin's nipple, plucked it, then rolled it between his thumb and index finger. He did the same to his left nipple. He kept jerking him off, squeezing that perfect cock hard and fast.

"Ungh!" Quentin groaned. "Ohfuckohfuckohfuck... coming. I'm...*Oh!*"

His cock pulsed in Mac's hands, spilling his load. Mac held Quentin's body as he trembled with the second pulse, then went slack. Mac pressed kisses on his head, his ears, his neck, anywhere he could reach with his lips.

"That was...yeah. Pretty damn perfect, baby."

"I'm s-s-sorry I d-d-didn't s-suck at it," Mac finally released the joke he'd been keeping in all that time.

It took a second before it landed, but then Quentin burst out in laughter. "That's fucking perfect. You thought of that minutes ago, didn't you?"

Mac grinned. "I d-d-did. Was w-waiting for the right m-moment."

Quentin pushed against Mac's arms and legs, and he untangled himself. He turned around, then sat on his knees in the bathtub, facing Mac. His smile transitioned into a burning look that shot straight to Mac's balls. "I want to make you come too, but not here. Wanna continue this on the couch, where it's nice and warm?"

10

Quentin didn't know what he wanted to do: kiss Mac silly, explore that fucking perfect body of his, or suck him off. Maybe he could do all three? He climbed out of the tub, strangely touched when Mac wrapped a fluffy towel around him first before grabbing one for himself. This man was such a caretaker, a nurturer. He was everything Quentin had ever wanted in a man...except for his body type.

No, strike that. Mac's body was hot as fuck, and just watching him made Quentin horny as all get-out despite his recent orgasm. It was more the fact that a man like him, a man that size, usually wouldn't...submit. Though truth be told, so far, Mac seemed more than okay with Quentin taking the lead, but maybe that was because he was so new at this? Surely once he was past that stage of figuring out which tab went into which slot, he'd conclude out he was the tab...not the slot.

Did that mean he shouldn't even try? No. Right now, even a few days with Mac were preferable over nothing at all. Being with him made Quentin strangely happy. Content, for lack of a better word. The way Mac cooked for him and took care of him brought a kind of peace to his soul he hadn't felt in a long time.

"Q-q-quentin..." Mac said softly.

Quentin's head came up.

"D-d-did you ch-change your mind?"

"Fuck, no. Just lost in my head for a sec."

"You l-l-looked sad."

There was so much he could say to that, so much he *should* say, maybe. But the words wouldn't come. Instead, he closed the distance between them, grabbed Mac's head, and pulled him down for a kiss. He loved how Mac let him manhandle him, even though he could easily resist. So he took Mac's mouth and kissed him deeply.

Mac's hands stayed on Quentin's shoulders, which was absolutely not where he wanted them. Nope, they belonged on his ass, pushing their bodies closer together. He unhooked his towel, then did the same to Mac's. Mac groaned into his mouth as his hard cock sprung free.

"Your hands...on my ass..." he panted between kisses. When Mac didn't respond fast enough, he took his hands and placed them right where he wanted them. That reminded him that he hadn't touched Mac's bare ass yet, so he lowered his hands there, and holy cow, his ass was full and firm and fit perfectly in Quentin's hands.

When he squeezed again, Mac jerked, rutting his cock against Quentin's belly, smearing precum all over him. How would he respond if Quentin...? Only one way to find out. He removed his right hand from that luscious globe, then let it dip into Mac's crack from the top till he reached...

Mac moaned loudly and gave another jerk with his hips,

then spread his legs farther. Now, *that* was interesting. Quentin repeated his move, his reward another low groan. Mac was rather sensitive there, wasn't he?

Fuck, he wished he had lube. It hadn't even crossed his mind to bring any. He'd never been the one-night-stand guy, and he'd figured that if he met someone, he'd simply buy it. Who the fuck would have predicted he'd get stuck in a snowstorm with the hottest guy ever? He couldn't go too far without lube, though, not with an anal virgin like Mac—at least, Quentin assumed he was.

He swiped his hole again, slightly pressing with his thumb, and Mac shivered. Quentin bit the man's lower lip, slowly pulled it out, then let go. "You like that, baby? You like it when I play with your hole?"

Mac's response was a quivering, "S-s-so g-good. M-more..." that made Quentin's insides go liquid. Something about that big man begging got to him, every single time. He was about to propose moving into the living room, since he was getting chilly, when Mac's phone rang.

Quentin wasn't expecting him to answer it, so he was surprised when Mac immediately released him. "I h-h-have to g-get this," he simply said, and with one regret-filled look at Quentin, he walked over to his jeans and grabbed his phone.

For a second, Quentin was distracted by his ass and the cock jutting out, but then he frowned. Why the hell was Mac picking up his phone while they were making out? Something was seriously wrong with his priorities, dammit.

Mac answered the call with a grunt, then listened. "N-n-not t-till it s-stops s-s-snowing," he finally said.

Who the hell was calling him right now, and why was Mac so nervous he was tripping over every word? His mood gone, Quentin got dressed. He didn't miss the disappointed expression in Mac's eyes but ignored it. If Mac had wanted to continue, he shouldn't have picked up. Apparently, it meant a whole lot less to him than it did to Quentin because there was no way *he* would've picked up. That was what voicemail was for. He didn't look back as he stalked into the living room.

When Mac came into the room as well a little later, he refused to face him, instead pretending to study the books in his self-help section.

"I h-h-have to g-go."

Now he did turn around. "You what? You can't go out now, not in this weather."

"It s-stopped snowing."

"But we're...it's..." Quentin sputtered.

Mac's face tightened. "P-p-please, Qu-quentin, don't b-be angry with m-m-me. I c-can exp-p-plain everything but n-not now."

Something in Mac's face told Quentin he was telling the truth and that he regretted leaving as much as Quentin did. It made him feel like an ass for jumping to conclusions again.

"What do you have to do?"

"C-clear the r-r-road. Then p-plow someone's d-driveway and h-haul off a t-t-tree that's c-come down."

"So it's a job," Quentin said.

Mac hesitated. "N-n-not quite."

"That's part of what you want to tell me?" Quentin understood.

Mac nodded.

"Okay, I'll come with you, then."

Mac's eyes widened in surprise. Then a smile broke out on his face. "Th-thank you. I'd l-love that."

"Okay, so I'll dress warm. Anything else I need to know?"

"B-b-bring your gun."

Bring his *gun*? What the ever-loving fuck was going on? Mac looked at him as if he expected Quentin to either freak out or pack his bags and leave. He'd reached his quota of overreactions for today, so he decided to bite back his response. "Okay."

Mac's relief showed him his answer meant a lot to him.

"Do we bring Lucy?" Quentin asked.

Mac shook his head. "N-n-never. She g-guards the house."

The man had multiple guns, a dog that needed to guard his house, and a property that was completely fenced off with some serious quality fences and locks. What the hell was Mac involved in? It started to look really bad, and yet Quentin couldn't shake the feeling that Mac wasn't the bad guy here. Despite how he'd seen people react to him and talk about him, his gut said Mac was on the right side of the law here. Still, he was curious as fuck about what was going on.

They both bundled up, and Mac packed some things from the kitchen into a backpack. They made their way to the garage, where Mac's truck was parked. Mac opened it and started the engine. "S-s-sit inside t-to stay w-warm. I g-g-gotta grab some e-equipment."

Quentin nodded and got into the car. Mac came back, hauling a chain saw and a large toolbox that he put in the back. He walked back out again, then returned with some chains and big bungee cords he threw into the back of the truck as well.

Mac only needed to clear the first bit of driveway manually so he could back out and turn, and then he was able to use the yellow snowplow attached to the front of his truck.

With an ease that showed years of practice, Mac cleared the driveway to his house, then the road that connected the street his property was on to the main route.

"Are there any other houses on this road?"

"N-no. The r-road circles around f-from route 189. There's a p-p-property n-next to m-mine, but it's b-been abandoned for years."

"Is that why you have to remove the snow yourself?"

Mac shrugged. "They'd p-probably d-do it eventually, b-b-but I can't wait for that. I always d-d-do it myself."

The sky was bright blue, making it painfully clear how much snow had fallen—literally, since Quentin's head hurt from the reflection of the snow. That had to be why Mac was wearing dark sunglasses that shielded his eyes.

"There's an extra p-pair of sung-g-glasses in the g-glove compartment."

Thank fuck for that. Quentin put them on and let out a sigh of relief. Much better.

The snow was both beautiful and intimidating as fuck. If he was staying in this area, he'd really need to learn how to handle storms like this because apparently, they were par for the course.

The main road had already been cleared—sort of. A thin layer of snow that looked slippery as hell still covered it, but Mac's big truck had no issue with it. Quentin thought of his sweet, old Corolla and shuddered at the thought of having to drive that on a road like this. Even with his new tires, he'd have slipped off the icy road in no time. This was four-wheel-drive country, obviously.

"We're h-here," Mac said. He turned into the driveway of a red farmhouse, several buildings visible from the road. Mac set the snowplow down and started clearing the driveway. It took him a few times going back and forth to remove all the snow, which formed two impressive walls along the driveway now.

When they drove closer to the house, Quentin spotted the tree that had come down. He had no idea what type of tree it was—or had been, more accurately—but it was huge, and it now lay sprawled on the ground, half of it on the roof of a side building painted in that same charming red.

"What was in that shed?" he asked Mac.

Mac sighed. "G-g-garage. His t-truck is in there and p-p-probably his t-t-tractor and some other e-e-equipment."

"That's why you had to clear the driveway," Quentin said, "because he's basically snowed in."

Mac parked the truck close to the half-collapsed structure. "Q-q-quentin, b-be careful. W—w-willis, he's n-not a nice m-m-man. He's b-bitter. Don't l-let him g-g-get to you."

Before Quentin could say anything, a dog started barking, and the front door of the house opened. The man walking outside was in his sixties, Quentin estimated, wearing rugged jeans and boots and a similar winter jacket, beanie, and gloves as Mac was sporting. Maybe everyone bought them at the same store?

The look the man sent Mac was anything but friendly. It was the same thinly veiled disgust Quentin had seen on that receptionist's face. Then the man faced Quentin, and surprise registered all over his face. "Who the hell are you?"

Quentin bit back his initial biting response and stuck out his hand. He'd try it with honey first. See if that would appease the man. He could always add a dose of vinegar and nastiness later. "I'm Quentin, and it's so nice to meet you. I'm a friend of Mac's."

As he had counted on, the man had taken his hand out

of reflex, but as soon as Quentin has declared himself a friend of Mac's, he dropped it like a hot coal with a distinctly impolite grunt. Okay, then. Mac had not been lying about the *bitter* part, but he omitted the *rude-as-fuck* aspect.

"You need to remove that tree," Willis snapped at Mac.

"How m-m-much?"

Quentin didn't understand the question, but Willis did because his eyes narrowed. "Fifty."

Mac huffed. "T-t-two h-hundred."

"That's way too much for a job like this. You're as greedy as your old man."

"T-t-two h-h-hundred. And if it t-t-takes me m-m-more than t-t-two h-hours, it's g-gonna be m-more."

"It's a fucking rip-off, and you know it, but it's not like I can do anything, since my truck is in there. Get the fuck to it, then."

With those charming exit words, Willis stalked back into the house, slamming the front door shut. One look at Mac's face dispelled Quentin of the notion of asking for clarification. That would come later, he assumed. For now, they had a job to do.

It took them three hours to take down the tree, Quentin following Mac's instructions to the letter. The man knew what he was doing, and he himself ranked below amateur on shit like this. So he did as he was told, holding branches up so Mac could cut them off, hauling smaller parts off to the side, and handing Mac whatever he was asking for. He also took pictures with Mac's phone every few minutes at Mac's request, though he had no idea why Mac had asked for those.

Mac was careful, making sure every part he sawed off was tied down to something and wouldn't come down on the garage—or on them. They both wore hard hats over their beanies, plus protective glasses. Quentin was sweating his ass off, and his muscles were already aching after the first half hour, but he dug deep and kept going.

An hour in, Mac signaled for a break and handed Quentin a sandwich he'd brought from home. Quentin stuck his tongue out at the sly smile on Mac's face, clearly a not-so-subtle dig at him getting cranky when he was hungry. The hot tea Mac had made was a delight as well.

When the entire tree was removed, they stood side by side, studying the damage. Mac took off his hard hat and scratched his head. "The whole r-r-roof needs t-to be r-r-replaced. That's g-g-gonna cost him."

Quentin winced. They'd seen the rather extensive destruction one huge tree branch had done to the man's truck—Willis was gonna be even madder than he'd been before. His tractor had been parked in the back and seemed to be okay, but Mac had said it looked like some equipment had gotten wrecked as well.

Rustling sounded behind him, and there stood Willis, his face resembling a thunderstorm. "What the fuck did you do to my roof? It wasn't this damaged before, asshole. You made it worse!"

He took a menacing step toward Mac, and at that moment, Quentin realized two things. The first was that Mac was the victim here. Dammit, Mac had fucking *known* this Willis asshole would make a claim like this. That was why he'd asked Quentin to take pics. For whatever reason, people in this town treated Mac like dirt and were taking advantage of him.

The second was that Quentin wasn't gonna stand by and watch that happen. He had no idea what he and Mac were, if they were together, if they had even the possibility of a future, but he did know that he was protective of this kind, sweet man.

Mac tried to say something but got stuck on the first consonant, his face tight with frustration. For the first time since he'd met him, Quentin interrupted him. He put a hand on Mac's arm to support him and kept his tone polite, if icy. "You're mistaken, Mr. Willis. All the damage you see was done by the tree, not by the removal."

"What the fuck do you know? Stay out of this and go back to California. You have no idea what you're getting into."

California, huh? Word about him had gotten around fast, apparently. "What I know is that I took pictures of the situation before, during, and after we removed that tree. That will clearly show nothing we did made it worse."

Willis's face distorted with fury. He came closer to Quentin, raising a fist in his face. "You need to stay the hell out of this, you faggot piece of shit."

Quentin felt Mac move but pushed him back with the hand he still had on his arm. Homophobic insults were nothing new, and the sad reality was that he'd learned to ignore those over the years. He kept his anger for the stuff that hurt way worse.

"My sexual preferences have nothing to do with this, Mr. Willis, so I suggest you keep them out of this. Other than that, we are done here. We're leaving, right now, and just so we're clear. You *will* pay Mac the three hundred dollars you owe him for this job."

"*Pay* him?" Willis's fury transformed into a sneer. "That just shows how little you know. I ain't paying him shit. He's still paying off the twenty grand he owed me."

"A-a-after t-today, f-f-four thousand f-f-four hundred,"

Mac said. "I will s-s-send you the r-r-receipt." He grabbed Quentin by his arm and dragged him to the truck.

Quentin kept his mouth shut until they were on the main road. "What the hell is that asshole talking about, Mac?"

11

This was it. This was the moment he'd been dreading ever since meeting Quentin. This was the moment he had to open up about his biggest shame.

"Q-q-quentin..." He couldn't find the words. How could he even hope to make him understand? God, he'd been *fearless*, confronting Willis like that, as if the man hadn't been three times his age, twice his size, and mean as hell. That faggot remark... Mac had wanted to beat the man up just for that, but Quentin hadn't even seemed shaken.

Quentin's hand came to rest on his thigh, and he shot him a quick look sideways. "Here's what we're gonna do. We're gonna go home. You're gonna make us some nice, hot lunch while I get to watch your sexy ass, and after that, when we're both warm and full and in a better mood, you can explain. And, Mac, I promise I will listen, okay?"

He nodded, his insides flooding with relief. How was it that Quentin, who had known him for such a short time, seemed to feel exactly what he needed? Quentin squeezed his thigh and kept his hand there for the entire ride home. Mac wasn't sure if it was meant as comfort or a proprietary claim kind of thing, but either one worked for him.

He made them omelets filled with fresh spinach, mushrooms, diced fresh tomatoes, some herbs and feta on top. Quentin devoured it—no surprise there. Mac loved watching him eat, since he so clearly enjoyed the food. He hadn't been kidding when he'd said he ate a lot. He stowed away as much as Mac did, and Quentin's body was, like, half Mac's size.

When he'd cleared his plate, Quentin looked at him, his eyes pensive. "Can we expect similar calls and jobs like this morning for the rest of the day?"

Mac very much wanted to say no, but it was a real possibility. Not only was he one of the few handymen in town, hell, even in the area, but he still owed a bunch of people, so they took every opportunity to let him work it off. "M-m-maybe."

"Do you need to open your... I don't know what to call it, the junkyard?"

"N-n-no. It's S-sunday."

Judging by the flash of surprise on Quentin's face, he hadn't even realized that. "Jeez, I totally lost track of the days. I need to call my mom. Anyway, would it maybe be better to talk tonight, when we know we won't get interrupted again?"

Mac sighed, both relieved and anxious to postpone the talk again. "P-probably."

"Okay, so that's what we'll do. If you get any more calls, I'll come with you, okay?"

"Thank you f-f-for speaking f-for me w-with Willis. S-s-stress w-w-w-orsens my st-st-stutter."

Quentin got up and put both their plates in the sink, then walked back and kissed Mac's head. "I know, baby. You're welcome."

Half an hour later, he got another call. Rick Monroe wasn't as much of an asshole as Willis, so at least he'd be treated with cold indifference rather than outright hate and disgust.

"What are we doing?" Quentin asked, grabbing two health bars to take with him while Mac was filling up a thermos with hot chocolate.

A wave of emotions rolled through Mac. When was the last time he'd been part of a "we"? Not since his mom had died. He swallowed back the lump in his throat. "W-w-we're t-towing a truck. He r-ran it off the r-road."

"Okay," Quentin said. "Let's go."

They didn't speak in the car, but it was a comfortable silence, not one of those periods where Mac would either wreck his brain trying to come up with something to say or would feel helplessly humiliated because he couldn't manage to say anything. Quentin loved talking to him, that much had become clear, but he was happy to enjoy silence too.

Monroe hadn't been exaggerating when he'd said his truck was a total loss. Monroe must have been speeding, spinning out of control in the bend, and he'd done a three-sixty by the looks of it before ending up against a tree.

Mac backed his truck up so he could attach a cable to Monroe's wrecked Silverado. What a waste. That car would've had a lot more miles in it if it hadn't run smack dab into that tree. The engine had to be toast after a hit like that.

When he got out, one look at the twisted front axel confirmed his previous diagnosis that the car was beyond saving. Both wheels stood at an odd angle, and little was left of the grill and the hood.

Monroe jerked his chin up as a greeting. "Mac."

Mac merely nodded as he made his way to the car. He walked around it to see what could be salvaged. It was a common model here, so that would help. The back tires were still good, as well as the exhaust—probably. He'd hit the tree straight on without getting stuck in a ditch, so the underside of the car would probably be okay. The engine itself was a goner. The best he could hope for were some spare parts, but most of it would be compromised.

"F-four h-h-hundred," he told Monroe.

"You sure about that? Seems to me it's worth more than that."

Mac sighed. He hated the stress of haggling over the price so much that he usually just gave in to save himself the frustration and embarrassment.

"What makes you think it's worth more?" Quentin asked with cool confidence as if he knew exactly what he was talking about.

"Well, it's...it's, erm, a relatively new truck, and he should be able to salvage a lot of it...and who the hell are you, exactly?"

With that outburst, it became crystal clear how Monroe had run his truck off the road. The alcohol smell was still strong on his breath. Fucking asshole. He already had two priors for DUIs, so a third one would cost him dearly. And still nobody in town hated *him* or called him names.

Quentin looked sideways and met his eyes. At first, Mac didn't understand the unspoken question, but then he remembered Monroe's rude question about who Quentin was...and he got it. He didn't care. Strike that. He cared a *lot*

—about Quentin and what they could have together. What he didn't give two shits about was this town or the people in it. This would just be one more strike against him for people who were always actively looking for more reasons to hate him. And so he nodded and smiled at Quentin.

Quentin smiled back at him, his eyes sparkling as if they shared something special and intimate—and maybe they did.

"I'm Mac's boyfriend," he said calmly. "And I'm also the guy who's gonna speak up when he's being treated like shit."

My god, he was fearless. And the power of that simple word...*boyfriend*. How could he ever have imagined what that would do to him, being *claimed* like that. It filled him with power, with warmth, with a sense of freedom he hadn't felt in forever. Mac beamed.

Monroe scoffed. "And what the hell did you wanna do about that?"

Quentin crossed his arms. "For starters, we could decide we're not interested in your car. We could go right back home and leave you here to find an alternative solution. I'm pretty sure that would end up costing you a lot more money than Mac's offer. So you can either accept his offer and get your car towed, and he'll drop you off wherever you want to go after, or you can continue being an asshole, and we'll leave you here to figure out something else. Which is it gonna be?"

Monroe's mouth actually dropped open for a second, and it was the sweetest feeling ever. The man swallowed back whatever angry response had been his first impulse. "I'll take his offer," was the curt reply.

"Good," Quentin said, and Mac wanted to kiss him, then hug him until that sensation inside him that felt like it was gonna explode had dissipated.

He didn't say a word, however, merely sent Quentin a look stuffed with everything he couldn't put into words. Maybe he didn't have to. Quentin winked at him with a sweet smile that spoke volumes.

Mac hooked up Monroe's truck and carefully pulled it off the tree and onto the road until he could hook it up to the tow. By the time he was done, he was soaked to the bone from trudging through the deep snow, though his boots had kept his feet warm and dry.

He was glad his truck had three seats in the front, and Quentin huddled close to him, which Mac didn't mind at all. They dropped off Monroe first, but not after Mac had him sign a receipt for the money. On the ride home, Quentin stuck close to Mac, leaning against him.

Lucy greeted them with happy licks and sniffs.

"D-d-damn, I'm c-cold," Mac said, shivering as he took his boots off.

"The power is back on," Quentin said. "Thank fuck. Let's get you out of these wet clothes."

Mac smiled at his fussing. "It's j-j-just my j-jeans."

"I don't care. Take them off so we can warm you up. Do you want to take a shower?"

"I'm f-fine. J-just need d-dry pants."

"Well, take them off, then. I'll grab you a towel and dry sweats."

God, he was so cute, being all protective and taking care of Mac. He didn't really need a towel, but he wasn't gonna say no to Quentin coming to his aid. He pulled off his wet jeans and hung them over a chair to dry. Quentin came back with a towel, kneeled at Mac's feet, and rubbed his legs. They weren't even that wet, more like clammy and cold, but the gesture was so sweet it made Mac's insides swirl.

Quentin carefully dried both his legs. "Is that better?"

"M-m-much." Mac made no effort to hide his hardening cock. Why would he? The effect Quentin had on him wasn't something he wanted to be ashamed of, ever.

"Can I grab a pair of sweats from your closet?" Quentin asked. "I didn't want to go rummaging in there without your permission."

"S-s-sure. I h-have no s-secrets f-f-rom you."

Quentin slowly rose to his feet. "I think we both know that's not true, but I appreciate the sentiment. Be right back."

Mac sighed. Quentin was right. Mac's secrets were standing between them—or rather, his shame was. What if Quentin never wanted anything to do with him after he'd confessed to the truth? Then again, he'd stuck with him so far, even after everything he'd witnessed. Maybe Mac should give the guy some credit for having more depth than walking out at the first sign of trouble.

He put on the warm sweat pants, mulling it over in his head. Quentin watched him silently as Mac heated water for tea and grabbed some cookies. He gave Lucy some dog treats and set the tea and cookies near the couch, where he curled up in the corner with his back against the armrest and his legs stretched out on the couch.

Quentin hadn't said a word, but he was looking a tad pale. No wonder, with the physical exertion he'd been through today. Mac was feeling his muscles, and he was used to it. Quentin was very much not, and yet when they'd gotten home, he'd taken care of Mac first. He held out his arms to Quentin, who immediately took him up on the unspoken offer and climbed onto the couch. He settled between Mac's legs, turned onto his side, and lay his head on Mac's chest.

"Damn..." He sighed as Mac pulled a blanket over both of them. He snuggled even deeper into Mac's side.

"S-s-so," Mac said. "B-b-boyfriend?"

12

When he woke up, Quentin was comfortable and toasty. His cheek was resting on something warm and soft, while he felt wonderfully safe being held in strong arms... His eyes shot open. Where the hell was he?

Mac. He was in Mac's arms, on the couch. He must have fallen asleep. No wonder, as his body had been about to shut down in protest at the utter torture he'd subjected it to. Even now, as he was barely awake, every muscle in his body hurt, and he let out a groan.

The hard body beneath him shifted a bit. God, what time was it? How long had he been sleeping? "You awake?" he whispered.

"I w-w-wasn't sleeping," Mac said, amusement lacing his voice. "You w-w-were."

"Oh." He rubbed his eyes, yawning. "How long was I out?"

"T-t-two hours."

His head shot up. Mac gazed at him with warm eyes. "I was asleep on you for two hours? Why the hell didn't you wake me, or you know, dump me on the couch and do something else?"

Mac looked almost insulted. "Why w-w-would I d-do that? I l-like holding you."

This man. This wonderful, sweet man. "I wanna kiss you badly right now, but I really need something to drink first."

"I d-drank your t-t-tea," Mac said.

Quentin shot him a look of warning. "Stay right here. Don't move. I'll be right back."

He untangled himself from the blanket and from Mac, shivering in the cold air that hit his body. "On second thought, maybe you could light the fireplace?" he said sheepishly. "I would, but I have no idea how to and would rather not set the whole place on fire."

Mac grinned. "B-b-better not."

Quentin quickly relieved himself, then drank a glass of water and made himself a new cup of tea. That, at least, he knew how to do. "Did you eat all the cookies too?" he called out to Mac.

"Of c-course not. I know b-b-better than t-to come b-between you and your f-f-food."

Smart man.

When he walked back to the couch, Mac had gotten the fireplace going, the crackling from the burning wood a lovely homey sound. Quentin put his tea down and grabbed a cookie from the plate Mac had brought in earlier.

"Mmm, these are so good," he said with his mouth full. He lowered himself onto the couch, wincing as his muscles protested.

"S-s-sore?" Mac asked.

"Yeah. My body is not used to this kind of work."

He finished his cookie as Mac sat down next to him and grabbed his feet, turning Quentin so his feet ended up on

Mac's lap. Seconds later, strong fingers dug into the cramped muscles of his feet and calves, and Quentin moaned in a combination of pleasure and pain.

"G-g-good?" Mac asked.

"Orgasmic. Hot damn, you have magical hands. I gotta put these to good use."

Mac smiled, but his eyes held sadness as well, and Quentin sobered. He put his hands on top of Mac's. "But first, we talk."

"I c-c-can t-talk and m-massage," Mac said.

"You like doing something with your hands while you talk?"

Mac nodded.

"Okay."

For a few minutes, they sat, Mac rubbing Quentin's feet and calves and Quentin patiently waiting for Mac to share his story. He would, Quentin was sure of that, but he apparently needed a little time to organize his thoughts or find the words.

Finally, Mac let out a sigh. "I'm n-not good at t-t-telling stories. M-maybe you c-can ask m-me questions?"

"Hmm, okay. How about you give me the two-sentence summary, and I'll ask about the details?"

Mac closed his eyes, and his chest rose with a deep breath. "M-m-my f-father is in p-prison for f-fraud. He s-s-swindled h-half the t-town out of m-money. I'm t-t-trying to p-p-pay back what he t-t-took."

Quentin's mouth dropped open. Out of everything he'd expected to hear, this didn't even come close.

Mac sat with his eyes closed, his brows furrowed, his shoulders up to his ears, his hands still on Quentin's feet. God, he looked like he expected a hit, like a little kid who was waiting for someone to lash out at him.

"Oh, Mac..." The words fell from Quentin's lips in an almost desperate sigh. "Oh, baby..."

He needed to feel him, to show him it was okay, they were okay. How could they not be after Mac had just revealed what kind of man he was? One who was honorable to his very core. And so he took Mac's hands and put them aside, then climbed onto his lap as Mac's eyes opened wide, his mouth a startled O. He wrapped his arms around Mac, laid his head on his shoulder, and nuzzled his neck.

It took a second for Mac to adjust, and then those big arms folded around Quentin and pulled him close. Mac let his cheek rest on Quentin's head, and for minutes they sat like that, quiet.

"How much did he take?" Quentin finally asked.

"Three hundred th-th-ousand, j-j-just in this area. But he'd d-d-done it before, we f-f-found out."

"Oh, god. How?"

"R-r-resort. He t-told them he had b-big inv-v-vestors. They c-c-could b-buy in, m-make f-four times their m-money b-b-b-back."

"He let them believe they were investing in a resort that was being built?" Quentin checked.

Mac hummed his affirmation.

"Why are you paying it back when he took it?"

"B-b-because m-m-my name was on the p-papers. I w-was eighteen, and m-my mom was already s-sick, and I t-t-trusted him when he t-t-told me to s-sign stuff. He s-s-said it was t-to protect the h-house if we r-r-ran into d-debt for my m-mom's medical b-bills."

Slowly, the pieces of the puzzle started to fall into place. "But he got convicted because you could prove you acted in good faith."

This time, it took minutes before Mac answered, but Quentin stubbornly waited, holding on to him.

"N-n-n-no. I g-got convicted t-t-too. I s-s-spent two years in p-p-prison."

Mac whispered the words, barely audible, but they stabbed Quentin in his heart. "Why? Why would you get sentenced for something you didn't do?"

"The p-p-people in t-town w-w-were so angry. N-n-no one s-s-stood up as my c-c-character witness. Only m-m-my mom, but the judge s-s-said she was b-biased."

"And you've been paying people back ever since."

"O-o-only t-t-ten thousand t-to go."

Quentin did a quick calculation in his head, then frowned. "It took you twenty years, well, eighteen since you got out of prison, to pay off everything?"

"N-n-no. I had to p-p-pay my mom's m-m-medical bills f-first. I s-started paying p-p-people off after she d-died and the b-bills were p-paid, eight years ago. H-h-he had a p-partner, so I'm only p-p-paying half of what h-h-he took."

"But..." Quentin let go of Mac so he could lean back and meet his eyes. "Where did the money go your dad took?"

"G-g-gambling. He g-gambled it all away. H-his share, and his a-a-asshole took th-th-the other half." Mac's eyes filled with tears. This big, strong man crumbled before Quentin's eyes. "M-m-my mom n-needed him, and ins-s-stead, he d-d-did this to her, t-t-to me, to us."

"But you were there for her," Quentin said. He grabbed Mac's face, made him look at him. "You were the one she leaned on. What a man you are, Mac McCain."

"Aug-gustus. M-m-my real n-name is Aug-g-gustus. P-people s-started calling me M-m-mac 'cause I always g-g-got stuck on m-my own name. And saying G-g-g-gus is r-really hard f-f-for me."

"Augustus," Quentin said, still holding Mac's cheeks. "What a beautiful name for a beautiful man. You're a good man, Augustus. A damn good man."

Mac's eyes spilled over. "N-no one has c-called me that in a l-l-long time," he whispered.

Maybe there was more that needed to be said, but Quentin was done with words for now. Mac—no, *Augustus*, he corrected himself—had just revealed the most painful thing ever. Going to prison for something he had no part in was one thing, but knowing his dad screwed over everyone in his town? That was a mighty big burden for a young man to carry. Yet he'd done it. He'd been there for his mom, had held his head high, and had been working his ass off to pay off his father's debts. No, he'd said enough to make Quentin understand.

"Baby," he said, then dropped a soft kiss on Augustus's lips. "If you were worried I'd see you differently, you were right. I do. You are the most honorable man I have ever met, and what you just told me makes me want to hug you and kiss you and do all kinds of things to you until we both run out of steam."

Augustus licked his lips, his tongue reminding Quentin of all the places he wanted that wet heat. On his lips. On his nipples. On his cock... How would Augustus look with his mouth around Quentin's cock? Or with the remnants of his cum in his beard? God, that was so fucking hot.

"Q-q-quentin." Augustus licked his lips again. "I want to..."

"Tell me what you want, baby. What do you want us to do together?"

Augustus's reply came on a deep exhale. "Everything."

. . .

Words had never come easy to him, not since he'd finally started talking at age three—with that horrific stutter he'd never gotten rid of. Words were fucking hard, and even more so when he was stressed or emotional. And dammit, he *was* emotional right now.

Quentin had *believed* him. He'd never even hesitated in his reaction, had completely, one hundred percent believed him. It was beyond anything he'd dared to hope as a reaction when he'd finally confessed his shame. He was an ex-convict, way past the stage where he had to check in with a parole officer, but forever a convicted felon. And yet Quentin was still here, looking at him with patient, if burning eyes.

"Everything, Augustus?" God, he loved hearing his name from those perfect lips. "You're gonna have to be a bit more specific than that."

But he didn't want to be. Didn't Quentin get that? He just wanted to *be* with him, to make him feel good and feel good himself, to express whatever that big feeling inside him was that demanded to be let out. So he shook his head.

"Whatever you w-w-want."

"It doesn't work like that, baby. Or it shouldn't. Hell, I don't know. Maybe it does for you, but I keep waiting for you to take over, to take the lead."

He frowned. "Why?"

"'Cause you're older and bigger, and I'm supposed to be the bottom, the weaker one."

He heard the words, but none of them made sense. It was like Quentin was speaking a different language. "I d-don't understand. You l-l-like to t-take charge. I d-don't. What's the p-problem?"

Quentin straddled him, bringing their faces so close he could feel the warmth of his breath. His eyes were kind as he spoke. "I know you've never been with a man, baby, but haven't you thought about the logistics?"

The logistics of what? Oh. Wait.

Sex.

Quentin was talking about sex. Sure, it had crossed Augustus's mind that one partner would have to *receive* and the other would give, but they could switch that up, right? Or was it custom to have one man doing the same position every time? That didn't make sense.

"I s-s-still don't understand."

"Have you ever heard of the term twink?"

Augustus shook his head.

"Well, that explains it. I'm what's known as a twink. Or at least, my body type is. Slender, boyish, on the smaller side."

Huh, okay. That was new information, that men would be somehow classified based on their body type, but whatever. Augustus still didn't get what that had to do with anything.

"Usually, generally speaking, twinks are expected to bottom."

There was that word again: bottom. What did he mean by... *Oh.* It clicked. The bottom had to be the guy on the bottom, meaning the receiving partner. And the other guy would be the...

"And you, considering how big and strong you are, would be expected to top."

Okay, then. Top and bottom. That made sense. But... wait. Because of their physical build, he was expected to top? Always? What the hell?

"Why? W-w-would it hurt otherw-w-wise?"

That seemed ridiculous. He'd expect it would hurt more the other way around, with the big guy on top and the much smaller guy on the bottom. Though their cocks were pretty similar in size. Fuck, his head hurt, trying to understand what Quentin wasn't outright saying.

Quentin was biting his lip now, a highly uncharacteristic sign of uncertainty. Augustus didn't like to see him this way, this insecure.

"P-p-please, Q-Quentin, what are you n-not telling me? I d-d-don't understand."

"Most guys I've been with wanted me to bottom. Only bottom. Men don't like it when I'm bossy or try to take charge."

It was like the sun broke through the clouds and everything was illuminated. It suddenly made sense to Augustus. This was Quentin's shame, his personal trauma. He was sharing what was keeping him back from being with Augustus. And for the life of him, he couldn't understand what had possessed other men to let Quentin go because of...of *that*, but he was eternally grateful if it meant he had a chance with him. If Augustus's past didn't deter him and all that was holding Quentin back was this, well, that was an easy fix, now wasn't it?

Augustus lifted both hands and caressed Quentin's smooth face, his soft cheeks. God, he was so fucking beautiful. "I l-l-like it when you're b-bossy. I l-like it a l-lot."

His heart somersaulted when Quentin's eyes lit up as if Augustus had just given him the most precious gift. "And if you w-w-want t-to, if you'd l-like to, you c-c-can t-top me. D-did I s-say that r-right? I w-w-would be h-happy f-for you to f-f-fuck me. P-p-please."

Quentin's eyes drilled into his as if he wanted to make extra, triple, super sure Augustus knew what he was saying, that there was no misunderstanding. So he let his eyes speak, allowed his eagerness and excitement to shine through.

"Oh, baby," Quentin finally whispered, covering Augustus's hands with his own. "I'm gonna make you feel so good, I promise."

Augustus nodded, smiling. "I know. C-c-can't wait."

Quentin took both their hands, then brought their mouths together. The kiss started soft, sweet. Augustus sighed into Quentin's mouth as his tongue traced Augustus's lips, then dipped inside and circled his mouth with slow, deliberate strokes. He put his hands on Quentin's ass, scooted him as close as possible, then ran them over his smooth back, sneaking under his hoodie.

Quentin tore away his mouth to yank off his hoodie, then impatiently dragged up Augustus's sweater as well. Augustus pulled it over his head, smiling when Quentin wasted no second in touching him. He stroked Augustus's pectoral muscles, then teased his nipples, which grew hard under his touch.

"Why didn't you get nipple piercings?"

"N-n-no one w-would see."

"Hmm. I would see them, and I think they'd look great on you," Quentin mused, rolling the buds between his fingers, making Augustus's cock grow rock hard. "Plus, I could play with them when I fuck you, and I would really like that."

"O-o-okay."

Right now, he would pierce anything Quentin asked him to. Hell, he'd even have someone pierce his fucking dick if that made Quentin happy.

Quentin continued his exploration of Augustus's upper body, his soft hands running over his arms, pinching his biceps, and tracing his tattoos, then caressing his pecs again, playing with his chest hair, following the trails down to his stomach and farther down, down, down...

Augustus held his breath when Quentin reached the waistband of his tenting sweats, where his cock was doing its damnedest to escape from the confines.

"Breathe, baby," Quentin teased, rubbing Augustus's package through the fabric. "We can't have you fainting for lack of oxygen. I've only just gotten started."

Quentin pressed his hand against Augustus's hard cock, and he bucked his hips, desperate for more friction. He bit his lip to keep a groan in.

"Don't hold back, baby. I want to hear what I'm doing to you."

Quentin slipped his hand under the waistband and wrapped it around Augustus's cock. An embarrassingly loud moan fell from his lips, and he threw his head back, canting his hips into that hand.

"Look at you. You're so responsive, so open in your reactions. I want to play with your body, baby. Hear all those low, sexy noises you make until you come apart in my arms. I want to make you crazy with want until you *beg* me to fuck you."

God, those words. Those wonderful, sexy, arousing words. They reached deep inside Augustus, lighting fires he never even knew could be lit, making him want something he never even knew existed.

"A-a-anything."

"Ah, baby, such trust you have in me. I'll take good care of you. I'm gonna make you fly, baby..."

Didn't Quentin know he already did? Augustus's body felt like it was somehow detached from his mind and at the same time the center of his universe. All he could do was *feel*. Quentin's hand, gently stroking his cock. His other hand, dragging down Augustus's pants and signaling him to raise his hips so he could take them off. His balls, heavy and hard, throbbing against his body.

Quentin climbed off for a few seconds and got rid of his own clothes before Augustus could even lift a finger to help him. He pulled Augustus down so he was lying on the couch on his back, then dove right back.

For the first time ever, Augustus had a naked man on top of him—and it was everything he'd hoped it would be when he'd started dreaming about doing this with Quentin. The difference between their bodies couldn't be bigger, with Quentin being so much smaller and softer and smoother, whereas Augustus was all hard and muscled and hairy everywhere.

He explored Quentin's back with his hands, then dared to dip down to his ass, those two luscious curves that fit so perfectly in his hands. God, his skin was so peachy-silk there, so...*edible*. Was that a thing? If not, it should be.

After another scorching kiss, Quentin started making his way down, licking and kissing and nibbling everywhere. He seemed tuned in to every little gasp, every small groan, every tightening of Augustus's muscles. He bit down on his right nipple, then slightly harder when Augustus moaned. Hmm, maybe he *should* get his nipples pierced so Quentin could tug on the piercings.

Quentin explored and discovered, tonguing Augustus's belly button in a way that had him desperate to hold on to something. Oh, for fuck's sake, this was...

All thoughts ceased when Quentin wrapped his long fingers around his cock again, brought his mouth down, and licked a drop of precum off. He took his crown into his mouth and suckled. Augustus bucked, a high-pitched moan escaping him. Nobody had ever done that, and ohfuckohfuckohfuck that was the most amazing sensation ever, those warm, wet lips around his cock, that hot mouth sucking him in deeper and deeper and...

"C-c-c-coming!"

He pinched his eyes tight shut as his balls pulled up and released, sending a shock wave of heat through him, ending in his cock, which unloaded in Quentin's mouth. Oh, damn, he was coming in his mouth... He opened his eyes, not wanting to miss that view, and was just in time to see Quentin send him a hungry look, licking his lips.

"That, baby, was just the beginning."

13

Augustus still looked dazed after his violent orgasm. No wonder. He'd come way faster than Quentin had expected. Probably also faster than the man had expected himself. Guess those women he'd hooked up with hadn't known how to give this sexy man a good time. Well, Quentin was about to remedy that. He wanted to fucking feast on this man's gorgeous body. But first he needed...

"You have any lube by any chance? Condoms?"

Much to his delight, Augustus's face didn't show any fear, only excitement. The fact that he wanted this as much as Quentin did was the biggest turn-on ever.

"L-l-lube's in m-my beds-s-side drawer. C-c-condoms t-too, but they're a-ancient."

Quentin smiled at Augustus, who was still spread out on the couch like a fucking buffet. And Quentin was *ravenous*. "When's the last time you had sex?"

"T-two years ago."

"Have you been checked since?"

"F-f-for what?"

God, the man was so adorably naïve in some aspects. "STDs. HIV."

Augustus nodded. "L-l-last year, f-f-for my life ins-s-surance."

"Do you trust me when I tell you I'm negative? I get checked every six months, and I always use condoms—a rule I'm apparently about to break, but since I didn't bring condoms and yours are expired and I'm done waiting to claim you..."

"P-please. It's f-fine."

His eagerness. That little catch in his voice, aside from the stutter, that signaled how excited he was. It was so addictive. "Stay here. Don't move."

Quentin jumped up from the couch, waking Lucy, who'd been asleep on the floor. She looked up with amusement at the naked man running through the house, then went right back to sleep.

Augustus did have lube in his drawer. As a matter of fact, he had a huge bottle. Even if he hadn't fucked anyone, he was at least very intimate with his right hand. Damn, he was gonna love being fucked...hopefully.

Quentin sobered as he hurried back. What if Augustus didn't like bottoming despite his eagerness to try? Not all men liked it after all, not even when they had a partner who knew how to make it good. Quentin did have topping skills, he'd like to think, courtesy of practice on mostly twinks even smaller than himself, but he'd never taken a man the size of Augustus. What if he hated it?

Oh, god.

"Q-q-quentin?" Augustus tugged on his hand. "D-d-don't doubt yourself."

"What if you hate it?"

He let himself be pulled back on top of Augustus, dropping the bottle of lube to the floor. Augustus wrapped his big arms around him. "Then w-w-we'll k-keep exp-perimenting until we f-find something we both l-like. L-l-love."

"How do you know the exact right thing to say?" Quentin asked, nuzzling his neck.

Augustus shrugged. "Your face is v-very exp-p-pressive. I can s-s-see what you're f-feeling."

"Yeah, but seeing it and wanting to see it and then choosing to say something are two different things."

Augustus put a finger under his chin and made Quentin meet his eyes. "D-d-do you w-want to hash that out, or d-d-do you w-want to fuck me?"

The man made an excellent point. Quentin gave him a quick kiss, then sat up and angled for the lube. "Promise me you'll talk to me, tell me when I'm hurting you, okay?"

Augustus nodded, his face turning adorably serious. "T-t-tell me what t-to do."

"For now, try to relax. We'll go slow. Pull your legs up for me, baby, and spread wide. I wanna see you."

Augustus did as he asked without hesitation. A deep sense of gratitude rolled through Quentin. This man was willing to be completely vulnerable, trusting Quentin without reservation in a way no one ever had. The wonder of that gift made his soul dance.

His eyes perused Augustus's body. He was so fucking beautiful. There was nothing fragile about his strong body, and yet the vulnerability was unmistakably there now that Quentin knew him. His arms and chest were broad and muscled, colorful tattoos circling both his biceps. Quentin loved the dark chest hair, tapering into a teasing happy trail that led straight to his thick cock. Everything about Augustus screamed masculine, and all Quentin wanted to do was make him *ache* for him.

"You l-look at m-me as if you w-w-want to eat m-me," Augustus whispered. His brown eyes were trained on Quentin, studying his every action.

Quentin's lips pulled up in a smile. "I do, baby. You have no idea what I want to do to you. You're so fucking stunning I don't know where to start."

With a quick move, he grabbed Augustus's balls. The man flinched but relaxed immediately again. Quentin rolled them in his hands, enjoying the weight, then let them go. "Everything about you is thick and strong, your balls included. They're perfect, like your cock."

He trailed his finger up and down the hard length. Augustus shivered.

"But right now, I'm really interested in your ass, baby." With his middle finger, he made his way to that perfect star that beckoned him. He gently tapped it. "Are you gonna be good for me and open up?"

He almost froze when he heard his own words. Was he pushing it too far? Letting Quentin take him was one thing, but would Augustus appreciate this kind of dirty talk? But Augustus nodded eagerly, not a trace of annoyance on his face. God, he was into this... Quentin's heart leaped up in his chest.

He squirted lube onto his fingers, then circled Augustus's hole, stroking it without pushing on it until he felt it soften and relax under his ministrations. Gently, he slipped his index finger in, stopping as soon as it was clamped tight in Augustus's muscles.

"Bear down on me, baby. Take a breath for me. There you go..."

The pressure on his finger decreased, and he slowly slid it in and out until he could insert it as deep as he could. Time to add a second finger.

Augustus's cheeks flushed, and he grabbed the couch, fisting whatever he could hold on to. Not in pain, though, Quentin concluded from the man's expression. More like something foreign that had the potential of being really good. "Look at you, baby, taking two fingers for me... You're being so good."

He felt inside, touching around for a bit until Augustus shivered violently with a moan of surprise. "Ah, there it is. You feel that, baby? That's your ticket to paradise right there."

He stroked it again, watching with a devious smile as Augustus's cock started leaking precum. He fucked him with meticulous, deep strokes of his fingers until every last tension in Augustus's channel was gone, then added a third finger. Augustus clenched around him for a sec, then audibly forced a breath out and relaxed again.

"One day, I'm gonna keep doing this until you beg. I'll keep teasing you, bringing you so fucking close to the edge without sending you over, just because I wanna hear you beg me..."

Augustus's eyes widened, and his cheeks reddened even more.

"But not today, baby. Today, I wanna be inside you. Do you think you're ready for me?"

Another one of those solemn, totally adorable nods.

Quentin gave one last stroke with his fingers and pulled out slowly. He coated his cock with some extra lube, then lowered himself on top of Augustus. "Arch your back and cant your hips. Yeah, perfect, baby."

He took a steadying breath. Oh god. He was really doing this. He was about to top this bear of a man. Shivers of anticipation danced all over his skin. He brought the tip of his cock to that hole and pushed. "Bear down on me, baby, just like before."

He slipped in after a second, stopping immediately so Augustus could get used to him. When he felt him relax around him, he gently went in deeper. Augustus shifted, angling his hips more, and his hands came to rest on Quentin's ass. When he didn't move right away, Augustus pushed against his ass, a wordless signal that made Quentin smile.

"You want my cock?" he dared to ask. Augustus hadn't been weirded out or turned off by his dirty talk so far, so he wanted to push it a little further.

"M-m-more..."

Quentin's smile widened. "Don't worry, baby. You're gonna get it all. Every damn inch."

He carefully kept thrusting until finally, he bottomed out. Completely embedded in Augustus, Quentin took a shuddering breath. This was everything he'd dreamed of. His cock was engulfed in a tight, slick pressure that made his blood roar in his ears.

When he looked at Augustus, a single tear was trickling down the man's right cheek, and Quentin's insides clenched. "Did I hurt you?" he asked. "Do you need me to stop?"

In reaction, Augustus's arms became like iron bars around him, preventing him from even moving an inch. "N-n-no...P-please...S-s-so perfect..."

Quentin went liquid inside. "You like this sensation?" he asked softly. He leaned on one hand so he could use his other to wipe the tear away as Augustus nodded.

Quentin retreated steadily, then surged back in with a more powerful thrust. Augustus moaned, unconsciously pinching Quentin's ass. Quentin repeated the move with more power, watching with deep satisfaction as Augustus's eyes all but crossed in his head. He was *loving* this. Augustus was loving the hell out of bottoming.

Something in Quentin's heart broke free. He surged in again, faster and harder, a deliciously dirty sound echoing through the room.

This man was *his*.

This *ass* was his.

No need to be careful anymore. This man was anything but fragile, physically at least. He could take anything Quentin dished out—and then some. Time to make him lose his everloving mind.

He sped up, positioning himself so he could use all his force to claim that ass, to fucking own him. His balls slapped against Augustus's rough skin as he slammed in, grunting in pleasure. Fire licked at his skin, his insides, his everywhere. He *wanted*... Oh, how he wanted.

Augustus's hands dug into his ass, hard enough he'd end up with bruises, but it only added to Quentin's need. He angled until he hit the right spot head on, conformed by an unintelligible, animalistic sound falling from Augustus's lips. He fucked him hard and deep until the proud, strong man below him was a whimpering, blabbering mess.

"P-p-please!"

He was begging. Augustus was *begging* him. For what, he probably didn't even know himself. But Quentin did. He fisted the man's thick cock with one hand, jerked him off hard. "Let go, baby. Fly for me."

And flying, he did. Augustus came undone, shouting, his head thrown back, his eyes pinched shut, his whole body shaking like a leaf as he spurted all over Quentin's hand and his own chest.

That sight was too much for Quentin, and his balls

pulled up tight against his body. Seconds later, he came, buried to his balls inside that strong body.

"Q-q-quentin," Augustus half sobbed. "Q-q-quentin..."

Too spent and tired to hold himself up any longer, Quentin dropped his weight on top of Augustus, knowing he could take it. His slick cock slipped out, but it was okay. Fuck, they were more than okay.

He scooted slightly higher, finding his favorite spot on that broad shoulder, nuzzling Augustus's neck and beard. "You were so perfect, baby, so perfect. God, the way you fit around me."

Augustus's right hand came to rest on his ass, the other on his neck, scratching softly. "I d-d-didn't know it c-could be l-like this," he whispered, his voice hoarse. "I've always b-been an outcast, b-b-but with you, I f-f-fit."

14

It didn't often happen anymore that Augustus got frustrated with his inability to speak. He'd gotten so used to it that he was usually content to have the perfect words in his mind alone, knowing they'd never be released into the world. But right now, he wished with all his might he'd be able to tell Quentin how he felt because it was so *big* and beautiful his heart was bursting.

"Q-quentin," he started, then sighed in frustration.

Quentin leaned up and looked at him, his lips curving into a soft smile. "I know, baby. I don't need your words. It was perfect. You were perfect."

"You w-w-were..." How did he describe this overwhelming sensation of being exactly who and what and where he was supposed to be? Of fitting in, for the first time ever in his life. Of feeling wanted and cherished and more beautiful than he'd thought possible because of the heat in Quentin's eyes. "You w-were everything."

Quentin stared at him for the longest time. "Was it okay, the way I talked to you?"

Augustus frowned. What was Quentin worried about? He tried to remember what he'd said specifically, but nothing stood out, except that it had been dirty and arousing as fuck and had made him want infinitely more.

"I sometimes forget that you don't know what's...normal in gay relationships. No, not normal, that was not the right word. Common, maybe? Traditional? Does that make sense?"

Augustus slowly shook his head. "What w-was d-d-different?'

Just then, Quentin's stomach rumbled. Augustus tried to hold back, but then he chuckled. "I'd better g-get my ass into the k-kitchen and make you s-s-some food."

Quentin sighed. "This is beyond embarrassing. Sorry."

Augustus kissed his head. "D-d-don't ap-pologize. I l-love taking c-care of you."

"You really do, don't you?" Quentin said with wonder. He dropped a quick kiss on Augustus's lips. "Let me clean you up." Quentin got up and went to the bathroom.

Augustus's ass was weirdly sticky, and something was dripping out of his ass. Right, that would be cum. What a strangely erotic sensation.

His ass hurt a bit, he concluded. Not unbearable by any standard. More like a sting, like how muscles felt you hadn't used in a while after exertion. Which would make sense, obviously, since he'd used muscles he had never been put into play before.

Quentin came back with a warm washcloth and gently cleaned Augustus's chest. He walked back to rinse out the cloth, then returned to wipe his dick and balls and lastly his ass. Augustus could've easily done it himself, but he liked it that Quentin did. Lying there, all naked and spread out for him, he'd never thought he'd feel this way, but he loved it. Like he was Quentin's, to do with as he pleased. It was a strange thought that made him happy.

Quentin meanwhile cleaned up himself, then pulled Augustus up from the couch. That move sent a bit of a smart through his ass again. Quentin's beautiful lips curved. "You feeling your ass, big guy?"

He nodded.

"Is it really horrible of me to say that I kinda like that?"

Augustus grinned, putting on his clothes.

"Aw, you're not cooking naked?" Quentin complained. "But I'd looked forward to watching your gorgeous ass while you cooked, imagining everything I want to do to it..."

Augustus's cock did a manly attempt at being interested, then gave up. Sadly, he was not twenty anymore like Quentin. "N-n-no naked ass in the k-kitchen. W-wouldn't want t-t-to spill s-something hot on m-my dick."

"Okay, good point." He slapped Augustus's butt. "Off you go, baby. Make us some food."

Augustus was halfway to the kitchen when it hit him. *This* was what Quentin had been referring to: him bossing Augustus around. That was what was supposedly not common.

He slowly turned around and found Quentin watching him, his eyes slightly widened, which affirmed Augustus's suspicion. Saying shit like this came naturally to Quentin, but for some reason, it shouldn't. But why the hell not?

Was it because being told what to do made you...inferior, maybe? Less than the other person? But that wasn't how it made him feel. He didn't mind it at all. Strike that. He *liked* it when Quentin got bossy. Maybe it was the way Quentin took charge, but it made Augustus feel like he was cared for, like someone valued him enough to invest in him. Plus, he actually loved taking care of Quentin, to make him happy. And a bossy Quentin was a happy Quentin; that much was clear. So Augustus was more than content to listen, to follow, to... He was searching for another word but couldn't find it.

"Sorry," Quentin said, tension dripping from his voice.

With three steps, Augustus closed the distance between them. He wanted to hug Quentin, to show him it was okay, but when he stood inches away from him, he reconsidered. Quentin's eyes showed fear. Not of Augustus hurting him, of that he was convinced. No, they showed something Augustus was all too familiar with. Fear of rejection. Quentin was afraid he was gonna get turned down, maybe even sent away for what he'd said and done.

And so Augustus did the only thing he could think of to show this beautiful man that he wanted Quentin exactly the way he was, that Augustus needed him to be himself. He sank to his knees at Quentin's feet, lifting his head proudly. His knees hit the floor with a thud, and another sting shot through his ass, but he held his head high, wanting to focus on Quentin's eyes.

"Oh, god," Quentin managed, his hand flying to his mouth. "Oh, baby... Do you realize what you're doing, what signal you're giving me? I'm... Augustus, are you *sure* about this?"

He nodded.

"Do you *like* it when I'm dominant?"

Suddenly the word he'd been searching for before came to him. *Submissive.* That was what he felt, what he wanted. Not inferior to Quentin, not less, but submissive by choice.

Dominant.

Submissive.

Wait, what was Quentin asking, exactly? Augustus knew jack shit about BDSM or whatever it was called, but he'd come across some porn that had seemed intimidating. And some of it had gone on his *hell no* list instantly.

But when he looked into Quentin's eyes, none of that mattered. He wasn't exactly sure what Quentin was asking and if he fully understood where Quentin would lead him, but dammit, he would *follow*. He had never felt like this, had never imagined he could feel like this, and it was all because of this man. He trusted him with everything he had.

"Yes." His voice rang out clear, no stutter this time.

Quentin bit his lip. "Augustus, do you understand where I'm going with this? I'm not just talking about being bossy or telling you what to do."

Augustus nodded. "You w-want to d-d-dominate me."

"Oh, god, you have no idea what I want to do to you."

"T-t-tell me."

Quentin blazed a trail with his index finger across Augustus's face, starting at his left ear, then lifting his chin higher and touching him everywhere. "I don't know, honestly. All I know is that I get such a thrill out of watching you submit to me."

He took Augustus's hand, placed it on his cock, which was hard as iron. "You feel that? That's what you kneeling for me does to me. I have so many dirty things running through my head, but I don't know if you're ready for this, for me. Hell, I don't even know if I can do this."

His knees were starting to hurt, but no way was Augustus changing position now, not when he knew how it affected Quentin. "W-w-why not?"

Quentin caressed his hair. "I've never done this before, not more than an occasional spanking and tying someone up with faux fur cuffs."

"B-b-but you w-want to do m-more."

"Fuck, yeah, so much more. But I never thought anyone would let me. I'm not exactly the type to be a Dom, you know."

A Dom. He'd said it. Quentin wanted to be a Dom. No, not just a Dom, Augustus's Dom. He let the word roll around in his brain, imagined himself being tied up, to a bed maybe? Quentin could...

An image filled his mind, of Quentin making him suck his cock. He'd be down with that. And spanking, maybe? He always liked to pinch himself when he jacked off, create that mix of pain and pleasure that made his release so much more intense.

He could get those nipple piercings for Quentin to play with and maybe even some piercings elsewhere. Or another tattoo. His tattoo and piercing artist had warned him when he got his first ink that it was addictive, and he'd been dead right.

"Where did you go, baby?" Quentin asked with a laugh in his voice. "I just watched your eyes go all dark and intense."

"I w-w-will let you. T-t-together. We'll both l-learn."

Quentin's smile transitioned into a look of wonder. "How did I ever get so lucky to meet you?" he whispered. He bent over and kissed Augustus, a fierce, fiery kiss that promised much more. "My first request: make us some food. Please. I'm fucking starving."

QUENTIN WATCHED SILENTLY as Augustus prepared them dinner—even though it was way past dinner time already. His heart was still racing, his mind so overexcited he had trouble focusing. What the hell had just happened? How was it even remotely possible that a man like Augustus wanted this and with him, little Quentin.

Baby Q, his friends had called him in high school because he'd always been the smallest and the guy with the babyface. The contrast with his best friend, Noel—six foot three and built like a damn tank—hadn't done him any favors either, though their friendship had been everything. Hell, more than one teacher hadn't believed him when he'd said he was in high school. At first, he hadn't minded because he figured he'd outgrow it, but when he'd been a senior and had still looked like he was twelve, he'd gotten frustrated.

Then college had happened, including a series of short-lived relationships with guys who were attracted to him because of his body type and the expectations that came with it. *Your ass was made to be fucked*, he'd been told more than once. Apparently, the fact that he had a dick too wasn't interesting. Sure, they'd jack him off, and he'd had some decent blow jobs, but more often than not, he was the one expected to be on his knees, offering up whatever orifice they requested.

He hadn't truly understood why that bothered him so much until he'd met Justin. Justin had been a six-foot-three muscled, tattooed bear of a man—everything Quentin loved. He'd also been into kinky stuff, and that had been a new experience. At first, Quentin had loved letting Justin experiment with him, but he'd soon discovered he had a problem. He was the one who wanted to *do* the spanking and the tying up and the doling out punishment, not to receive it. When he'd finally mentioned it to Justin, his boyfriend had laughed him out of the room.

Justin had been scathing in his parting comments that Quentin had better forget about the idea of being a dominant or even of topping. *No one will ever look at you and think I wish that guy would fuck me. Trust me, every gay man alive wants a piece of you...but not that piece. They want your ass, not your dick.* Those cruel words had broken Quentin's heart.

Of course, that had been the end of his relationship with Justin, but he'd still hoped the guy had been wrong.

He'd met some guys who were willing to let him try something, but they'd all been twinks like him. Total fuckboys who just wanted to have a good time and were happy to don a pair of pink faux fur cuffs if that got them laid. Quentin wanted *more*. He wanted so much more. He'd dreamed of it until he'd lost hope and had told himself to forget it.

Now it seemed he'd found it, though it was still hard to believe Augustus meant what he'd said. Did he truly understand what he, what they were getting into?

A hand landed on his neck. He jerked. "D-d-don't fret. We'll f-figure it out," Augustus said, then kissed Quentin's head.

Quentin's heart warmed. He was such a sweetheart, such a kind, tender man. "I know, baby. What are you making for us?"

"Homem-made m-mac and cheese. It'll b-be done in a m-minute."

"It smells delicious. I'll set the table."

Being here with Augustus was homey, as if it was the most natural thing in the world for the two of them to be here, together. He'd never felt this familiarity with anyone else, maybe because he'd always felt the need to keep his mask on. With Augustus, he could be himself.

"D-d-do you w-want to tell m-me about your f-f-father?" Augustus asked when they'd started eating.

Quentin nodded after only a short hesitation. As much

as he wanted to talk about the other stuff, about Augustus kneeling for him and where to go from there, they had to take it slow. Hell, they were already going at breakneck speed, considering they'd had sex within two days of meeting for the first time. For Quentin, who'd done the hookup scene for a while, it wasn't that big a deal, but with Augustus, everything was different. This was not a hookup, no wham-bam encounter. This had the potential of being *more*, of developing into something worthy of big and scary words. So they'd talk about stuff first. Stuff that mattered, like their past.

"My father is from around here. From Northern Lake, actually, which is why I set up a research project there. I'm hoping to find out what happened to him. My professor doesn't know that part, and neither does my mom, but I'm skipping a few steps."

He took a deep breath, organizing his thoughts. This, too, had been a dream he'd had for years. He'd always felt like a part of him had been missing, not knowing what had happened to his father.

"My father was a sales rep for a company that made bottled water. He was traveling for work to California, where he met my mom, who was a waitress at a restaurant he had dinner at a few times. They had a one-night stand, but when he was tasked with setting up a new plant in California, they got involved. A year later, my mom got pregnant with me. They never married, but she told me he was supportive of her keeping the baby and helped her out with money. He's also listed as my father on my birth certificate."

"W-w-what happened? You s-said he w-walked out on your m-mom?"

"His job in California ended, so he had to go back to New York. They stayed in touch until I was three, and he visited us a few times, my mom told me. He asked her to move to New York, obviously bringing me, and she was seriously considering it. Then he fell off the face of the planet. Gone. His phone was disconnected, he'd moved out of the address she had for him, and that was it. She figured he was tired of her, and stopped looking for him."

"D-d-did you hire s-someone to f-find him?"

"No." He could have, and it wasn't like he hadn't thought about it. "Money has always been tight, so we couldn't waste it on trying to find a man who clearly wanted nothing more to do with us."

Augustus's eyes were kind. "B-b-but you're here, l-looking for him."

Yeah, Quentin should have known Augustus would see through his tough attitude. With a sigh, he put his fork down and pushed back his empty plate. "I need to know why he ghosted her, what made him change his mind."

Augustus's eyes became even softer, and his big, calloused hand covered Quentin's. "Y-you w-w-w-want to know if he r-r-rejected you."

"Yeah," Quentin whispered. "I know I'm setting myself up for massive rejection and disappointment, but I need the closure. All these years, I've wondered if maybe something happened to him, you know? Maybe he had an accident and died or had had amnesia or…"

He stopped talking, his face flushing with the embarrassment of the childish, naïve stories he'd made up over the years. Augustus squeezed his hand, his silent look of understanding more of a comfort than eloquent words could have been.

Quentin sighed, his body feeling heavy and achy all of a sudden. "It's foolishness, this whole endeavor. Rationally, I know that. But emotionally, I'm still that little boy who's hoping his dad will come back."

He hated that his throat closed up when he said that. Hated that stabbing pain in his heart. Hated that even as he uttered the words, he still hoped that it had all been a misunderstanding. But most of all, he hated that despite telling himself a million times he was gonna get hurt, he couldn't change course. He needed to know.

"Hope is n-n-never f-f-oolish," Augustus said, and it hit Quentin so deep that he slid off his chair and crossed over to Augustus, who instantly pushed his chair back to make room for him. Quentin nestled himself on that firm lap, on those thighs that were like tree trunks, and he laid his head against the big man's shoulder.

They sat like that for a while, Quentin's thoughts wandering in all kinds of directions until something hit him. "Your father, is he still in prison?"

Augustus made a sound of disgust. "N-n-no. He s-served t-t-ten years and g-got out on g-g-good behavior r-right before my m-m-mom died. He d-disapp-p-peared. N-never even s-showed up at her f-f-f-funeral."

Quentin couldn't hold back the gasp, and he pushed against Augustus's shoulder so he could sit up and meet his eyes. "You're shitting me. He's *out*?"

Augustus nodded, shrinking a little, probably from Quentin's tone, which had been way sharper than he'd intended. It was just that he had so many questions now. Like, why the hell was Augustus paying off his father's debts?

He put his hand against Augustus's cheek, his beard soft under his fingers. "Have you seen him since? Or even spoken to him?"

Augustus's answer was silent as a breeze. "N-n-no."

And suddenly Quentin understood his remarks about hope. Deep inside, even Augustus still had hope his father would come back. Hope is never foolish, Augustus had said, and he would know. Quentin nestled back against him, and they sat like that for a long time.

15

Augustus loved having Quentin on his lap. He hadn't thought it possible for someone to look this delicate and fragile while at the same time being so strong. Quentin reminded him of Legolas, the elf from Lord of the Rings. He had that same innate grace, that fluidity of movement, so effortless and beautiful. But at the same time, he was just as deadly.

The way he'd stood up for Augustus with Willis and Monroe, Augustus had never seen anything like it. His mother had tried to have his back, but she'd been a soft-spoken woman by nature, not one to raise her voice. Quentin was fearless, on fire, and it did something to Augustus deep inside. To see someone defend you like that, how could you not fall in love?

He might not be experienced when it came to love and sex and relationships—and that was an understatement—but he wasn't stupid. He'd read enough books, had watched enough movies to know that it was way too soon to talk about love. Love didn't happen just like that. Except it was hard to describe what he felt inside as anything else, so that was something he would have to think about.

For now, they had different priorities. Quentin's body had gone slack against him, and Augustus guessed he was minutes away from falling asleep. "Do you w-w-want to go t-to bed?" he asked.

Quentin yawned, and it made Augustus smile. "Yeah, I'm super tired, and my body is aching everywhere."

Augustus frowned. Had it been too much for him? Quentin wasn't used to this physical exertion, especially not in the cold. "I have s-s-some p-painkillers if you want."

Quentin sat up, then stretched out with another yawn. "Nah, I'm good. But thank you. I just need to sleep."

He couldn't invite him into his bed. That, too, was too fast, wasn't it? Then again, they'd had sex. His body might not be troubled by the snow shoveling and the physical labor he'd done today, but he still felt Quentin's lingering presence in his ass. Not that he wanted painkillers for that. Hell no. He liked being reminded of what they had shared. It was a promise for more, and that thought alone made his heart skip a few beats.

"I n-need to do a l-l-last round of checkups around the p-prop-perty," he said. "But you don't have to w-wait for that. You should b-be w-warm enough in your room, since I p-p-put an extra comf-f-forter on your b-bed."

Quentin slid off his lap and stood before him, hands on his hips. "If you think I'll be sleeping on my own tonight, you are not as smart as I thought you were."

Heat exploded in Augustus's belly. "I didn't w-want to p-présumé."

Quentin stepped in and cupped his cheek with a gentle hand. Augustus couldn't help but lean into it, feeling that touch way deeper than just on his skin. The effect Quentin had on him was like magic.

"We have a lot to talk about, baby, you and me. And we will, I promise. But we both need to sleep, and I would very much like to do that together. But I also want to make sure I'm not crossing your boundaries, so you'll need to speak up if I do something you don't want."

Augustus nodded almost automatically but then reconsidered. Quentin had said speaking up, and that was not as easy for him as it sounded. He didn't like talking. He never had. If he could get away with nonverbal communication, he would. If Quentin counted on him to speak up and do it fast when needed, he could be in trouble because it usually took a while to overcome that barrier to use his voice.

"I don't l-like t-t-talking," he said softly.

Quentin's eyes narrowed in confusion, but then understanding washed over his face. "You need something else than words."

He seemed to think about it for a few seconds, and Augustus waited patiently. He had no doubt Quentin would figure something out.

"How about we do this?" Quentin released his cheek and tapped his shoulder three times in a row with his fingers. "You can use your hands, your foot, make a sound with your tongue, or snap your fingers, but as soon as you make that succession of three, I will stop immediately."

Augustus nodded, then realized this was not something he could agree to without words. Sometimes, Quentin would need the words from him, and this was one of those times. "Yes. That w-will w-w-work."

Quentin curled both his hands around Augustus's cheeks and leaned in for a velvety, intimate kiss. "Good. Now, let's sleep." Augustus opened his mouth to point out he still had to do his safety round. Quentin waved his hand. "You go check on whatever it is you need to check on. I'll wait here for you, and if I fall asleep in the meantime, well, you'll just have to carry me to bed, now won't you?"

Augustus grinned at him. Somehow, that didn't seem like a threat at all.

He dressed quickly, then whistled for Lucy to come. He chuckled when he saw the silent complaint in her eyes that she needed to go outside when she'd been so warm and comfortable inside. Still, when he opened the door, she darted past him and happily jumped around in the snow for a bit.

He did his usual check, making sure all the cameras around his property were on, that the gates were closed, and that the snow was undisturbed of footprints. Not that he expected any trouble on a night like this, but he'd learned to be careful.

Revenge was a powerful motivation to do stupid stuff, and so was anger, bitterness, hatred toward the person they blamed for ruining their lives. In a way, he understood, but that didn't mean he tolerated vandalism on his property or the multiple attempts to break in and steal things from him. Since the sheriff's department offered him little courtesy, let alone protection, he was on his own here, hence the multiple security measures he'd taken to keep people out. It seemed to work as it had been a while since he'd had any problems.

When they got back inside, he dried Lucy off with one of the old towels he had stacked near the front door, then took off his jacket and snow pants and used that same towel to mop the floor and remove all the snow that had fallen off his boots. He hung the towel in the mudroom, then walked into the living room.

Quentin lay stretched out on the couch, a blanket pulled up to his chin. His eyes were closed, and Augustus took a few seconds to study him in the soft light from the dying fire. It couldn't last, he knew that. He had nothing to offer Quentin, nothing to make him want to stay. But he would take him as long as he could have him, as long as Quentin wanted him.

He scooped him up from the couch, startled for a second when Quentin's eyes opened. He looked at Augustus with heavy-lidded eyes and a sweet smile on his lips. "Mmm, I like it when you hold me like this," he all but purred. "You're so big and strong."

Augustus held him close to his chest as he carried Quentin to his bedroom, reveling in the very caveman-like emotions inside him. Who would've thought it could do so much to him to be admired for his physical strength? It aroused a primitive feeling inside him, the urge to protect Quentin, to take care of him, to make sure he was safe. How that coexisted with this deep need to submit to him, Augustus wasn't sure, but they would figure it out.

His bedroom was chilly, and he shivered as he gently lowered Quentin onto his bed. "Do you w-want anything from your s-suitcase? P-p-paj-jamas? Toothb-brush?"

"I can't be bothered right now. I guess that means it's your job to keep me warm tonight. You up for that, big guy?"

Augustus nodded. He could do that. He swallowed as Quentin sat up on the edge of the bed, then got up and undressed as fast as he could. He didn't have much time to admire his body because Quentin was under the covers within two seconds after getting naked, but the thought that he was waiting for him there made Augustus swallow again.

"Get naked," Quentin said, and it wasn't a question.

Augustus picked up Quentin's clothes first, folded them

quickly, and hung them neatly over the clothes rack he had in his room. His own clothes followed, and he reveled in the sight of someone else's presence in his bedroom, a warm feeling unfurling in his belly.

"Get your ass in bed," Quentin told him, and Augustus hurried over to obey.

As soon as he was under the covers, Quentin practically positioned himself on top of Augustus, and he held him close, sensations thundering through him at the skin-to-skin contact. His cock, which had been half-hard since picking Quentin up from the couch, sprang to full attention, and for a few seconds, he was worried about Quentin's reaction. But Quentin merely chuckled and gave his cock a gentle squeeze, which had Augustus gasping.

"You'll have to wait till tomorrow, but we're not done yet," Quentin said, his voice low and sexy.

It sounded like a promise, which only fueled the fire inside Augustus. He accepted that nothing would happen tonight, and after Quentin fell asleep within minutes, he lay awake for a long time, too excited to sleep.

It wasn't just the physical excitement, though it was a tad hard to find sleep when your body wanted release. It was the emotional satisfaction of having someone in his bed, in his arms. And not just anyone, but Quentin, this beautiful, gorgeous man who made Augustus feel things he never felt before, who made his body experience things he'd never had before, who made him have *hope* again.

Hope was never pointless, he'd told Quentin, and how true was that. For so long, he had felt like he'd had no way out, like he would forever be stuck and buried in this place, in this town, between these people who hated him so much.

But Quentin offered him a way out, and Augustus would take it, even if it was only temporary. Even if it was only an escape through sex, through an emotional connection, through being whoever and whatever Quentin needed him to be. He would find hope and comfort in that human connection for as long as it lasted. Maybe it would be enough to sustain him until he was done here.

16

Quentin woke up in an empty bed the next morning and decided he didn't like that one bit. When he checked the time on the alarm clock, however, he realized it was almost nine thirty in the morning. Since it was a Monday, Augustus had probably gotten up early for work. He couldn't fault the man for that. Didn't mean he wasn't a little disappointed.

He got up, groaning when his muscles reminded him of the physical labor he'd done the day before. After getting dressed and quickly brushing his teeth, he made his way to the kitchen, where he found scrambled eggs, bacon, sausages, and some fresh fruit waiting for him. He heated the hot food, meanwhile nibbling on the fruit.

Augustus was such a sweetheart, taking care of him like that. Quentin wasn't spoiled by a long shot. Hell, he'd never even had the opportunity to become spoiled. He'd grown up without money. He and his mom had lived from one day to the next, never certain if they'd have enough to fill their bellies, let alone pay the rent for their trailer.

But they had survived, and thanks to a very helpful

career guidance counselor in high school, Quentin had scored scholarships to the University of California, first for his bachelor's and then for his master's degree in sociology. It hadn't been a full ride, but with student loans, he'd been able to do it. No one had cheered louder than his mom at graduation, and where others might have felt the weight of expectations, Quentin had basked in her pride in him, in her endless hard work and desire to see him build something out of his life.

Now, he had his eye on a prestigious PhD position at the university, but Professor Danson had told him he needed to pad his résumé with more independent research. So he had helped Quentin score a research grant to study small-town dynamics in Northern Lake. Never in a million years had he ever imagined he would run into a man like Augustus here.

As he ate his breakfast, he pondered about his next steps. He had a week before he officially started his project, which would last four months. He'd booked a room through Airbnb in Brookville, a town about twenty minutes from Northern Lake. It had been the cheapest place he could find, since lodging in Northern Lake itself was expensive, even in winter.

He had prepared himself, like he always did, so he'd known winters could be harsh here. But knowing it could snow and actually being confronted with the results of a snowstorm were two completely different things. God, he had been woefully underprepared for two feet of snow. If not for Augustus and his unexpected offer of hospitality, he would've been fucked ten ways till Sunday.

His first priority was to find a new car. That would be tricky, since he'd already discovered his price range was low compared to the cars being offered in this area, most of which were all-wheel drives in reasonable condition. No one wanted to get stuck in a crappy car or slide off the road in weather like this, which Quentin wholeheartedly understood after his own experience. Didn't mean he had a couple of grand extra all of a sudden to pay for an upgrade in transportation.

Once he had a car, he would be able to travel to Northern Lake and check out the accommodation he had rented. He'd only paid for the first week, which had been a bit of a risk, considering how few affordable options there were in the area, but he hadn't wanted to tie himself down to a location for the full four months without having seen it.

So a car and then checking out Northern Lake. That was his to-do list for now. And when he was in Northern Lake, he could see what he could find out about his father. He'd have to build up rapport with the local community. As soon as he'd made some connections, he could casually work his father's name into the conversation and see if that triggered any recognition.

He rinsed his plate and put it in the dishwasher, then bundled up and went outside. As soon as he opened the back door, Lucy came running for him, happily barking and dancing around his legs. He smiled as he bent down and petted her, rubbing her head until she ran away again.

"Where's Augustus?" Quentin asked her as if she could answer him. She barked once, and his smile widened. He followed her excited lead as she ran out a few paces in front of him, then waited for him to catch up. That process repeated itself a few times until he saw Augustus.

The big man had backed up his pickup truck close to the half-collapsed shed, where the massive tree branch had caused such damage. He'd removed the tarps from the metal structures he had created, and in the light of day, Quentin got a much better look at them. They were stunning, intriguing forms and lines that drew him in and made it impossible to tear his eyes off them.

Augustus was brushing one off with a duster, and Quentin observed as he uncovered a deer. The animal was beautiful, its simple, elegant lines created by raw pieces of welded metal.

"It's amazing," he said softly, and Augustus glanced over his shoulder at him.

"Yeah?" he asked, the joy clearly audible in his voice.

Quentin stepped up next to him, following the line of the deer's antlers with his index finger. He shivered when the frigid temperature of the metal registered with him. "This is pure art."

Augustus sighed deeply, the smile vanishing from his face. "I l-l-lost four p-pieces. A few others g-g-got d-damaged, but I can r-repair those. This one esc-caped unharmed."

Quentin put his head against Augustus's shoulder. "I'm sorry. They must've taken you many hours to create."

"It's what k-keeps me s-s-sane. The work I do here is m-mind-numbing. I don't m-mind hard w-w-work, and I've always l-loved f-figuring out how things work, f-fixing stuff. But this w-was n-never my ch-ch-chosen career."

Bitterness sharpened his voice, a simmering anger that Quentin had no trouble picking up on. "I bet you didn't have much of a choice."

Augustus let out a harsh laugh. "No one w-wants to hire a f-f-former conv-vict. Esp-p-pecially not when he's s-stolen all their life s-savings."

"This was your grandfather's, right?" Quentin asked as he gestured to the junkyard around him.

"Yeah, m-m-my mom's d-dad. He bel-lieved in my in-n-nocence and left it to m-me when he d-died."

Augustus's voice betrayed the deep affection he felt for his grandfather, and Quentin's heart overflowed with empathy. He'd had too many losses to deal with, this man. His grandfather, his mother, his father, who had set him up, then left him to face the consequences. It was almost too much to bear for one man, and yet he had done so with a dignity and stubbornness Quentin couldn't even fathom.

"Thank you for breakfast."

Augustus made another sound, much gentler and happier. Quentin put his index finger on Augustus's chin and turned his face toward him. "Can I get a good-morning kiss?"

Ah, that brought out such a sweet smile on the big man's face. Quentin had to rise to his toes to kiss him, but he took his time kissing him, licking Augustus soft lips and teasing his piercing before slipping his tongue inside and roaming his mouth. He tasted of strong coffee, and Quentin drank him in, not satisfied with that first taste. He pressed himself against Augustus, moaning into his mouth when those solid arms came around him and dragged him close.

Just like before, Augustus was happy to let Quentin set the pace, and the weight of that responsibility thundered through his veins, making his blood roar and his heart beat fast. They must've kissed for minutes when he finally pulled back, his mouth throbbing and leaving Augustus's lips swollen and glistening.

He swiped them dry with his thumb, then patted his own mouth dry as well, since it stung in the bitter wind. "That was a good start of the day after that delicious breakfast," he said, which earned him another smile from Augustus. "I need to see if I can find a car today. Any suggestions on where to start?"

Augustus nodded. "I asked ar-round. There are two c-c-cars we can l-look at this aftern-noon."

Quentin raised his eyebrows in surprise. "You set that up already?"

Augustus shrugged. "I knew it would b-b-be a p-priority for you, and I f-figured I would know m-more about what car w-would be b-b-best than you." Suddenly he appeared worried, and he shuffled his feet as he said, "I didn't overs-s-step, d-did I?"

Quentin considered it. With anyone else, he would have labeled it overstepping. He didn't like it when others made decisions for him without consulting him. But it felt different in this case. Augustus was right that he had known it would be a priority for Quentin, and he was also on the money that he knew far more about cars than Quentin did. The only worry he had was that he hadn't told him his budget.

"You didn't, but everything I've seen so far was outside of my budget."

That resulted in another shrug from Augustus, and this time, Quentin wasn't so easily persuaded to overlook him taking the initiative. "The cars we'll be looking at are within my budget, right?"

Augustus cast his eyes down now, shuffling his feet again. How it was possible for a man who in theory appeared as menacing as this guy did to look so adorable, Quentin would never understand. "They're s-s-safe cars. G-good c-cars."

Quentin narrowed his eyes. "I'm sure they are, but that doesn't tell me if they're within my price range. What good is it going to do me to see a car I can't afford? I'm on a tight budget for the next few months, and there's only so much money for transportation, considering what I'll have to pay for lodging and food."

"Ab-bout that," Augustus said and then fell silent.

Quentin wasn't sure if he needed time to find the words or the courage, but he waited until Augustus spoke again.

"You said your research p-project was in N-n-northern L-lake. That's a thirty-m-minute drive f-from here."

"Only thirty minutes?" Quentin asked, surprised.

Augustus looked up, then nodded. "There's a d-direct road from F-f-frostville to Northern L-lake. We happen to be on the s-s-same country road."

That was much closer than Quentin had expected it to be. He thought it would've been at least a forty-five-minute drive, if not a full hour. That made it only slightly farther out than the lodging he'd found.

Wait, was Augustus going where Quentin thought he was going with this? Was he suggesting for him to stay here rather than pay for an Airbnb? His first instinct was to say nothing and wait if Augustus would offer. It would be presumptuous of him to bring this up and possibly put Augustus in a position where he had to offer now, even though it hadn't been his intention. After all, Augustus hadn't actually said the words. It was purely Quentin's interpretation. Maybe even speculation.

But then Quentin reconsidered. If this thing between him and Augustus, whatever it was, was growing in the direction he wanted it to go, communication would be key. He had to learn to suck it up and be direct, no matter how scary it was.

"Are you implying I could stay with you?" he asked softly.

Augustus nodded. "If you w-want. I wouldn't ch-ch-charge you anything, so you would have the m-money to b-buy a better car. A s-s-safe car, a dep-p-pendable one that will l-last you through the winter. I w-would cook for you, and you wouldn't have to p-p-pay me anything for it. You know I l-like cooking for you. And we would have t-t-time t-to..." He swallowed, his Adam's apple bobbing. "To be tog-g-gether. To spend t-t-time together. If that's what you w-w-want."

It was probably the longest speech Augustus had made so far, and every word wriggled its way deep into Quentin's heart. He'd had some smooth-talking admirers over the years, good-looking guys who had praised him with silky words, with effortless compliments. They'd commented on his looks, his body, his witty sense of humor, all with the goal to get in bed with him.

But not once had he been as touched by a proposal as the one Augustus had made just now, halting and stammering and fighting for every word. Somehow, it meant so much more than all the perfectly delivered compliments he'd ever gotten. It made his answer so incredibly easy.

"Okay," he said. "I'll stay."

Augustus's eyes widened, and the softest gasp fell from his lips as if he couldn't believe what Quentin had just said. "S-serious?"

Quentin smiled at him. "Serious."

"I thought I w-would have to conv-vince you."

Quentin leaned in for another kiss, his eyes sparkling. "I recognize a good proposal when I hear one."

The sheer joy on Augustus's face warmed his belly, stirring something in his heart he'd never felt before. But before he could say anything, the sound of car tires on the snow made them both turn around.

"C-customer," Augustus said, all joy disappearing from his face.

And Quentin, who had planned to get back inside as quickly as humanly possible to prevent transforming into a snowman, took Augustus's hand, sensing the tightness in his body and the stress on his face.

"I'm here," he said simply, and the way Augustus squeezed his hand confirmed he'd made the right call.

17

Augustus spent the whole morning clearing the junkyard of snow, at least where the snow hindered his work. Business had been slow, luckily, most folks in town too busy to dig themselves out to ask for his help with anything else. That wouldn't last, but at least it had given him the opportunity to get his workplace back in order.

The only customer had been Huey, a friend of his grandpa, who had shown up when Quentin had still been out. He was one of the few men in town who was still nice to him. Augustus had introduced him to Quentin, and old Huey had barely batted an eye, god bless him. Then again, Huey's daughter was married to a woman, so he hadn't expected much else from the man.

He'd saved as many of his sculptures as he could, and Quentin had helped carry them into another shed, where they had covered them with tarp, since he wasn't entirely sure that roof would hold. After that, he'd taken out the chain saw and had cut the big branch that had crushed his workshop. It had taken him well over an hour to cut the damn thing into pieces, then haul them off to the side with his truck. At least he'd have firewood for next winter.

Quentin had gone back inside at Augustus's urging. He appreciated him being outside by his side, but he'd seen the slow, painful movements. Quentin hadn't recovered from the day before. Augustus had been on his own for years, so he didn't need him. Oh, he needed him on a different level, but not for the practical, physical stuff.

When he walked in around noon, Quentin had installed himself at the kitchen table with his laptop, looking ten kinds of adorable and nerdy with a pair of glasses. Augustus stopped, this strange emotion welling up inside him, soft and warm but so big it took his breath away. He was so beautiful, Quentin. Like an otherworldly creature, precious and perfect.

He smiled at himself. Look at him, all going gooey inside. Give him a few more seconds, and he'd be spouting poetry or some shit. Quentin did that to him. He made Augustus feel so much more than he'd ever thought himself capable of. Moreover, Augustus *liked* it. He liked how he was so much more aware of his own body, of his emotions, of this need inside him to please Quentin.

Because god, he wanted to please him so much. How it was possible, he had no idea, but somehow, this man had become the center of his universe. His sun, that was what Quentin was. He was the sun, which had brought light and warmth into Augustus's life.

See? Poetry.

To prevent himself from becoming even more of a puddle of goo, he softly stepped behind Quentin and wrapped his arms around him. "You l-l-look very s-s-smart and s-sexy with your g-g-glasses."

Quentin chuckled as he pressed his warm cheek against

Augustus's, then shivered. "Damn, you're cold, baby. Do you need me to make you something warm?"

Augustus smiled. "You'll b-burn the p-p-place down," he teased.

Quentin leaned into his touch. "I'll have you know I'm an expert at heating soup. Me and Campbell, we understand each other, you know?"

He deserved so much more than crappy food like that. Maybe Quentin needed him as much as vice versa, and that thought warmed Augustus inside. He kissed Quentin's soft cheek because it was right *there*, looking all smooth and perfect, and then let go of him.

"I'll m-make us l-lunch."

Within ten minutes, he had big club turkey sandwiches ready, accompanied by the chicken soup he'd dug up from his freezer. With an apple for after, that had to be enough, even for a bottomless pit like Quentin.

Conversation flowed easily while they ate, and Augustus relished it. He'd so rarely experienced this, people who actually *talked* with him, who had the patience to listen and hear him out.

"I'm n-n-not used to t-talking so much," he said.

Quentin looked up from his bowl of soup. "I'm not surprised, considering the assholes that surround you here."

Augustus waved his hand. "Even b-b-before."

Quentin took a spoonful of his soup, looking pensive. "Most people find it hard to be faced with a disability. They don't know how to react. It makes them uncomfortable, and they want to either pretend it doesn't exist, compensate for the pity they feel with over-the-top attention, or try to fix it."

He closed his eyes for a second, then shook his head, and a wave of irritation crossed his face. "And now I'm lecturing you. Sorry. You know this better than I do from your own experience."

Augustus nodded, though he hadn't taken offense at Quentin's words. He felt *seen* by Quentin, comforted by his passionate words, which showed understanding. "Y-you know this f-f-from research?"

"Partially. We did do a course in college about disabilities and how they affect social roles and dynamics, but my best friend, Noel, is hearing-impaired. I've seen over the years how people treat him, and it's made my blood boil on more than one occasion."

"You haven't asked if I have t-t-tried to f-f-fix it."

Quentin met his eyes dead on. "Because it's not something that needs to be fixed. *You* don't need to be fixed. You're not broken, baby. If it bothers you and you want to seek treatment to see if that can help, that's awesome, but if not, then that's okay too."

It wasn't fair. How could one man be so perfect? It made it impossible not to fall for him, but Augustus shouldn't. Quentin wasn't here to stay, and the more he allowed his heart to get involved and get attached, the harder it would be on him when Quentin left.

"Thank you," he said, enjoying that warm, happy feeling in his belly a little longer.

After lunch, he closed up shop, hanging a sign that he was closed and people could call him if they needed him. Then he and Quentin got into his truck to check out the first car he'd found for him that morning. It was an hour's drive away, but Bill, the man who sold it, had worked for his grandfather. Augustus could trust him not to screw him over, which couldn't be said for a whole lot of other people who might want to sell him a lemon.

"What kind of car is it?" Quentin asked after they'd sat

in silence for a while. He'd been looking out the window, letting out little sounds of awe at the majestic mountains, now covered in snow, they drove through.

Augustus mentally braced himself. "S-subaru F-forester. S-seven years old."

Quentin's head whipped to his side. "Seven years old? I can't afford that."

"It's a g-good brand and m-m-model. Very r-reliable. Cheap in m-maintenance. And it's an all-wheel d-d-drive."

"I'm sure that's all true, but how does that help me when I can't afford it? What price range are we talking about here?"

"T-ten k, g-give or t-t-take."

It was higher, most likely, but there was no need to mention that. He'd said *range*, after all, not exact price. Besides, Augustus might be able to get the price down by offering some incentives.

"Oh, for fuck's sake, Augustus, that's five thousand more than I can spend. Probably closer to seven more, but whatever. Same difference."

Was it weird that he liked it when Quentin got angry with him? It felt so normal, like they were a real couple. Not that he wanted him to be upset with Augustus, but he loved that Quentin had no qualms about expressing it.

"You won't have t-t-to p-pay rent," he reminded him. "That w-w-will save you m-money."

Quentin let out a deep sigh. "Yeah, but not five thousand dollars over six months."

"F-free f-f-food?" he offered. "And I c-can f-f-fix it if you have c-car trouble again."

"For ten thousand dollars, that car damn well better be trouble-free for the next five years," Quentin grumbled, but his tone had changed.

It was his pride now that was in the way, and that was something Augustus knew all about. Pride had helped him keep his head high despite everything his neighbors had done to him, every insult to his face and behind his back, every sneer in his direction. Pride was powerful and could be a motivator, but it could also hold you back.

"I know it's h-hard t-to accept h-h-help," he said. "It h-hurts inside."

Quentin turned halfway in his chair, leaning against his window. "It makes me feel like a failure."

Augustus nodded. Oh, how he understood that. "I d-don't think you're a f-f-failure. I w-want t-t-to help you s-s-succeed. You're s-so s-s-smart, and you d-deserve to d-d-do well. I d-don't like you d-driving around in an old c-car. It's n-not safe. Not in the w-winter. Not when you're this r-r-remote."

A quick glance sideways showed Quentin looking at him with gentle eyes, all traces of frustration gone from his face. "I love that you want to take care of me, but how did you envision this? It's not even that I don't like spending the money. I don't have it. My grant is paid out in installments, so I can't plonk down ten k in cash, and fuck knows I'll never get a loan because my credit score is shit."

Augustus shrugged. This was the easy part. "I'll p-pay."

"You'll pay."

He nodded.

"You have ten thousand dollars lying around?"

The incredulity in Quentin's voice was thick, and Augustus couldn't blame him. To Quentin, it had to sound like a fortune. "Y-yes. It's m-my emergency f-f-fund."

"Augustus, baby, this does not qualify as an emergency. What if your washer stops working or you need to replace your furnace or some shit?"

"I c-can f-f-fix almost anything, and if n-not, the t-t-townspeople w-will have to w-w-wait a l-little longer for their m-money."

He pulled up in the car dealer's parking lot, which looked very much like his own junkyard, except Bill traded more in used cars than Augustus liked to do. It required way more talking than he was comfortable with.

He shut off the engine, and Quentin unbuckled and turned toward him. "Are you sure about this? It's hard for me to accept this, and I will pay you back, but I'm worried about wiping out your safety net."

Augustus beamed at him. "You're w-worth it."

The smile that broke through on Quentin's face made him look stunning, and Augustus's belly did a few somersaults before settling again. Then Quentin leaned in and kissed him, and his whole system went haywire again. Oh, no doubt about it, he'd *so* made the right call.

18

Quentin had to admit that his new car drove like a dream compared to his ancient Corolla. No wonder, since it had almost been as old as he was, so the Subaru was a massive improvement. The all-wheel drive was pretty handy as well, giving him a good grip on the country roads. They had been cleared of snow for the most part, but he'd still seen some slick spots.

And my god, this area was as beautiful as it was intimidating. He looked to his left every few seconds, not daring to take his eyes off the road too long, but the view was irresistible. The sky was a brilliant blue, contrasting sharply with the white, snow-covered mountains. They seemed undisturbed, pristine, and maybe they were. This was a sparsely populated area, so other than the occasional hiker, few people would venture here. The ski resorts were a bit farther north.

It was one of the reasons why Northern Lake had been so perfect for his research project. Sure, he had ulterior motives to spend a few months there, but the size of the town—or rather, the lack thereof—made it perfect for studying small-town dynamics. And in a few minutes, he would get his first look at Northern Lake.

He put his foot a little farther down on the accelerator to climb a hill, and when he'd reached the top, he gasped. There it was, maybe another mile to go. It was exactly the way he had imagined it. Picturesque, secluded, surrounded by mountains and lots and lots of snow.

He'd done his research, obviously, and he had picked a few starting points. Every town, and especially one this remote, had a few options where locals could hang out. Quentin's first job was to find out what these were in Northern Lake. It could be a local library, if they had one, a bakery, or a bar. Sometimes it was a restaurant, a gas station, or some local shop that functioned as a convenience store.

He slowly drove through the town, staying on the main road, looking to his left and right as much as possible. Ah, *Mary's Convenience and Café*. That sounded like the perfect place to start. He passed through town entirely to make sure nothing else caught his attention, then turned around and set course for Mary's. It had a small parking lot in the front, and he easily found a spot.

He opened the door, and the smell of cinnamon and vanilla greeted him. He smiled. Homebaked goods. God bless small towns. He'd stepped into the convenience part, a small store with shelves that held the standard selection of products. They had everything one could need on a day-to-day basis. Nothing luxurious, nothing exotic, but all the basic staples were available.

He nodded at the teenager managing the register and got a friendly smile from her in return.

"Good morning," she said. "Is there anything I can help you with?"

Quentin could tell from her tone she had spotted him as an outsider, a newcomer. It was subtle, but the offer of help would have been made in a different way had he been a local; he was sure of it.

"I'm just looking around, but thank you," he said.

"Are you visiting Northern Lake?" the teenager asked. "You got lucky with the snowfall. The ski resorts are doing good business right now."

Ski resorts. Right. They were close, maybe half an hour from here. Northern Lake must get its fair share of tourists, even in the winter. In the summer, nature lovers were drawn to the Adirondack Mountains, and this place would have tourists all year round.

"I'm not here to ski, but thank you. The café is that way?" He pointed to the hallway to her left, from where telltale noises of spoons clattering in mugs came.

She nodded quickly. "Yes. Make sure to try the hot chocolate. Mary makes it with a dash of vanilla, and it is heaven. She also made fresh apple pie this morning."

Quentin's stomach rumbled softly in agreement with her suggestions, and he gave her a smile as he walked toward the café. "That sounds amazing. Thank you."

The café had only seven tables, and they were larger than what one would see in bigger cities, most suitable to seat at least six. A group of five women sat at one of the tables, chatting and laughing with each other, with large mugs and empty plates in front of them.

There was no sign that said he had to wait to be seated, so he found a spot at a table in the corner with his back toward the wall. It was the perfect vantage point to observe, and he placed his bag on the seat next to him and pulled out his note bloc and a pen.

He hadn't sat there even a minute when a soft, plump

woman came over to his table, sporting a warm and open expression. "Good morning, and welcome to my café. I'm Mary. What can I do for you today, honey?"

Honey. Had she called him that because she'd surmised he was gay? Or had she misjudged his age, which wasn't outside of the realm of possibilities either? Something to think about.

"It's a pleasure to meet you. Your hot chocolate and apple pie came highly recommended, so I'd like to try those, please."

He was rewarded with a big smile. "Did Kacy tell you? The girl behind the register?" When he nodded, she said, "That's my middle daughter. She has a weakness for anything sweet."

Quentin grinned. "So do I, so that came in handy."

"All right, then. I'll get that right in for you. Would you like your apple pie hot or cold? Ice cream and whipped cream?"

"Hot please, and yes to everything. I'm hungry."

Mary chuckled. "Growing boys like you are always hungry. I've raised two sons, and when they left home, my grocery bill was cut in half, I swear."

"I know, ma'am. My mom says the same."

She smiled broadly as she waved her hand at him. "Look at you being all polite. Your mama raised you well, honey. But you can call me Mary, just like everyone else."

He felt the eyes of the women at the other table on him, and a glance sideways confirmed that they were watching his interaction. Wasn't it wonderful when everything went just the way he had expected?

"Thank you, Mary. I'll make sure to tell her."

"I'll get that hot chocolate and apple pie for you right away, honey. Won't be but a few minutes."

Mary walked away, which gave Quentin the opportunity to study the women. They were still stealing glances his way, and he smiled at them. They greeted him back with a small nod, then left him alone and continued their conversations.

A few minutes later, three more women came in, chatting animatedly as they took off their jackets and joined the group. A table was pushed against the other one, creating one large setup, and the women hugged each other, then sat back down. With the addition of the newcomers, the noise level rose considerably, and he caught snippets of conversations about the snow, power outages, and teenagers who had been put to work.

"They can get a little loud," Mary said as she put a steaming mug of hot chocolate in front of him. "They gather here every Wednesday morning."

Quentin's mouth watered as the rich smell of the apple pie reached him. "God, that smells delicious. I take it they're locals?"

Mary nodded quickly. "It started out as a mom thing, mothers catching up while their toddlers were in pre-K for two hours. But they continued to do it, and over the years, other women joined while others moved away. It's been going on for, gosh, close to fifteen years, I would imagine."

"That's amazing. And how nice of you to host that."

Mary winked at him. "Sure, it's nice, but those women love their sweets as well, if you know what I'm saying. I always bake extra on Wednesdays. Enjoy your pie, honey."

He spent an hour in the café, sipping at his hot chocolate and devouring his apple pie because that had been too scrumptious to eat slowly. He caught quite a bit from the conversations, which were mostly about mundane topics like the weather, how long it would be till spring, about some woman named Beth who had cancer, and about kids and pets and husbands. None of it was earth-shattering, but it was easy to notice the warmth and familiarity between them. Quentin unobtrusively observed and made notes, ensuring to never look at them too long.

He'd have to come clean about his project soon. Outsiders couldn't hang around in towns like this one for too long before arousing suspicion, and he wanted to avoid all negative gossip about him. But he should be good for a week or two, which would give him the opportunity to observe them before they knew what he was studying. And it would help him get the lay of the land, to discover what the focal points were in this town, though he suspected he'd already struck gold with Mary's café. But for now, this was a great start.

Augustus had stressed he needed to fill up his tank, so on the way out, Quentin stopped by the gas station that was situated just outside of town. He winced at the price, even though it was far less per gallon than he paid in California. But this car had a much bigger gas tank, so the total was still a lot higher than he had hoped.

Augustus had made good on his promise to pay for the car, and he had, not just the five grand that Quentin had counted on but the whole amount. He'd told Quentin to take a few weeks to see how he was on money before paying them off. The fact that Augustus had assumed Quentin would pay him back had rested his worries for now. He wouldn't have accepted charity, something his mom had drilled into him.

He could've easily paid for the gas outside, but why not go inside and catch a little more small-town charm? This time, it wasn't a teenager behind the register, but a man who looked like he was in his midforties and carried the weight of the world on his shoulders. His eyes were friendly but oh-so tired.

"Just the gas or do you need anything else, son?"

Quentin swallowed. *Son.* A casual word and the man meant nothing by it, but it was a painful reminder of the other reason he was here. God, he hoped to find some answers. The idea that his father could be here in this town was strange. The man behind the register could be his father, for fuck's sake. He looked a little too young for that, but who the fuck knew?

"Just the gas, thank you."

He quickly paid, and he had just put his change in his wallet when the bell above the door rang through the little store. A guy in faded jeans and a black leather jacket strode to the register. Quentin took him in. He was a few years older than him, Quentin guessed, with a pair of sharp, piercing blue eyes and the body of a quarterback, tall and packed with lean muscles.

"Langley," the man behind the register greeted the newcomer. It was barely friendly, Quentin noted, the man's face tight.

"Xander."

That tone held an edge as well. Did these two have some kind of history? That would be hard to manage in a small town like this where there was no way of avoiding each other, at least, not for long. What was their story? Had they had a falling out, maybe over a woman? Quentin's imagination went full throttle as he gave them both a friendly nod and walked toward the exit.

"I told you a thousand times my name is Alexander, not Xander," the guy behind the register snapped. Quentin was halfway to the door, but his voice low was loud enough for Quentin to hear.

"Yup, and I've told you I'll keep ignoring that as long as you ignore the truth."

Oh, this was not about a *woman*. This was about something else entirely. Quentin stopped long enough to throw a quick look over his shoulder. The tension between those two men was enough to light a fire—and it wasn't purely hate. Then again, hate and passion were closely related, weren't they?

He walked out as slowly as possible, looking over his shoulder a few times, hoping to catch another exchange, but Langley didn't say a word as he put money on the counter. Once outside, Quentin spotted a pickup truck parked at the other gas pump. That had to be Langley's. So he had stopped by for gas, just like Quentin. But Alexander—or Xander, apparently—had been a hell of a lot friendlier to Quentin than to Langley. God, he hoped he would find out what their story was. This, right here, was why he loved what he did. It was like a puzzle, and he loved figuring those out.

He was in a good mood as he drove home, thinking of ways to have some *fun* with Augustus when he came home. Surely they had to celebrate that he'd officially started his research, right?

19

Augustus had always been a live-in-the-moment guy. It was hard to think about the future when it felt like you had no future, when you were stuck in hell with no way out. Over the years, he'd learned to take it day by day, even hour by hour. Fuck, there had been days when he'd had to fight to take it a minute at a time, not sure if he would have a reason to live if he looked past that time frame.

But now, everything was different. With Quentin here, he couldn't wait to take his lunch break. And after lunch, he counted down the hours until he could close and head back inside, where Quentin was waiting for him. Quentin had made daily trips to Northern Lake the last week, but he'd always been home during lunch so they could share that time together. And on more than one occasion, they had shared a little *more* than just lunch.

Augustus had learned things about himself, about his body that he had never known. Quentin had shown him the beauty of rimming, and boy, that had been a revelation. He still wasn't sure if he preferred to do the rimming or to be the willing recipient, but it was a close call. There had been blow jobs and hand jobs and the wonderful sensation of Quentin's cock filling him to a point where everything else ceased to exist. His mind would go blank, everything fading away until all he could see, all he could feel and hear and think was Quentin.

He looked forward to every minute they spent together, and that was an entirely new concept for a man who had lived day by day for the last twenty years of his life. It was like he had put it before: Quentin was his sun. He had brought light and hope and warmth and all these amazing emotions and feelings.

The only aspect where Augustus was still happy to live in the moment was the future of their relationship. Oh, he hoped. He hoped more than he'd ever be able to put into words, but never more than that. He hadn't mentioned to Quentin the possibility of them lasting beyond the period of his research. He hadn't dared to.

He couldn't tie him down, couldn't hold him back, not when Quentin was so young and had such a brilliant future ahead of him in California. He could become a *professor* if he worked hard, and how could Augustus compete with that? All he had to offer was a shady past, a junkyard, and a crap ton of baggage. So he'd kept quiet, meanwhile enjoying every moment they spent together.

They'd had a few inches more snow two days ago, and Augustus stomped off his boots as he went inside after doing his evening checkup. Quentin had already let Lucy out, so he could lock up for the night. Once inside, he took off his boots and hung up his jacket and gloves.

It was dark in the house, he noticed when he stepped

into the kitchen. Quentin had turned off most of the lights, leaving only a few on. Where was he? Had he gone to bed already?

He looked around, and his heart skipped a beat. Quentin was sitting in one of the reading chairs, buck naked, his slender body draped all over the chair, giving Augustus full view of every tantalizing inch of skin. That sight alone was enough to make him drool, but then Quentin casually raised his hand.

"You in, baby?" he asked, holding up a set of ropes.

Oh, *that* had been in the Amazon package that had been delivered a few days ago. Augustus had wondered, but he hadn't asked. Quentin was entitled to his privacy, even his secrets.

Ropes. He had no trouble deducing what those were for. They'd talked about this a week ago, when they had gone through a whole list of options together, deciding which ones they wanted to experiment with. It had been at the top of both their lists. *Bondage.*

Augustus nodded, letting out a deep breath. "Yes."

Quentin would need words for this. Verbal confirmation. Quentin had learned to read Augustus well, and since Augustus had relied on nonverbal communication for a long time, they had quickly found a good way to communicate. Quentin had suggested two additions to the three taps he'd instructed Augustus on before: one to signal he was good, two to slow down, and three to stop. But for certain things, he still demanded words, and Augustus understood.

Quentin slowly rose from his chair with that grace that never failed to captivate Augustus's attention. "You realize this means you will be at my mercy."

It wasn't a question but a statement, and Augustus felt comfortable just nodding.

"And that I can do whatever I want to you."

Quentin took a step closer, and Augustus swallowed as he nodded again.

"You'll be helpless, fully surrendering to all my whims."

Despite the arousal that put his body on high alert, Augustus smiled. The word *whims* was in sharp contrast to Quentin, who Augustus had never seen do anything on a whim. But he understood the game they were playing, the roles they had in this exchange, and he didn't need to see his fully aroused body to know this excited him to no end.

"G-g-ladly," he said. "I will g-gladly s-surrender to you."

The look on Quentin's face changed. Where it had been sexy before, dominant and almost wild, it now grew softer. "You say the most beautiful things, baby. Your words are a treasure to me."

No one had ever said that to him, and it was a compliment that Augustus would remember forever.

Quentin closed the distance between them, then stood in front of him, their bodies only inches apart. The contrast between them was stark when they stood like this, Augustus's body dwarfing Quentin's. Yet it was crystal clear who was in charge, who called the shots. And so he waited until Quentin would give him further instructions.

Quentin dropped the ropes on the floor, then slowly brought his hands up and pulled Augustus's hoodie over his head. He had to help him a little, and his T-shirt followed next. The soft sigh Quentin let out as he put a flat hand on Augustus's chest made Augustus swell with pride. Quentin took pleasure in his body, and he showed it every way he could.

He stood still as Quentin caressed his chest, then trailed down toward his abs. He shivered but otherwise stayed motionless. Quentin continued his exploration as if it was the first time he touched Augustus's body, as if he wanted to memorize it all over again. He ran his hands over his stomach, then stepped behind him and did the same to his back, touching him everywhere. His biceps, his lower arms, then back to his chest as he once again stood in front of him.

His nipples had hardened, and a soft smile played on Quentin's lips as he put both hands back on Augustus's chest, rolling his nipples gently between his thumb and index finger. The line between pleasure and pain was thin, and when Quentin pulled a little harder, Augustus hissed.

"Mmmm, such beautiful sounds," Quentin purred, his voice as sweet as honey. "What sounds are you going to make for me tonight, baby? Do you think I can make you beg again?"

He hadn't begged him since that first time, when he'd pleaded with Quentin to fuck him, but they had barely scratched the surface of everything that was possible. Considering how overwhelming the sensations already had been, begging was a very real possibility. Quentin had a mean streak in him, reveling in making Augustus suffer.

No, *mean* wasn't the right word. It was... Augustus didn't know how to describe it. Pain, humiliation, but mixed in with so much pleasure that he loved it, even as he hated it. How the fuck that was possible, he had no idea, but that was Quentin. He had managed to introduce Augustus to all kinds of new experiences.

Quentin's hand dipped below his belt, boldly slipped into his underwear, and circled his cock with a strong grip. Augustus grunted, as much in surprise as in pleasure. God, the way Quentin simply *took* shouldn't be as arousing as it was. He had his safe signals, they both had, and until either one of them used them, Quentin could do whatever he wanted. And Augustus would *let* him because what a turn-on it was to give this man free rein.

Quentin didn't say another word as he unbuckled Augustus's belt, then swiftly stripped him out of the last of his clothes, including his socks. It was weird to be naked in front of Quentin while he took him in with that intense gaze, and for a few seconds, Augustus felt vulnerable, painfully so.

But then Quentin looked at him with those hot eyes, his gaze so full of need and lust that Augustus's cock jumped up. The slight smile on Quentin's lips showed it hadn't gone unnoticed, and that was confirmed when he dragged his fingernail along Augustus's length. He tensed up, bracing himself for what would happen.

There it was, and he had to fight to stay still. Quentin loved playing with the head of his cock. He would scratch it with his fingernails, teetering on that razor-thin edge of pain and pleasure. Or he'd scrape it with his teeth during a blow job. Squeeze it just a little more tightly than was comfortable. And Augustus would suffer and groan and grunt and bear it because…

Because *why*? He still hadn't figured that part out other than that he wanted to please Quentin. Ultimately, Quentin would bring him more ecstasy than he'd ever experienced, so one could argue it was worth it, but that was not why he did it. The satisfaction he experienced went way beyond physical pleasure, and it came from the act of obedience itself.

He'd spent a lot of time thinking about that the last week, but he still hadn't come to a conclusive answer as to why he liked that so much. Maybe he never would. Maybe it was one of those mystical things in life he had to accept, like whether one loved broccoli and Brussels sprouts or absolutely hated them.

"As you've probably guessed from the ropes, we're going to try something new tonight." Quentin's voice was soft as he walked around Augustus, his hands touching him everywhere. A pinch here, a scratch there, a slap on his ass, a twist of his nipple. All his nerves were fired up, sensitive, and eagerly awaiting what came next.

"Since you'll be tied up for a while, we're going to do this in the bedroom so you're comfortable."

Augustus nodded, even though Quentin didn't need his permission. It was new, so maybe a little extra confirmation that he was all in for this wasn't a bad idea.

"I can see you're already excited," Quentin said, shooting a pointed look at Augustus's leaking cock.

Augustus shrugged. There was little sense in trying to hide his arousal, let alone deny it. He was excited. Why lie about that?

Then Quentin wrapped his slim hand around his cock and pulled, and Augustus winced as the pressure increased, until he had to take a step forward, then another one, and then he got the hint. Quentin led him to the bedroom by his cock, and fuck if that wasn't arousing in and of itself.

Quentin had prepared the bedroom, the comforter and pillows removed from the bed but extra sheets put on, which hopefully meant he intended to make a mess of the best kind. God, Augustus had never run as many loads of laundry as he had the last few weeks. They went through almost a fresh set of sheets daily. He'd even ordered two extra sets on Amazon.

Quentin gestured to the bed, and Augustus climbed onto it, checking with a look whether Quentin wanted him on his back or on his stomach. Stomach it was, and he lay down, spread-eagled, his body relaxing.

Quentin stood beside the bed, uncoiling the ropes, and Augustus turned his head so he could watch him. Quentin's tongue peeped out between his lips as he slowly created a knot that tied Augustus's hands to the bedposts. Quentin tested it, pulling firmly a few times, then nodding as to assure himself he'd done it correctly.

A quick slap on his ass, which for some reason never failed to attract Quentin's attention, and then he switched his preparations to Augustus's ankles. Augustus couldn't see him, too restricted by his tied hands to move around. The rope looped around his right ankle, then again. There was tension on the rope as Quentin tied it to the bedposts, at least, that was what Augustus assumed he was doing. It took long, though, much longer than with his wrists.

"Shit, hold on a second," Quentin said, sounding frustrated. He hurried past Augustus to the night table where he picked up his phone. A few swipes and he studied something with furrowed brows. "Did I do it wrong?" Quentin mumbled, but Augustus was pretty sure it wasn't meant for him.

Quentin stalked back to the end of the bed, phone in hand. The ropes were removed from his ankle, then wrapped around it again. "I had it this morning. This goes over here, and then that one goes under there. So why is it not holding?"

Augustus held still, not wanting to make it even more difficult for Quentin, who clearly had trouble with the knots. He muttered something, then untied Augustus's ankle again, only to start all over. Finally, he seemed satisfied and moved on to Augustus's other leg.

"There, that should do the job," Quentin said, his voice

thick with satisfaction. He dropped his phone back on the nightstand, then appraised Augustus with burning eyes. "You look positively edible, baby. Too bad I'm not in the mood to eat you. Yet."

Augustus's stomach rolled. Funny, he hadn't even thought beyond the part of getting tied up. What was Quentin going to do to him now that he had him restrained?

20

Quentin had to make an effort to keep his breathing even. He had done it. Adrenaline fired through his system as he watched Augustus spread out for him on the bed. The sight of that powerful body immobilized by the ropes was not just arousing. It was powerful, exhilarating, and also scary as hell.

The last two days, after the ropes had arrived, he'd practiced making the knots, but it wasn't as easy as it had looked on the websites. Even with the step-by-step instructions, he had still struggled, frustrated by a lifelong lack of spatial awareness. It had been his nemesis all through high school math as well. He just couldn't read drawings, diagrams, graphics of any kind. Give him words, and he was fine, but any kind of pictures fucked him up. Noel had spent hours explaining that shit to him, and he'd still only scraped by on those exams.

But he'd managed it, right? He did the last check, making sure that enough space remained between Augustus's skin and the rope so he wouldn't cut off his circulation.

Once he had assured himself he'd really done a good job, Quentin blew out a slow breath. Now came the next part.

He had planned this. Meticulously, in fact. He didn't like to leave things to chance anyway, but in this case even less because Augustus depended on him not only for his pleasure but for his safety as well. Quentin had to be worthy of the trust this man had put in him.

"Remind me of your safe signals," he said, his voice cracking a little. "What's the signal for green?"

Augustus snapped his fingers once.

"Yellow?"

He slapped them on the bed twice. Maybe that was easier than snapping? And faster, probably.

"Red?"

He did the same, but three times.

How could Augustus seem so calm and composed? This was all new to him as well, and moreover, it wasn't just the D/s part that was new to him but the whole gay part as well. Though Quentin had to admit Augustus had taken to both like he'd done it all his life. His surrender came so easily, so naturally, and it made Quentin even more aware of the weight of his responsibility.

His hand trembled, but he extended it anyway, pausing only for a second before he let it land on Augustus. Augustus jerked from the unexpected contact, then grew still again. Should he talk to him? The advice he'd read on the blogs had been contradictory. Some people—and it had been both Doms and subs who had argued this—said that if you were both new to the lifestyle, talking was important. It helped establish an open communication, and Quentin could see the truth of that.

But others had claimed that was nonsense and that explaining everything you were about to do diminished the impact of the scene. That sounded pretty reasonable as well, so which should he believe? Which advice should he follow? In the end, according to most Doms, it came down to following your gut, and that was not as easy as it sounded.

He trailed his hand down Augustus's back, reveling in the sheer strength of the muscles he caressed. If he wanted to—and if he hadn't been tied down—Augustus could knock him out with one strike. Not that he would ever get violent with him; that, Quentin was sure of. But he *could*, and it made his submission all the sweeter.

The man's ass was a work of art. Compared to the rest of his body, it was just a tad rounder, had a bit more meat to it. It was still strong and muscled, honed by years of physical labor, but it held just that little extra jiggle. And god, the way he *felt* inside, the tight grip his ass created on Quentin's cock when he fucked him... Quentin swallowed at the thought.

But no, he couldn't skip steps. This mattered, and he had to get it right. He continued his gentle exploration of Augustus's body, touching him everywhere, tickling him a little when he saw that got a reaction out of him, and of course, carefully avoiding any intimate areas. Oh, he could see them, since Augustus was beautifully spread wide, his crack, hole, and balls on full display.

He ran his hands over Augustus's ass but skipped his crack. He stroked his thighs but never his balls. And when Augustus moved his hips in an effort to seek friction for his cock, one sharp slap on his ass cured him of the notion that that was okay. When he was satisfied that Augustus had surrendered to whatever was coming, it was time for the next part of the program.

He'd placed the lube within reach and now drizzled some of it between Augustus's ass cheeks, making him squeal with shock. He giggled, feeling almost high with exuberance. "Oops, was that cold?"

To his credit, Augustus didn't say anything but merely relaxed his body again. That deserved a reward, and Quentin dragged his index finger down Augustus's crack, slowly, teasingly, briefly halting at that tempting pink star, then continuing down. Augustus made one of his beautiful sounds, something between a grunt and a moan, low and needy.

Quentin repeated his action and was rewarded with a similar sound. Quentin wasn't sure if it was because Augustus had so little experience or if it was his character, but he loved how uninhibited he was in his reactions. He seemed to have no shame for how he reacted, for how Quentin made him feel, or for the sensations in his body. Quentin had never had a bed partner like that, and he wanted to see all Augustus's reactions, hear all his sounds. God, he wanted to make him *sing* for him.

Pleasure was ruling now, so a little pain was inevitable. Quentin went by pure instinct as he circled his hand around Augustus's balls, already somewhat squashed under his weight. Augustus tensed, and Quentin squeezed a little harder.

A beautiful grunt erupted from Augustus's mouth, and Quentin tightened his grip. This part he knew because he'd practiced on himself. It wasn't the same, and every man's pain threshold was different, but it had given him a good idea of how far he could go. And Augustus's tolerance for pain was pretty damn high.

He held his tight grip, and after a few seconds, Augustus keened. "Q-quentin..."

Mmm, it wasn't quite begging, but it was close, wasn't it? He let go, smiling when Augustus blew out a breath of relief. He went back to teasing his crack, making sure to skip his hole every single time. As soon as Augustus moved against his touch, seeking more, Quentin went for his balls again, and it didn't take long for the man to catch on.

It was mean, maybe, punishing him for reactions he could hardly help when Quentin teased his helpless body, but Quentin didn't care, and he was pretty sure Augustus didn't mind either. He had his safe signal after all, and so far, he wasn't showing any indication of wanting to use it.

Augustus fought hard to keep himself from reacting. Quentin felt it in how tense his muscles got. He held out for minutes, and Quentin was about to give up and reluctantly admit defeat when Augustus lost the fight against his urge to move. He snapped his hips back, and Quentin's slick fingers tapped against his entrance.

This was what Quentin had been hoping for. His left hand went for Augustus's balls, even as his right index and middle finger pushed inside him with force. It was a brute attack on the man's senses, pain in two places, but also the pleasure of finally having something inside him. Augustus jerked, his arms and legs putting full tension on the ropes, and the ropes on his wrists gave way.

"Dammit," Quentin cursed.

Had he gotten the knots wrong after all, or had he not tightened them enough? Maybe he had underestimated Augustus's strength? Frustration coursed through him that after all his preparation and effort, he had still failed.

"S-s-sorry," Augustus said. "I d-didn't m-mean to p-pull them l-l-loose. I'll hold them s-still. Or you c-can retie them. Whatever you w-w-w-want."

The fact that he was willing to spend so many words on this meant he realized the depth of Quentin's frustration.

That was sweet, but it didn't change the reality that Quentin had fucked up.

He withdrew his fingers from Augustus's ass and released his balls. "It's not your fault. I didn't tie them tight enough. I should've known you were stronger than my feeble attempts at creating a knot."

He hated the hurt in his voice, hated that he wasn't able to stay as calm and composed as he should be as a Dom. How could he have ever thought he was ready for tying someone up? He was an absolute beginner, and he should've known better than to try something like this, especially with another novice.

He rolled off the bed. "I'm sorry," he said, his voice sounding as hopeless and tired as he felt on the inside. "I shouldn't have tried to do something I don't have the skills for."

God, the urge to run away was so intense, but he couldn't. First of all, Augustus was still tied to the bed with his ankles, and even with his hands free, it wasn't easy for him to untie his legs. But second, Quentin wouldn't run away. It wasn't who he was, no matter how shitty he felt.

So he took a deep breath and untied Augustus, his fingers trembling. "You're free," he said, but much to his surprise, Augustus stayed in the same position. He only lifted his head and turned it toward Quentin.

"I d-don't want to be f-f-free. I l-liked being t-t-tied up by you."

God, he was so sweet, but Quentin still shook his head. "My knots were useless against your strength. You weren't really tied down."

"D-doesn't m-m-matter. You t-tried, and it was g-good enough for me. I didn't w-want you to s-stop."

It was hard to argue with so much kindness, but Quentin

couldn't lie, not even to make Augustus feel better. "I'm not ready for this," he said softly. "I had to look up how to make secure knots, and I don't think that's a good enough skill level to do shit like this."

Augustus frowned, and he moved for the first time, putting his hand under his head and rolling onto his side. "Why n-not?"

"Because you deserve better. And because it's not safe to play when I don't know what I'm doing."

"Why n-not?" Augustus asked again.

"What do you mean, why not? I just told you. It's not safe. I could hurt you."

Augustus pushed himself up into a sitting position, shaking his head. "H-hurt me? How? With r-r-ropes? They were not t-t-too tight. If they had b-been, I would've t-t-told you. How can r-ropes that are too l-l-loose hurt me?"

Quentin opened his mouth to contradict that statement but then closed it again. The man was right. "I meant it more in general. Not just about tonight, but going forward. I shouldn't be experimenting with you and playing with you if I don't know what I'm doing. I need lessons of some kind, someone to teach me how to do this safely."

Augustus got up from the bed and stepped in front of Quentin. "You m-make it t-too difficult. You're s-s-smart enough to know when it b-becomes uns-safe, and so am I. I can s-s-say stop or g-g-give the s-s-ignal, and I kn-kn-know that you will r-respect that."

"Always," Quentin promised him.

Augustus nodded. "So why uns-s-safe? They're ropes, n-not metal chains or s-s-something I couldn't get out of if n-n-necessary."

"But that is not the point. The whole idea is that you should be tied down, that you should be at my mercy."

"I don't kn-know anything ab-bout this, so maybe I'm wrong, b-b-but isn't that an ill-ll-llusion anyway? I am t-t-ten times stronger than you and t-twice your s-size. You would have to g-g-go through a hell of a l-lot of trouble to imm-mm-mmobilize me to the p-point where you c-c-could overp-power me physically."

Quentin swallowed. He didn't like that line of reasoning at all. What was Augustus trying to say? That Quentin's feeble attempts at domination were never going to work? "So I should just give up?" he asked, his voice sounding a lot sharper than he had intended.

Augustus's eyes widened for a second. "N-n-o," he said softly, then again, "No. You d-don't unders-s-stand. My subm-m-mission to you isn't a ph-ph-physical thing. It's a m-mental thing. I ch-choose to submit to you, n-not because you're s-s-stronger or smarter or have me t-tied down, but because I w-want to. I want you t-to be in ch-charge. I w-w-want you to d-d-do to me whatever you w-want. Even if I can walk away, even if I c-c-can break free, I don't w-w-want to."

And as Quentin tried to process the truth of the words Augustus had just fired at him, the bear of a man in front of him did the unthinkable. He sank to his knees again, kneeling low until his mouth was pressed against Quentin's bare feet. His breath danced over Quentin's skin, warm and reassuring. Augustus never looked up as he dropped a kiss to Quentin's left foot, then his right.

"I'm *always* at your m-m-mercy," he whispered. "S-sir."

21

It didn't feel demeaning to Augustus. Here he was, on his knees for another man, hell, almost flat on the floor, literally kissing his feet...but he'd never felt more powerful. He'd never felt more free. He'd spoken the truth, and the rest was up to Quentin. He *was* at Quentin's mercy, and that was exactly where he wanted to be.

Something wet dripped on his shoulder. A tear. Quentin sniffled, and Augustus listened hard but stayed motionless. He wouldn't move until Quentin told him to. He *owed* him that after what he'd promised him.

"Augustus," Quentin said, and it felt like a caress.

Another tear dripped on his shoulder, trickling down his back.

"Baby," Quentin whispered, and it sunk deep inside him, the *rightness* of that word.

He kissed his feet again, those knobbly feet that were so out of proportion with the rest of Quentin's body, maybe the only part that wasn't perfect and graceful. It made him even more endearing in Augustus's eyes.

"Stay," Quentin commanded, and his voice had changed.

Gone was the insecurity, that edge of pain and disappointment. In its place was the old Quentin, the self-assured, almost cocky Quentin, who had thundered into Augustus's life and had turned everything upside down. Oh, he would stay at his feet as long as he had to. As long as Quentin wanted.

Quentin shuddered, and he moved, though how, Augustus couldn't see with his eyes closed and his mouth still pressed against those feet. Then sounds reached his ears. Slick, wet, rhythmic. Quentin jacked off above him, his legs swaying in the same cadence as his hand.

Augustus could picture him in his mind, the blush on his cheeks, the way his eyes darkened and got all intense. He had this focused look where his eyes bore into Augustus and saw every bit of him.

He relaxed as best he could while Quentin continued his unhurried rhythm. His breathing sped up, his breaths turning into soft pants, and he swayed a little more. Augustus held posture, even when it became uncomfortable, even when his muscles tensed, then trembled and burned. His body *hurt,* but his mind escaped, finding a peaceful place where he didn't feel a damn thing except the bliss of pleasing Quentin.

Quentin growled, a throaty sound that made Augustus's dick twitch. He was leaking all over the floor, but he didn't care. Nothing was more important than this, than staying where he was and making Quentin happy.

"My beautiful Augustus," Quentin said, his voice a raspy purr, thick with arousal. "My perfect baby."

Seconds later, splashes of hot cum landed on his back, on his shoulders, and in his hair, but he'd already received his reward. Hearing Quentin call him his perfect baby, that was why he did it. That was why he would endure anything

Quentin wanted. Anything his Sir wanted. He didn't need to understand why those simple words meant so much to him, only that they did.

"Stay," Quentin said again and stepped back, and Augustus obeyed, not moving except to put his head on the floor. He kept his eyes closed. The rush of being perfect for him was exhilarating. He wanted to hold on to that as long as he could.

"Spread your legs."

The hardwood floor was cold underneath him, and he shivered while he opened his legs wide. Frigid air danced down his ass, his crack, whispering over his hole. His empty, empty hole, which still felt the afterburn of Quentin's fingers. What was he..."

Oh.

Something wet drizzled down on him, too warm to be lube. Spit. Quentin was letting a string of spit rain down on Augustus's crack, and he shivered again. God, was he planning on fucking him after all?

He fought to stay still. His cock was so hard, and the floor was right *there,* and all he needed to do to get friction was move a little. Just a tiny shift of his hips. But no, he wouldn't. Moving meant disobeying, and that was not an option.

A whimper rose, and it was him, the sound escaping from him instead of sheer begging.

Please, please, please. I need...

Quentin. He needed Quentin.

And then Quentin's body dropped on top of him, and his legs were roughly shoved even wider, and he went with it. His ass was held open, and Quentin pushed inside him, not going slow this time but surging in, ruthless and so big.

Augustus made a sound, a pitiful wail of pain and pleasure, of ecstasy and protest, of being too full and so empty simultaneously. He wanted Quentin to stop and to move, to fuck him hard, to do anything to make this feeling of being too big for his skin, too cold and too hot at the same time stop. He needed...

Quentin put his full weight on him, snapped his hips back, and drove deep inside him. Augustus *howled*. God, yes. Quentin held still for a moment, then another one, and Augustus smacked his flat hand on the floor once. *Don't stop. Please don't stop. Don't make me say it.* He didn't even have time to brace himself before Quentin pulled back and slammed back in.

He didn't hold back this time. No tender lovemaking, no going slow. No sweet words and careful thrusts. This was a man on the edge, going all out with vicious, rough strokes that set Augustus's body on fire. He spread his legs wider, distributed his weight evenly to brace himself against the onslaught, and he took it.

He soaked in every harsh grunt Quentin made, every wet slap of flesh hitting flesh. He drank in his smell, the way his pants made his skin prickle, the bruising grip on his arms. Quentin held him down. Augustus could've easily bucked him off. One move and Quentin would be the one on his stomach. Or on his back. But Augustus submitted. He surrendered, even as tears of joy trickled down his cheeks.

God, it *hurt*, but in the best way. His muscles screamed with fatigue, his ass stung, and his knees fucking ached from being smashed hard against the floor. But his body sang, his balls full and tightening, his cock so hard it could obliterate nails. Every circuit in his body was firing, nerve endings he'd never even been aware of sending signals of pleasure and pain, pain and pleasure, until the two became one, and he exploded.

Lightning flashed behind his closed eyes, and his ears buzzed as his balls unloaded. His body trembled and shook, and he came without ever touching his cock, his eyes tearing up with the force of his orgasm. His cock spurted, then again, and he bucked and arched reflexively. Quentin pinned him down even harder and slammed in one more time, roaring as he came hard, flooding Augustus's ass with his cum.

Quentin's mouth found a spot on Augustus's shoulder, and he sank his teeth in, marking him as his body shook and trembled with his orgasm. Finally, he collapsed on top of him, and they lay together, chests heaving and lungs panting.

"That," Quentin said, what had to be minutes later, and Augustus *still* hadn't moved, "was the single best fuck of my entire life."

Augustus's face broke open in a wide smile. He was dirty and cold, and god, *everything* hurt, but hearing that had been worth it. His smile didn't waver as Quentin scrambled off him, doing a little sighing and grunting of his own. Yeah, floor fucks were definitely not the most comfortable. Augustus could attest to that. But holy fuck, that had been hot. Insanely sexy. Mind-blowing.

"How are you doing, baby?" Quentin asked, and Augustus took that as a sign he could move.

He carefully rolled onto his back, wincing as his muscles protested. He'd had his eyes closed for so long that he had to blink a few times before they would focus again, and when they did, Quentin looked down on him with amusement sparkling in his eyes.

"You have..." he started, and then he giggled in that sweet, happy way that made Augustus's belly dance. "You have the imprint of the floor on your skin."

Augustus sat up, then glanced at his chest. Quentin was right. The wooden floorboards were pressed into his skin, leaving an exact replica of the pattern. He shrugged. "T-t-totally w-worth it."

Quentin's face lit up. "Yeah?"

"Mmm."

"Was it good?"

"P-p-perfect."

He laughed when Quentin extended his hand. Did he really think that he could pull Augustus up? He grabbed it, then let Quentin bear his full weight. It only took a second before he toppled over, and Augustus caught him, falling backward with him and breaking his fall by letting him land on his chest.

"You did that on purpose," Quentin accused him, pushing himself up again and meeting Augustus's eyes. He was laughing, though, so Augustus grinned as well.

"T-totally w-worth it."

22

It was like an idyllic scene from a movie. Maybe even an old Norman Rockwell painting, aside from the fact that they were two men, of course. They lay on the couch in front of a glowing fire, Augustus stretched out with his head in Quentin's lap. He'd taken his shirt off at Quentin's request. It was warm enough so close to the fire, and he loved having free access and touching him everywhere.

He was tired, Quentin could tell. His movements were slower than usual and his eyes sad and troubled. Quentin hadn't asked him if something had happened. He'd learned that when Augustus was this bone-tired, his reluctance to speak became stronger. It was like he lacked the energy to fight against it and gave in to his desire to stay silent. Asking him what was going on would only make him more stressed, so he wouldn't. He would simply hold him and be there and wait until he was ready to talk. Or not.

He would read to him on nights like that, hours of quiet togetherness until Augustus's eyes grew heavy and his body slack. Or Quentin would talk, and Augustus would listen. He'd been guilty about that at first and more than a little awkward. It felt unnatural and selfish to talk and never ask questions, but Augustus had made it clear he loved listening to Quentin. After that, Quentin had gotten over his reluctance, and they'd spent a few nights like this.

"I saw those two guys again, Langley and Alexander," Quentin said. "You know, at the gas station?"

Augustus gave an almost imperceptible nod, but Quentin was tuned into him now. "Well, you said we were a little short on milk, so I figured I'd pick up a gallon of two percent at the gas station."

Augustus raised one eyebrow.

"Okay, so I was hoping to run into them. Can you blame me after that first time? I was so freaking curious about what the story was between them."

Instead of answering, Augustus merely quirked his eyebrow again. Quentin had learned it wasn't disinterest that made Augustus go into silent mode, and since he understood the reasons, he had no trouble accepting it. The eyebrow meant "tell me more," and so he would.

"They were arguing when I came in. Something about Alexander having money problems and being too stubborn to ask for help. He's the guy who owns the gas station. Langley was ripping him a new one, but he stopped once they spotted me. Unfortunately. I was really curious, and I would've loved to hear more."

"L-l-lovers?"

"Maybe. There's definitely sexual tension between them. If they haven't had sex already, they will at some point."

"M-mary's?"

Quentin nodded. "I spent some time there again as well.

It was Wednesday, so the women were hanging out. They were friendlier than last time, smiling at me and shit, so I'm making progress. And Mary already greets me by name when I walk in, and so do her daughters. Both her middle and youngest daughter work in the store."

He ran his hand through Augustus's dark hair, so silky under his fingers. Augustus made a soft sound of contentment, and his eyes drifted shut.

"I haven't told them about my project yet, but I will next week, I've decided. I've been hanging out there for two weeks now, so it's time. It will get suspicious anyway if I keep coming back without a reason."

"O-o-kay?"

Quentin hummed. "Yeah, I think they'll be okay with it. You never know, but they seem to be pretty friendly and open to strangers."

Unlike Frostville. God, this town was fucking awful. News of their relationship had clearly done the rounds because he was getting the same treatment as Augustus now. A few days ago he'd gone into the mini supermarket for some quick groceries, and everyone had stared at him. Nobody had said a damn word. What the fuck was *wrong* with these people?

No wonder Augustus was exhausted. He'd borne their hostility for years now, and even though he seemed to take it all in stride, it had to eat at him. The unfairness of it made Quentin's blood boil. Something had to have happened today, an incident that had made his burden heavier than usual.

Augustus had looked so sad, so hopeless. Maybe not asking about what had happened today was smart because at some point, Quentin would lose his cool about the whole situation. His temper wasn't easily triggered anymore, but it was still there...and it could be formidable.

He mindlessly played with Augustus's lip piercing. "How long have you had this?"

Augustus held up his hand, all fingers stretched wide.

"Five years? Your septum piercing too?"

He nodded.

"The first things I noticed about you were your piercings and your tattoos. Well, the ones I could see with you all bundled up anyway. You looked like a badass mofo, man. I was more than a little scared of you."

Augustus's eyes opened, and he turned his head a little to the side and met Quentin's eyes. "S-scared?"

"God, yes. I cursed that AAA guy ten ways to Sunday when he left me here. You were like the big bad wolf."

Augustus smiled, then leaned into his touch and licked his hand.

Quentin grinned. "You're more of a puppy, aren't you? You appear mean, but you're just a little puppy on the inside."

He stroked the colorful tattoos on Augustus's right arm. He had a bold, red tribal pattern wrapped around his biceps and a much bigger black lion covering his shoulder. "Why a lion?"

Augustus shrugged. "R-r-respect. He's the k-k-king."

"True. He's at the top of the food chain, I guess."

"So the tattoos and the piercings, that was your way of saying 'fuck you' to your townspeople?"

Augustus's eyes grew sad. "I had h-h-hoped f-for f-forgiveness. A s-second chance. Even w-w-when I s-started p-paying off, n-no one offered m-m-mercy."

His pain pierced Quentin's heart. This man and the boy inside him had suffered so much, and no one had ever offered compassion other than his mom. "Your mom loved you very much," he said softly.

Augustus pointed at a small tattoo, almost hidden between the much bigger ones he had on his other arm. A bear on his shoulder on this side and another tribal pattern. But in between were three small letters in a feminine script. *Mom.*

"Was that her own handwriting?" Quentin asked.

Augustus nodded, and sadness radiated off him in waves. All Quentin could offer were clichés, but he'd say them anyway. "She would have been proud of the man you've become."

Augustus's expression changed, and a spark danced in his eyes. "Sh-she w-would have l-l-liked you."

"You think?" Quentin had never thought about it, but now that he did, Augustus's quiet confidence that his mother would have liked Quentin warmed his heart.

They sat for a while, Quentin touching him everywhere, following the lines of his tattoos, the planes of his muscles, then his jaw, ruffling his beard. Augustus leaned into his touch, and his soft sighs fueled Quentin's desire to take care of him, to help him relax.

With every touch, Augustus's body relaxed a bit more, the tension seeping out of him until it transitioned into a different kind of tension. Quentin hadn't planned to do anything, figuring Augustus was too tired, but maybe he could distract him? Make him feel better? And of course, get some pleasure of his own as well.

He came back to his lip piercing, flicking it a little. "We should get your nipples pierced."

"You'd l-l-like th-that?"

"Hell yeah." Quentin slid his hands lower across that broad, hairy chest, finding those little buds and pinching them. Augustus bucked off the couch, growling in protest at the rough treatment. "Mmm, yes. I could tug those piercings, have you make sounds for me you've never made before..."

Augustus arched his back, straining himself to move with Quentin's hands, and Quentin smiled, then released him. The big man's breath was shaky as he settled back on the couch. Quentin stroked his chest with light hands now, smoothing and soothing.

"Would you do that for me, baby? Would you have them pierced for me?"

The words rolled off his lips like honey, sweet and seducing, and Augustus's eyes darkened. "Yes."

Deep satisfaction blazed through him at that soft answer. Was there anything this man wouldn't do for him? He had *kneeled* for him, for fuck's sake. Twice. And he'd meant it. He'd done it with all his heart, knowing what it symbolized.

But Quentin couldn't help but push a little harder. Go a little further. Augustus was so beautiful when he submitted, so stunning when he suffered for him.

He smoothed his hands down Augustus's chest, then leaned in so he could travel lower and lower. Augustus groaned, eagerly raising his hips, inviting Quentin to dip under his waistband, under his briefs. Quentin was sure Augustus would've invited him under his skin if he could.

His cock was warm and at half mast, but once Quentin wrapped his hand around it, it hardened instantly. Augustus's lips parted, and this time, his moan was soundless, a hitchy breath that hovered on his lips.

Quentin rolled half on top of him, bringing his mouth to Augustus's ear, even as his hand increased the pressure. "What about your cock, baby?"

Quentin's thumb traced the head of Augustus's cock, then pushed down harder, making him instinctively pull back. "Would you pierce that for me? A nice, fat Prince Albert?"

Augustus's eyes grew wide and dark, and he licked his lips. As if that wasn't enough of a hint to how he felt, his cock hardened even more in Quentin's hand. He *liked* that idea.

"Mmm, I think we could have so much fun with that. Or a frenum piercing..."

Augustus held his eyes, and the desire in them spoke volumes. Quentin smiled, bent over for a slow kiss. He licked Augustus's lips, tugged gently on his piercing, then slipped his tongue into his mouth.

He welcomed him on a moan, and Quentin surged in, their tongues meeting and sliding together. Augustus's eyes fluttered closed, and he pressed himself against Quentin, rolling his hips into Quentin's touch. Quentin pulled back a little, still holding Augustus's cock but lightly as he intensified the kiss. But Augustus lifted himself again, chasing his touch.

Quentin gave in, stroking him firmly, and Augustus let out another beautiful moan. He was still so eager, so uninhibited. Quentin kneaded, stroked, then grabbed his balls and squeezed. Augustus gasped, his body freezing as Quentin kept him teetering on the brink of pain. He coaxed him back by releasing and caressing, by sliding and rubbing. Then he pinched the hard head of Augustus's cock, and the man hissed. He caught the sound, swallowed the grunt of pain that followed as he did it again.

Oh yeah, they would definitely need some more piercings. He let go of Augustus's mouth and shimmied lower on his body, tracing a path southward with his lips, his tongue, his teeth. Augustus shuddered, grunted, bucked, his fists balled and his body as tense as a bowstring. God, the *sounds* this man made. This beautiful, raw man. *His* man.

He pushed up for a second, irritated by his own shirt. He wanted to feel him, press his hot skin against Augustus's. Nothing between them. Nothing.

His shirt drifted to the floor, and then he yanked his jeans off, his socks, and with some maneuvering, his underwear. It wasn't that he wanted to fuck him. He just needed to feel him, to be as close to him as he could.

Augustus watched him with heavy-lidded eyes, his lips partly opened, still swollen and wet from their kiss. Quentin didn't say a word as he dragged Augustus's jeans down, aided by him lifting his hips, then again for his underwear. His cock slapped against his stomach, heavy and wet, and as soon as Quentin had thrown the clothes onto the floor, he dove on it.

He sucked him in all the way, ignoring Augustus's raspy shout of shock, holding him with his right hand to prevent him from slamming in too far in reflex. He pushed back his legs, and Augustus complied, spreading wide for him, then placing his feet on Quentin's shoulders when he gestured him to. He let go of the man's cock long enough to spit into his fingers, then went right back to work. He wasn't gentle when he pushed against his entrance, but Augustus had gotten good at bearing down. Besides, Quentin had fucked him that morning in the shower, and he was still a little loose.

He pressed and was let in, and then he shoved harder, deeper, unrelenting, until he had two fingers buried deep into that silken heat. His mouth sucked while his fingers fucked, and Augustus made incomprehensible sounds now, babbling and protesting and moaning all at the same time. The man was falling apart, and Quentin soaked it up.

The powerful body underneath him trembled, Augustus clenching and unclenching his fists as he bore Quentin's onslaught. Quentin didn't let up and plunged his fingers deep inside his ass, hitting his prostate straight on. Augustus jerked and squirmed, rocking back, then forward again, confused as to what to do to make it better.

Then he grabbed Quentin's hair, pulling him down on his cock, and Quentin let him, taking him in until he gagged, until his nose was buried in the man's pubes, breathing in his sweat, his scent, his everything. Augustus's grip tightened, becoming painful. Tears sprang in Quentin's eyes, but he held on.

"Q-q-quentin," Augustus said. A warning.

Quentin let go for a second to catch his breath, then sucked him in again. Augustus roared, the sound filling Quentin's body, his heart, his soul. His mouth overflowed with cum, and he swallowed, coughing, then again. Before Augustus was even done spurting, Quentin released his cock and yanked his fingers out of his ass and moved up, his hand circling Augustus's throat as he kissed him. Hard. Brutal. Wet. The last cum now dripping into Augustus's mouth.

The kiss softened. Quentin melted against him. The desperation in him subsided, and calmness returned. His stomach unclenched, and even though his own cock was still rock hard, it was okay. It hadn't been the physical release he'd needed, but something else. Something deeper. Connection. And he'd found it, as always, through pain and pleasure.

Should he feel guilty? Had it been too much for Augustus, too raw? An apology was on the tip of his tongue until he broke off the kiss and pushed himself up. Augustus lay underneath him, smiling, his eyes glazy now, his body a boneless puddle. He was happy, and not a trace of the burdens he'd borne earlier had remained.

"Th-th-thank you," he whispered, and Quentin beamed.

"You're welcome."

23

It was a cold day with a bright blue sky but a biting wind that kept most people indoors. Augustus didn't mind the lack of customers. As much as he could use the money, he appreciated spending some time by himself, his head peaceful as he stripped down the two cars that had been brought in earlier that week.

As long as he kept moving, he would stay reasonably warm. His feet never got cold thanks to a pair of expensive but well-insulated work boots. He'd splurged on a pair of long johns, specifically designed for outdoor enthusiasts in the winter. In combination with his windproof, water-resistant pants, they ensured his legs stayed warm.

The only challenge, as always, was his hands, but so far, his work gloves had done their job. He had to take them off sometimes when they got in the way for tasks that required precision or fine motor skills, but it had only been for a few minutes each time. No, Augustus appreciated a cold day like this because it usually meant a peaceful day, even if he had to spend it without Lucy, who had gone inside to escape the cold.

Quentin had left half an hour earlier, as always taking his time to kiss Augustus properly before he took off to Northern Lake. His research was going well, and the excitement in his voice and body language when he talked about it was hard to miss. He truly loved doing what he did, and it made Augustus a little envious.

He sometimes wondered what his life would've looked like had his father not screwed him over. He'd been sent to prison a few months after graduating high school. Would he have gone to college otherwise? Probably not.

It had always been implied he would take over the junkyard from his grandfather, and it had never occurred to him to protest that. Sure, in the last two years of high school, he'd looked into going to college. His grandfather had said he had an aptitude for fixing things, for working with his hands, and he didn't mind it. But he'd had good grades in school, at least for those subjects where he didn't have to speak. Languages were impossible, but he loved writing reports for history or social studies, and he had aced math and science.

His high school counselor had discouraged him from college, though. She'd kept stressing it would be hard for him with his speech impediment, repeatedly telling him that college required speaking up, oral presentations, things like that. It had scared him enough to never even consider it again.

Besides, there had been no money for college, and that same counselor had told him getting scholarships would be a hard sell because of his lower grades for certain topics and the fact that he'd never played sports. The latter wasn't for lack of trying, but despite being decent at football, they'd never wanted him on the team. An outcast, that was what he'd been his whole life, never fitting in.

It made his connection with Quentin so special, so magical. Quentin didn't only treat him like he would anyone else, but they *fit* together. With him, Augustus felt normal, accepted. Seen. Quentin *got* him.

In the four weeks he had been here, he'd managed to learn to read Augustus like a book. Quentin sensed when he was tired, when speaking was hard, and he had never once complained. Instead, he would help Augustus find distraction, relaxation, relief. He was a miracle worker, and Augustus had become good at stuffing down all thoughts of Quentin leaving.

He'd done some learning of his own as well. Like, why Quentin hated guns. The trailer park he'd grown up in had been violent when he was a kid, and his best friend had gotten shot by accident when two neighbors got into a gun fight. He'd been nine years old…and he'd died. Ever since, he'd hated guns, even though he'd learned to use them, he'd told Mac, who had held him as Quentin had gotten emotional. As much as he hated to see him hurting, he loved that Quentin shared it with him.

The sound of a car on the road made him look up. He followed the noise, frowning when it came closer, then turned into his driveway. He put the radiator he had just removed from the wreckage down on the tarp he'd placed on the ground, then walked toward the entrance.

As soon as he recognized the car and the man who got out, his stomach dropped. Willis. What did he want now? He straightened his back as he strode toward him, silently comforted by the weight of the gun in his jacket's pocket.

Willis stood waiting for him, his arms crossed and his face scowling under a woolen beanie that was pulled low over his eyes. Augustus didn't say anything. Willis would have to start. They stared at each other for a bit, but

Augustus didn't give in. He wouldn't give the man the satisfaction.

Finally, Willis made a grunting sound. "The insurance company stopped by to look at the damage from that tree. They say you made it worse with the way you removed that tree. If you had done it properly, you could've saved me two thousand dollars in damage."

Augustus still didn't say anything. Fury bubbled up inside him, and it fucking *cost* him to keep his face blank. How dare this man accuse him of causing the damage when it had been his own stupidity? He was known as a cheapskate who would never spend money on preventing disasters, like cutting down a dying tree to keep it from toppling over and crushing his barn.

"I'm gonna have to hold you responsible for that extra damage, so you owe me two thousand dollars."

It was the biggest load of crap Augustus had ever heard, and they both knew it. But even as he realized that, a wave of hopelessness came over him. How would he defend himself from this? How far would Willis go this time to extort money from him?

"And don't bother sending your little *boyfriend* after me because I know he's not here."

A muscle ticked in Augustus's jaw, but other than that, he managed to keep his face in check. If Willis knew Quentin wasn't here, he must have been watching them. That was not a comforting thought. His cameras still worked because he had checked them just that morning before he'd gone outside, so if Willis tried to pull something, at least Augustus would have evidence—if that would even do him any good.

"B-b-bullshit," he said finally, and he struggled to even get that word out. "I'm n-not p-p-paying."

Willis laughed, a scornful laugh that made Augustus feel like a middle schooler again, getting bullied by his classmates.

"Not quite so eloquent and feisty without your boyfriend, huh? It only proves what a wimp you are, letting someone else do the talking for you. The insolent little shit."

Augustus thought he was used to it by now, the endless taunts, the derisive comments about his stutter, the sneers, and the bullying. And maybe he was, but Willis's sharp words about Quentin fired up the anger inside him in a way he hadn't felt in a long time. He'd thought he was beyond getting this worked up about it, but having Quentin dragged into it made it different. Not that he would show Willis that.

"St-st-still not p-paying," he said, noting with satisfaction that a flash of surprise washed over Willis's face. If the man had really thought Augustus would give in, he was in for a nasty experience.

But then Willis straightened his shoulders, and his face contorted in a mask full of hatred. Augustus almost stepped back in recoil. "I was hoping it wouldn't have to come to this, but if you can't be reasonable about this, you leave me no choice but to involve the law."

Involve the law? Oh god, what had Willis done?

The look on Willis's face was pure glee as he took his phone from his pocket and pressed a button. It didn't take long for the call to connect, because only seconds later, Willis said, "Sheriff, good morning."

Augustus had to close his eyes to steady himself. The sheriff. Willis had called Sheriff McAuley on him. This would not end well. He knew from experience. Still, he had no choice but to let it play out. No way was he paying Willis two thousand dollars just to avoid this. If he did that once, everyone would find out he could be blackmailed.

No, he had to stand his ground here and face the consequences.

The call was quick. "Sheriff McAuley will be here in five minutes," Willis said after ending the call. The closest sheriff's office was twenty minutes away in South Falls, so McAuley must already have been in Frostville, awaiting Willis's call.

They didn't say a word as they waited, but Augustus's head was spinning with possible scenarios. Willis didn't have the proof, no matter what he'd claimed about the insurance company. Augustus had taken the pictures, and he still had them, so he could show what the situation had been before he'd even started. So what was Willis after?

He had to know that claim would never fly, so he had to have a different reason, an ulterior motive. The sheriff would be on Willis's side, but even then, McAuley had never gone beyond the law. It had been a fine line at times, a gray area, but whether it was out of a true sense of wrong and right or out of fear of losing his job, the sheriff had never crossed that line. Willis had to know that. Everyone knew it. So what was he after here?

It only took four minutes for the sheriff to arrive, and Augustus's hands got clammy as the cop's car pulled up. McAuley had held the job for close to thirty years, Augustus reckoned. He could've retired years ago, but he hadn't wanted to, and since he kept getting reelected and there really wasn't that much for him to do aside from the occasional crash, DWI, or drunken brawl, there had been little incentive for him to quit. He had two more years until his term was up, and he would make it with ease.

"Mac," the sheriff said, his tone as cold as the air around them.

Augustus only nodded at him. There was no sense in trying to be friendly.

"Mac, Mr. Willis here called me this morning about the dispute he has with you over the destruction of his property. I've looked at the evidence, and I would really advise you to pay him and settle this out of court, son. Otherwise, with your record, things could get nasty."

Augustus breathed in, then out. He focused on the way his chest expanded with the next inhale, holding it a few seconds, then slowly releasing, his chest retracting again. He'd learned this technique in prison, of all places, taught by a helpful nurse who had taken pity on him after he'd had a few panic attacks.

He waited until he was sure he could keep his voice steady, even if the stuttering would get bad. "I d-d-disagree, Sh-sheriff. I have p-p-pictures that p-prove the s-s-situation before I st-started w-work, and I c-continued to take p-pictures throughout the p-p-process. They sh-show that I have d-done a thorough job and that the d-damage was already d-d-done before I a-a-arrived on the scene."

God, he *hated* this. He hated that they made him talk, hated that they made him explain things, hated that they forced him to do the one thing he feared more than anything else.

"Now, Mac, let's be reasonable here. I'm confident we can find a middle ground. Mr. Willis is asking for two thousand dollars in damage. How about you pay him a grand, and we'll consider the case closed?"

He didn't even need to take a calming breath before answering. "N-no."

The sheriff crossed his arms, a look of irritation on his face. "Mac, you have to be willing to compromise. I told you, if this goes to court, it's not going to go well for you as a convicted felon."

It always came down to that, didn't it? A convicted felon. Never mind that he done his time. Never mind that it had been twenty years ago and that it hadn't even been his crime in the first place. Never mind that he'd taken the fall for his own father. And never mind that ever since, he had done whatever he could to make things right, to pay everyone back. In the eyes of this community, he was and always would be a convicted felon.

"I'll t-take my ch-ch-chances," he said.

Willis and McAuley shared a look that spoke volumes about how they had expected this to go. Had they really thought it would be that easy to blackmail him out of a grand?

"Do you mind if I looked around the junkyard for a bit?" McAuley asked, and Augustus narrowed his eyes.

He was almost tempted to shake his head at the balls of that question. It never failed to amaze him that after all these years, everyone still thought he was stupid. They should know better by now, but apparently, the general opinion that had formed when he'd still been a kid had rooted deep enough to never be challenged ever again. That McCain kid? Oh, he's stupid. Plain retarded. Here they were, thirty years later, and no one had been willing to change their mind.

"I d-do m-mind," Mack said. "I d-d-do n-not give perm-mission."

He was far from an expert, but he'd been blessed with a helpful parole officer. The man had probably done it out of pity, but he had made sure Augustus knew the exact laws and rights that applied to him as a convicted felon. And since he was well past his parole time, McAuley couldn't search the premises without a warrant, and he had no legal grounds for one.

"Why would you mind? Do you have something to hide, son?" McAuley asked, and this time, Augustus couldn't keep himself from reacting with more emotion.

He scoffed, and both men looked at him in surprise as if they had never expected him to see through their bullshit. "Get a w-w-warrant," he told McAuley, whose face darkened.

He took a step closer to Augustus, but that, too, failed to intimidate him. Didn't the man understand that after two years in prison, he wasn't fazed by a cop? He'd confronted guards, fellow inmates, men who wanted a piece of him, and he had come out the other side. A nearly sixty-year-old man didn't frighten him in the least.

"Look, Mac, I'd hate for you to get into trouble, but it's been reported you have guns on the premises. I shouldn't have to tell you that as a felon, you're not allowed to have a firearm. I would strongly advise you to surrender your firearms to me right now, so I won't have to come back with a warrant and seize them. If I do that, I have no choice but to press charges, and you'd be sent back to prison for at least six months."

Augustus took a step back, then another one. The rage that exploded inside him was so blazingly hot that he didn't trust himself not to get physical. He'd always known people hated him. Hell, he had been an outcast from his first day in kindergarten and had suffered anywhere from teasing to outright bullying all through his school years. And after he'd done his time, no one had ever treated him with kindness. He knew the gossip and had bravely faced the scorn, the ridicule, the gossip, and the derisive remarks.

But never in his wildest dreams had he expected someone to threaten him with sending him back to prison.

How could they hate him that much? What had he ever done to deserve a wrath that had lasted twenty years by now? He'd done everything, tried everything, but they would never forgive him, would they? They would never let this go, would never give him a second chance. No matter what he did, he would always be the outcast, the felon, the man who had taken their money, even if it had never been him but his father.

And now McAuley was threatening him with prison. He couldn't go back. Not ever again. He had survived the first time, but barely. If he hadn't found protection in the unlikely form of another inmate, his cellmate of all people, he wouldn't have lasted. He would've probably killed himself within the first few months. But Gabe, his cellmate, who had been ten years older than him and had already served five years for armed robbery, had taken him under his wing. Augustus had never understood why because Gabe had never asked for anything in return, but Gabe had protected him throughout those two years. They had still been horrible, but he had *survived*.

That wouldn't happen a second time. If he were sent back to prison now, he would die.

"How c-can you h-h-hate me this m-much?"

The question was out of his mouth before he could swallow it back, before he could prevent himself from showing they had gotten to him.

But instead of the scorn he had expected to see on McAuley's face, the sheriff seemed embarrassed for a moment. Almost ashamed. "This has nothing to do with hate, son. I swore an oath to uphold the law."

He covered himself quickly, but Augustus had seen it. Maybe he'd reached that line the sheriff wasn't willing to cross, even if it was a thin, blurry one.

He took a deep breath, sucking back his anger all over again. "I d-do have weapons on the p-premises. I also have the n-n-necessary p-permits, and if you had b-bothered to ch-ch-check the reg-g-gister, you would've seen they are all r-registered with New York St-st-state."

McAuley looked confused. "I don't understand. You can't legally own a fire weapon as a felon."

"I app-p-plied for a C-certificate of R-r-relief of Disab-bility and was granted one, years ago. That certificate a-allowed me to apply for a g-gun permit and rec-c-ceive one. Check your d-database, Sh-sheriff. I guess you were s-s-so convinced you had m-me that you never b-b-bothered to even look."

"I... I didn't know. That you had a certificate, I mean." McAuley was full out flustered now, but even the satisfaction of knowing that he'd bested him didn't take away the stabbing pain inside Augustus.

He turned to Willis. "I'm not p-paying. S-s-ue me. We b-both know you w-w-won't win."

He took another few steps back. "Now g-get the h-h-ell off my prop-p-perty."

24

It was the fourth Wednesday Quentin spent in Northern Lake. It was also the fourth Wednesday he was visiting Mary's café. They had been talking about him, the Wednesday ladies. He deduced that from their reactions when he came in: covert glances and subtle elbows alerting each other to his presence.

He sent them a friendly smile. It fit what he had expected based on his research. He was an outsider, a newcomer, and by now, they realized he wasn't a tourist. Of course they'd want to know more.

Mary was as nice as always, and if she was curious about what was keeping him here so long, she didn't ask. He ordered another hot chocolate but with pecan pie this time. No matter what he ordered, it had always been delicious. No wonder the café was usually busy when he stopped by.

"I'll get that right in for you, honey," Mary said, sounding as maternal as she had that first day.

After she was gone, the other women shared looks, a lot of nodding and gesturing in his direction, and Quentin bit back a smile. He had no trouble interpreting what was happening. They were engaged in a silent battle to figure out who would approach him. Seconds later, a woman who had to be in her early fifties, with silver streaks running through her dark hair, got up from her chair and walked over toward him. Bingo.

"Hi," she said and extended her hand to him. "I'm Joanna Pullman. We've seen you here a few times, and we were wondering if you were new to town."

It didn't escape Quentin's attention that the café had grown silent and that all eyes were trained on them. He took her hand. "It's so nice to meet you. I'm Quentin. I'm hoping to be around for a couple of months."

"A couple of months?" she asked, letting go of his hand. "What brings you to the area?"

He'd called that one. Quentin gestured at her to take a seat, and she looked over her shoulder to the other women.

"Or I could join you," Quentin suggested with a soft smile. He hoped he wasn't too forward because that could burn bridges, but Joanna turned her attention back to him and smiled.

"Yes, why don't you join us," she said. "I'm sure the others would like to meet you as well."

They made room for him at the table, and Quentin's heart rate jumped at this opportunity. He had to tread carefully here. He could not fuck this up. The women quickly introduced themselves, a whirlwind of two Susans, a Patricia, a Laura, he thought, and a few names he'd forgotten as soon as they said them. He had time to learn their names. For now, it was important they got to know him a little and that he could establish a basis of trust.

"So, what does bring you to our area?" Joanna repeated her earlier question.

"I'm from California," Quentin started, and that resulted

in a couple of gasps around the table.

"California?" One of the women—Laura?—said. "You're a long way from home."

"I have to admit it's been quite the shock. The weather here is no joke. I respect you guys for enduring this winter after winter."

They chuckled amicably. "This winter has been pretty mild so far," one of the other women commented. "Aside from that big storm a month ago, it's only been dustings."

"That storm freaked me out," Quentin said, making sure to widen his eyes a little more. "For someone who has never seen snow in his life, that was a lot of snow as a first introduction."

That resulted in more laughs and some good-natured remarks about people who weren't used to snow. None of it was unfriendly, and he fed their pride in surviving the harsh winters here by complimenting them a few times.

"What brings a boy from California all the way to upstate New York?" Laura asked.

The woman to her right gently slapped her arm. "We're not upstate New York. Don't let the real upstate folks hear you."

Quentin frowned. "This is not upstate New York?"

The women started talking at the same time, but then one managed to take the lead. "Technically, it's midstate, though no one ever calls it that. To someone from the city, we're definitely upstate, but to someone from Buffalo, this is not upstate. A little farther south, if you get close to Albany, we call that the Capital District. I guess we're smack dab in the middle here, so we just say New York."

"Well, whatever it's called, it's beautiful here. The mountains are amazing, especially with the snow," Quentin said, and that earned him proud smiles. He understood that he couldn't procrastinate any longer. They had asked the question of why he was here several times now, and to change the topic again or delay responding would be rude.

"I've come to Northern Lake for a research project. I work for the University of California, and I'm running for a study on small-town dynamics."

The café grew silent again, all the women staring at him with what he hoped was friendly surprise. Mary stopped by just then and placed his hot chocolate and pie in front of him.

"Small-town dynamics? What do you mean by that?" Joanna asked when Mary had walked away again.

"I have a master's degree in sociology, which is basically the study of groups of people. My thesis was about the difference in dynamics between neighbors in big cities and small towns. My professor liked my analysis of the small town in California I studied, and he encouraged me to do further research. Since we wanted results from somewhere else, I came here."

"I've lived in the city," one of the women said. She hadn't spoken up so far, and she seemed to be the youngest of the group. "I left a good career on Wall Street to move here, and I haven't regretted it a single day. The city will eat you up and spit you out."

It took a few seconds for Quentin to realize that by *the city* she meant New York City specifically. "I can imagine," he said. "I couldn't survive in a big city either."

"City folks don't even know each other's names," someone spoke up. "Every time you read some poor schmuck died and wasn't found till two weeks later, it's always been in a big city. That would never happen here. We look out for each other."

The others hummed in agreement, and Quentin smiled.

"That's the kind of dynamic I'm studying."

"And when you say studying, does that mean you'll be observing us for months?" Joanna asked, and her voice held a hint of distrust there, of displeasure.

"No, absolutely not," Quentin hurried to reassure her. "That would be a gross invasion of your privacy. I was hoping to do some interviews with local residents."

Joanna's previous friendliness was back. "Oh, okay. So you mean that you would sit down for, like, an hour with each of us and ask us questions?"

Quentin nodded. "Yes. I'm hoping to interview as many of you as possible and then compare all the results and see if I can draw any conclusions."

Of course, it wasn't quite as simple as that, but he didn't think they'd want to hear him give a course on Statistics 101.

The women looked around the table to each other, and he saw nothing but open reactions. It seemed his approach had worked, and a rush of excitement flowed through him.

"I'm sure all of us would be more than happy to talk to you, and if you give us a few days, we can ask our neighbors and friends as well. This is a friendly town, and we're proud of our community," Laura said.

"That would be amazing. I would appreciate it so much. I had hoped for a friendly reception, but you never know."

"Do you have contact information for us? A phone number where we can reach you or an email address? That way, we can contact you if we have a list of people ready and willing to talk to you."

Laura was a practical woman, and Quentin appreciated that. He quickly wrote down his name, email address, and phone number on his note bloc and ripped off the sheet, then handed it to Laura. "Thank you so much. Laura, was it, right?"

Laura beamed at him, clearly pleased he had remembered her name. "Yes, that's right. Let us do some asking around, and we'll get back to you, Quentin."

She glanced at the paper he had given her, and something must've caught her eye because she kept looking at what he'd written. A small frown appeared on her forehead. "Your last name is Frost?"

Quentin's heart skipped a beat. Did she recognize it? Did she know his father? Could he really have gotten this lucky that the first person he talked to actually knew him?

"Yes. My father was from this area originally. From this town, actually. I don't know if any of you know him, Leonard Frost?"

To his right, a spoon clattered on the table, Joanne stared at him with shock painted all over her face. A glance around the table showed she wasn't the only one. An uneasy feeling settled in his stomach. What had just happened here? They had been so friendly and welcoming until... Until he had mentioned the name of his father.

"Did I say something wrong?" he asked, and his voice trembled a little.

The glances the women exchanged this time were different. Unfriendly. The heaviness in his stomach grew worse. Something had gone horribly wrong, and he had no idea what.

Laura rose from the table and ripped the note with his name on it in small pieces. "On second thought, I don't think anybody is willing to talk to you. Let's go, ladies."

Quentin had never felt smaller in his life as when he watched the women grab their jackets and walk out of the café. He was left with his hot chocolate and pie, both untouched. What the hell had happened here? His father's name had triggered something, but what?

Tears burned in his eyes as he pushed his chair back. Obviously, he wasn't staying here. He didn't know what had gone wrong, but it was clear he wasn't welcome anymore.

Mary stood a few steps away, arms crossed and brows furrowed. Her face didn't show the animosity of the other women, but not the friendliness from before either. It gave him the courage to ask, "What did I do wrong?"

She gently shook her head. "Honey, the name of Leonard Frost is a notorious one in this town. It's clear from your reaction you didn't know, but you may want to do some research into him."

He swallowed. "Research into what?"

She pressed her lips together as if debating whether to say more. Her frown intensified as she studied him. Finally, she said, "People have a long memory here, Quentin. It may have been twenty years ago, but they haven't forgotten."

With that, she walked away, and Quentin knew he was dismissed. He held his head low as he hurried back to his car. He hightailed it out of Northern Lake.

What the hell had his father done that a whole town hated him?

Wait. The whole town hated him. Just like Frostville hated Augustus.

She had said it had been twenty years ago.

The dots connected, and he had to pull the car over on the shoulder because his hands were shaking too hard to drive. It couldn't be. It couldn't have been his father.

But the time frame fit. The reactions of the women made it clear he'd done something horrible. It explained why he had disappeared. He'd been in prison. There was no other explanation.

His father had been the accomplice of Augustus's father.

25

Augustus had been impatiently waiting for Quentin to come home for lunch. After the shitty confrontation he'd had with Willis and Sheriff McCauley, he was hoping Quentin would be in the mood to distract him a little. One look at Quentin's pale, tear-stricken face made it crystal clear that sex would not be on the schedule.

Not that that was his biggest concern, not even close. What the hell had happened? He quickly closed down the junkyard and hung a sign he would be back in an hour, then hurried inside.

He found Quentin on the couch, pulled up into a fetal position, his arms wrapped tightly around Lucy, who endured the physical affection she would usually growl at. She, too, had sensed something horrible had happened.

Augustus's first instinct was to sit down next to him, hold him in his arms, and ask him what had him so upset. But it was way past their usual lunchtime already, so Quentin had to be hungry. He might not feel like it, but he had to eat something. Whatever was bothering him would only be exacerbated by hunger and low blood sugar.

Augustus heated the mac and cheese from the freezer. Just one portion for now. He could wait. Quentin could not.

He kneeled next to him, and the deep sadness in Quentin's eyes cut into his soul like a knife. It had to be really bad to cause him to look like this.

"You n-need to eat a l-l-little," he said softly.

Quentin shook his head before Augustus was even finished. "I'm not hungry. I don't even think I could eat right now."

Augustus hesitated. Was he wrong to push this? He couldn't force him to eat, but maybe he should try once more. "We'll t-talk after. You n-n-need f-food. You're p-pale."

Quentin's eyes met his, those green eyes that were always so bright and full of life but were now so sad and hopeless. "Please, b-baby. Eat."

Augustus wasn't sure if Quentin had seen the validity of his argument or that he'd given in to avoid another fight, but whatever it was, it had worked. Quentin pushed himself into a sitting position, but when he reached for the bowl, Augustus pulled it away. Instead, he scooped a little of the mac and cheese on the spoon, blew on it so it wasn't too hot, and brought it to Quentin's mouth.

Quentin opened, taking the spoonful from him, and Augustus breathed out with relief. He fed him, spoon by spoon, until Quentin had a little color back in his cheeks and his eyes had lost some of that hollow look.

When he had finished it all, Augustus asked, "D-do you want m-m-more? A s-sandwich?"

Quentin folded both hands around his cheeks, then leaned in and kissed him softly. "A Coke, please. Thank you. Thank you for taking care of me."

His voice broke on that last word, and worry filled Augustus all over again. Whatever had happened, it was *bad*. His stomach clenched with fear for Quentin.

He made himself a cup of tea and a peanut butter and jelly sandwich, then grabbed Quentin his Coke and settled down on the couch next to him. For a while, they sat there, Augustus eating his sandwich and Quentin sipping from his Coke. He didn't need to ask what had happened. Quentin would tell him when he was ready to talk. Augustus had long finished his sandwich when Quentin turned toward him, lifted his eyes up at him, and asked, "What was the name of your father's accomplice?"

He frowned. His father's accomplice? What did that have to do with anything? "L-leonard F-f-frost. Why?"

Quentin swayed a little, and Augustus grabbed his shoulder to steady him. Why would Quentin ask about his father's accomplice? And why would that get him so upset? It didn't make sense.

Had someone said something to him about it? He'd been in Northern Lake. There had been some victims of the resort scam from that town, but Augustus hadn't contacted them for repayment. They had been swindled by Frost, since Northern Lake was his hometown.

It clicked, and his stomach rolled violently as the truth hit him. "He's your f-f-father. L-l-leonard Frost is your f-f-father."

Quentin nodded, his face going pale all over again. Oh god. How the hell was this possible? What were the odds? And yet here they were, two sons who were facing the consequences of their fathers' sins.

"I d-d-didn't kn-know," he said. "I s-s-swear, I didn't kn-know he w-was your f-f-father.

"I know," Quentin said, his voice hoarse. "In the car, I

realized I'd never given you my last name. And even if I had, you might not have connected the dots. I didn't, not until I asked about him in Northern Lake."

Augustus winced. That would not have gone over well. "Were they m-m-mad?"

Quentin's eyes welled up, and then a single tear trailed down his cheek. "The Wednesday morning ladies invited me to sit at their table. I told them about my research, and they were willing to answer my questions. I had it all set up. And then I dropped my father's name..." The last word ended on a choked sob, but when Augustus reached for him, Quentin held up a hand. "They walked out on me. They left me there, all on my own. One lady—Laura—ripped up the paper with my name and phone number on it. They're never gonna want to talk to me ever again."

Oh no. Augustus's heart hurt for him. He felt it on a physical level, the stab of pain as he imagined that scene. "I'm s-s-sorry," he said, and it wasn't enough, but then again, his words were never enough. His words were always inadequate, never capturing what he really wanted to communicate.

"I know. I know you understand better than anyone. You have faced this for twenty years. I shouldn't complain, not after dealing with it once. But it hurts so much."

This time, when Augustus held out his hands, Quentin gave in, and Augustus pulled him on his lap, wrapping his arms around him. He didn't say anything, but he didn't have to. Quentin knew. Whatever Augustus could offer him, Quentin *knew*. There was no comfort for this pain. There was nothing Augustus could say that would make it hurt less, and so he wouldn't even try. He would hold him and be there, and that was all he could do.

"Do you have any idea where your father is now?" Quentin asked after what had to be minutes later.

"No. I n-never tried to f-f-find him. After he didn't sh-sh-show up for my m-mom's funeral, he was d-d-dead to me."

Quentin sighed.

"Did you ever meet him? My father, I mean?" he asked.

"I d-did. He c-came around all the t-t-time before that shit went down. I never p-paid much att-t-tention to him. I was in high sch-sch-school, trying to gr-graduate. I wasn't interested in w-whatever b-business my f-father and he had." His grip on Quentin tightened a little. "You don't l-l-look like him."

Quentin's laugh was without joy. "I'm the spitting image of my mom. Thank fuck for that."

His mom. God, this was so complicated. "Will you t-t-tell her?"

"Yeah. We're very close, and I could never keep this from her. Besides, I think she deserves closure, just like I did. It's a far cry from the closure either one of us had hoped for, but that's life. You know better than anyone else that it can kick you in the teeth just when you think things are going well."

Wow, Augustus did not envy him that difficult conversation. Imagine telling your mother that the man who fathered her child had been a criminal and that when she thought he had walked out on her, he had actually been in prison. Closure had never been that bitter.

It was long past time he had to open the junkyard up again, but no way was he leaving his position on the couch. Quentin needed him, and everybody else could fuck right off. Besides, after what had happened to him and Quentin, chances were he would do some real damage to the first person who looked at him the wrong way now. Better to stay inside and take care of Quentin.

"I'll m-make us some t-tea." He lifted him off his lap and rose to his feet. After a few minutes, he returned with two steaming hot mugs and a plate of cookies, which he handed to Quentin. Augustus set the mugs down on the coffee table and settled right back on the couch, Quentin between his legs. Quentin rested against his chest, his cheek against Augustus's right pectoral, nibbling on a cookie.

"I'll need to contact my professor as well," Quentin said.

His research project. Augustus hadn't even thought of that, but that had become impossible now. "What w-w-will you t-tell him?"

Quentin took his hand and laced their fingers together, then pressed a kiss on Augustus's hand. "This is the end of my research project here. I'll have to talk to him if I can set it up somewhere else. I guess I could, since it's not tailored toward Northern Lake. That was just the town I picked. Theoretically, I could do it anywhere else as long as it is a small town."

"Anywhere else b-but here," Augustus whispered.

Quentin squeezed his hand. "Yeah. Anywhere else but here."

"You're l-l-leaving, then."

This time, Quentin didn't answer as quickly, and when he did, his voice was filled with pain. "I don't want to leave you, but I have to go. I can't stay here, not after what happened."

Augustus's chest had never felt this tight, and his heart had never beaten this painfully. "I underst-st-stand. There's no f-f-future for you here."

Quentin pushed himself out of Augustus's arms, got up, and kneeled between his legs. "There's no future for you here either, baby."

Augustus hadn't expected it to hurt that much, to have

someone else pointed it out to him. It was the truth, and it wasn't like he didn't agree with it, so why did it stab him to hear Quentin say that?

"I can't l-leave. Not bef-f-fore I've paid off m-my debt."

Quentin's eyes flashed. "They don't deserve your money. They don't deserve to be paid back. They're horrible people who are nothing but mean to you, and they are not worthy of you being this honorable to them. God, I would almost say they deserved to be cheated out of their money, since they are such sorry excuses for human beings. Maybe it was karma's way of settling a score."

Augustus almost smiled. If nothing else, he would never forget the rush of having someone like Quentin in his corner. It had been a precious gift, Quentin's loyalty. His attention. His *love*. Oh, they hadn't said the words, but Augustus knew. This wasn't casual for Quentin either.

"You don't m-mean that," he said mildly. "No one ever d-d-deserves to be a v-victim."

Quentin's eyes softened, but only a little. "Maybe, but I'm not fully convinced they didn't call this upon themselves. But whatever. Point is, you don't owe them anything anymore. Baby, you've done everything you could. When will it be enough?"

Augustus inhaled deeply. It was tempting, so tempting. And it wasn't like he couldn't see the reasonability of Quentin's assessment. Hell, he'd had the same thought many times over the years. But he'd always come back to the same thing, and this time was no different. It wouldn't be enough until he'd paid what his father had taken from them. If he left this godforsaken town... No, *when* he left this godforsaken town, it would be with his head held high, his honor intact, and every last cent of his debt paid off.

"I c-can't. I can't l-leave until I'm d-d-done. Two m-more

years. T-t-two more years and I will h-have paid off e-e-everyone."

Quentin leaned forward, bringing their foreheads together, and closed his eyes. "I can't wait here with you for two years. I can't. I would die on the inside. I don't know how you can stand it, but it would eat me bit by bit."

"I kn-know. I wouldn't w-w-want you to s-suffer for me."

He meant every word. He *did* understand that it was more than Quentin could take, facing two more years of this hostility. But even if he had offered to, Augustus would've turned him down. He couldn't let them do it. He couldn't let this town wound Quentin as deeply as they had wounded him. Quentin deserved better. His future wasn't here.

"You have to g-go b-back to C-c-california. That's where you b-b-belong."

It hurt to say the words. Every word he pushed over his lips stabbed his heart, but he still said them. He had to.

"What about us? I don't want to leave you."

Desperation laced Quentin's voice, the same desperation that made it so hard for Augustus to breathe. He'd always known that he and Quentin were temporary. They couldn't have a future together, not when he was stuck here with no way out. But he'd counted on having more time. They were supposed to have three more months together.

Words had always been a struggle for him, especially those spoken in public. But never had he had to fight harder to get words out as when he pulled Quentin back into his arms and whispered, "You h-have to g-go. Your f-f-future is n-not here."

26

"Mom, I have to tell you something."

That was how Quentin's phone call with his mom had started fifteen minutes ago, and half of that, she had spent crying. He'd waited a day with calling her. His emotions had been too conflicted, too messed up. But she'd deserved the truth, and he'd set up the call.

Right before he'd called her, he'd had a brief moment of doubt. Had she known and not told him? Was that why she had never tried to find his father? But then he rejected it. She would never keep something so important from him. Her reaction proved he'd been right. It had blindsided her. Still, she'd thanked him for telling her.

"I'm so sorry for you," she said, her voice still hoarse from crying.

Quentin let out a sigh. "I still haven't decided how I feel about it. You knew him. I never did. I don't know if it's possible to be disappointed in someone you've never met."

"Maybe not disappointed, but you have every right to be angry with him."

"It wasn't like he deliberately fucked up my research project," Quentin said with a hint of a laugh.

"No, but he fucked up much more than that. If he hadn't been this stupid, he could've seen you grow up. You would've had a dad."

"True, though in hindsight, I have to wonder if I had been better off. Clearly, his character left something to be desired."

"I still can't believe he did that. It doesn't fit with how I knew him."

They were quiet for a while, and Quentin wondered how to bring up the second part of the conversation: Augustus.

"How did you find out about him anyway?" his mom asked, and he had his opening.

"Mom, I met someone here." He didn't say anything else, because she would...

"You have? I'm so happy for you. Tell me everything about him."

See? That was his mom. He'd heard horror story after horror story about teens coming out to their parents and facing rejection, but his mom had never even batted an eye. Quentin had been eleven when he told her he liked boys, and she'd given him a hug and told him that was fine and that he could come to her if he ever had any questions.

"His name is Augustus, and he's wonderful, Mom. He's..." How did he describe Augustus? It was hard, even for him, to find words to capture what he had come to mean to Quentin. "He's special, Mom. He's sweet and honorable, and he *gets* me. I can be myself with him."

Quentin had never told her what had happened with Justin. Not the specifics anyway, but she'd known it had been a bad breakup that had blown his self-confidence. She hadn't asked, respecting his privacy, and he hadn't wanted to tell her, not sure if this was something she needed to know. But she had been there for him, and the one advice she'd kept giving him was to find someone who would allow him to be himself. She'd understand how much Augustus meant to him.

"How did you guys meet?" she asked.

"Mom, his father was Leonard's accomplice."

He wouldn't ever call him father again. The man didn't deserve that honorific.

"What? How is that even possible? How did you manage to find him?"

Quentin explained the sheer coincidence that had brought the two of them together. He also told her about Augustus's efforts to pay back his debt. Or at least, what he saw as his debt.

"There's no way I can continue my research project here," he told her. "I'm gonna have to call Professor Danson and ask him what to do, but my guess is that I have to go back to California. He will end the grant if I can't carry out the research I received it for."

"Well, you don't know for sure until you've talked to him, but that does sound reasonable. They can't pay you money for work you're not doing."

That was so typical of his mom. She'd always worked hard her entire life, having at least two and sometimes three jobs at the same time. She'd never accepted a dime of welfare, had always insisted on earning an honest wage, even when it had exhausted her to the bone. If nothing else, she had shown him what work ethic was.

"No, I agree. But it would mean I have to leave here on pretty short notice."

"Oh, honey, but what about Augustus?"

Quentin rubbed his temples. Augustus was outside, working, which he had checked before he'd called his mom. It wasn't that he had secrets from him, but he could be more honest about his feelings when he wasn't within hearing distance.

"He's not coming with me. He can't, he says. He won't leave until he's paid off his debt."

"You have to admire his sense of honor."

"That's what makes it so hard to get upset with him. How can I fault him for doing what he believes is the right thing? Mom, these people here are horrible to him. They have bullied him his entire life, and it's only gotten worse since he got out of prison. It's a hell he's living in every day, and according to him, he has no way out."

"And you can't stay," she said. "So now what? What have you guys decided on?"

"I don't know. There is no solution, is there? If he can't leave and I can't stay, what else is there?"

"Oh, honey..."

They were silent after that, neither of them knowing what to say.

"Take your time to make a decision, honey," his mom finally said. "If your connection with Augustus is as true and deep as you say it is, it is too valuable to give up on that easily. Maybe you can find a compromise."

Quentin sighed. "Maybe," he said, even when he had no idea how that would ever be possible.

As if by unspoken agreement, he and Augustus didn't bring it up during lunch. In fact, they didn't speak much at all, but the silence wasn't oppressive. There was no tension between them, no discord. Just a sadness, sadness that brought a new level of intimacy between them, as if it united them in their grief.

After lunch, Quentin gathered his courage and called his professor. That conversation was a lot less friendly than with his mother, though once he'd come clean about what had happened, his professor did understand the improbability of him completing his research successfully.

"You should've been honest about this, Quentin," he told him. "If I had known you had ulterior motives to pick that town, I would've denied you the grant."

"You're absolutely right, professor. I should have been transparent about this. But can I just point out in my defense that I had no idea about this? I couldn't have known what reaction mentioning my father's name would have."

"No, I'll give you that. And I am sorry about how it turned out. It can't be easy for you to be faced with a truth like that."

Quentin breathed out with relief. He'd always had a good relationship with Professor Danson, and this proved why. The man was strict and demanded hard work, but he was also fair and reasonable.

"I'll admit it's been quite the shock. For my mom as well." He swallowed, closing his eyes. "I assume I need to return as soon as possible?"

He hadn't told the man about Augustus. Of course he hadn't. That part, at least, was still private. It had already cost him a lot to come clean about his father and what he had done, but he wasn't dragging Augustus into this. But leaving him out also meant that Professor Danson had no reason to suspect Quentin wanted to stay. And he didn't. Or at least he wouldn't, if not for Augustus.

"I'll give you a few days to pack up and arrange everything you need to, but I'll need you back here next Monday. We'll talk about it further then."

It sounded like he still had options. He'd already been

awake half the night, worrying about the consequences for his future. Would losing this research project mean missing out on that PhD position? He couldn't wait another week to hear about that. It would drive him mad in between.

"Do I still have options, Professor? I know I messed up, but you know how hard I've worked for that PhD job."

He didn't say anything more than that. He wouldn't need to. Professor Danson was smart enough to figure out the rest.

"I can't make any promises, Quentin. Your work so far has been exemplary, and you're certainly qualified for that position. I'd hate to see you lose it over one transgression. So let's see if we can find you another short-term project to ensure you meet all the requirements. I'll do whatever I can, but keep in mind that is no guarantee that we will be successful."

"I understand, Professor. Thank you so much for your willingness to help me. I promise I'll work my ass off to deserve your trust in me."

"I know you will. Take some time to process and recover. I take it you're driving back?"

Quentin thought of the all-wheel drive Augustus had bought for him. He would have to trade it in for something cheaper. "Yes. I promise I'll be there by Monday."

"Drive safely."

Quentin slowly took his AirPods out. Not everything was lost just yet. He still had a shot at getting the job. All he had to do was prove he was qualified. And with Professor Danson willing to stick his neck out for him, he stood a chance.

But he would have to leave. He had two, three days at the most, and that was it. If he didn't leave, he'd lose every chance at that job, and he would never get another opportunity like that. If he violated Professor Danson's trust in him now, he was done for. The man would never recommend him for a position ever again. No, this was his last opportunity. He had to take it.

He had to leave Augustus behind.

27

Dinner was as subdued as lunch. Augustus didn't have the words. He rarely had them, at least not *spoken* words, but this was even worse. His insides churned and stormed, but no words were adequate to capture the tumult in his heart.

He was too tired to cook anything healthy, and so he fired up the grill and made burgers. They ate silently, then cleared away the dishes and tidied up the kitchen. He made tea and grabbed some cookies, knowing Quentin would want something sweet after dinner. He always did.

Quentin already lay stretched out on the couch, and Augustus put down the tea and cookies, then hesitated. Was he still welcome in Quentin's arms? The rules had changed, hadn't they? They weren't fighting, exactly, but he wasn't sure how to act.

Quentin opened his arms. "Come here, baby."

Augustus crawled into his embrace, putting his head against that bony shoulder. Quentin held him close, then kissed the top of his head. "You don't have to say anything."

Augustus closed his eyes and thought of that old No

Doubt song. She'd been right, Gwen Stefani. There was no need to say the words when you already knew the outcome and when all they did was hurt. It hurt to say them, and it hurt to hear them. Nothing they could say would change the outcome.

For an hour, they cuddled, sitting up every now and then to sip their tea and, in Quentin's case, eat his cookies, and then they'd find each other's arms again. The silence brought peace to Augustus's head and maybe even a bit of healing. This couldn't be the end of their story. Their connection was too strong, too special to end like this.

They could do a long-distance relationship until he was done here. They could video call, and Quentin could come visit. Augustus would have to pay his ticket because there was no way Quentin would have the funds. That meant a slight delay in his pay schedule, but surely that would be worth it.

Quentin shifted and found his lips. The kiss was soft, slow. Augustus melted into it, his stomach dancing when Quentin cupped his cheeks with endless tenderness. Their tongues slid against each other, teasing and probing, then soothing and comforting.

A low fire sprang up inside him, gradually building higher. His lips were swollen, but he didn't want the kiss to stop, didn't want Quentin to stop. Heat pooled in his belly, in his cock. His right arm was immobilized by Quentin's weight on it as they lay side by side, face-to-face, but his left hand searched under Quentin's hoodie, finding that warm, smooth skin.

He rubbed him as they kissed, slow circles that traveled lower and lower. When he reached his waistband, Quentin gyrated his hips against him. Augustus moaned into his mouth. Would he ever get used to the way

Quentin made him feel, to the way his body reacted to his touch?

Quentin turned onto his back, pulling Augustus on top of him, and he went willingly, reveling in how they fit together. His insides were roaring with need now, with a blazing fire that kept getting bigger and stronger with every kiss, every brush, every caress. Quentin had free rein now, and he slipped both hands under Augustus's jeans and underwear and kneaded his ass possessively.

Sweat broke out all over Augustus's body, and he pushed himself up a moment and dragged his hoodie over his head while Quentin did the same. Their eyes met, and they smiled in understanding as they got up from the couch and took off the rest of their clothes. Back to the couch or were they taking this into the bedroom? Augustus looked at Quentin, who pointed toward the fireplace. He nodded. It was much warmer here.

Quentin stretched out on the couch again, and this time, Augustus didn't wait for him to give the signal. He lowered himself on top of him, and they both let out a sigh of contentment. Augustus wasn't sure what the plan was, but the skin-to-skin contact alone was enough to make him tear up. He needed this. He needed him.

Quentin found that tender stretch of skin behind his ear and licked it, then sucked gently. God, how could one spot be so sensitive? His cock jerked in reaction. Next, Quentin nibbled on Augustus's ear, his teeth scraping all those soft spots that made his insides go all weak.

"I want you inside me tonight," Quentin whispered in his ear, and Augustus froze.

Had he heard that correctly? He pushed up and met his eyes. "I th-thought you h-h-hated it."

"Not hate. I don't prefer it, but tonight, with you, I want to. I want to feel you, baby. I want to feel you for days."

He understood that need. He'd felt it himself, before, that deep craving to be claimed by Quentin, owned in a way he would still feel the next day. "O-okay."

Quentin wrapped his hands around his neck and pulled him down in another wet, thorough kiss. He explored every bit of his mouth as if he was mapping it...as if he wanted to remember forever. Augustus let him and then did some exploring of his own while his hips found their rhythm, gently grinding into Quentin's. Their cocks left smears of precum on each other's bodies, and it felt dirty and right at the same time.

When Quentin finally broke off the kiss, they were both panting. "Show me you love me," Quentin said, and Augustus wasn't even surprised he knew. How could he not when Augustus was barely able to keep himself from shouting it out? So he nodded and smiled. There was no more need to keep it in. It was okay to love him, even if he would lose him again.

He dropped his mouth lower, but Quentin's hand held him back, his finger lifting Augustus's chin up. "You know I love you too."

He did. A love as big as he felt, the magical connection they had, could not go unanswered. They belonged together.

He nodded again, unable to speak. But he didn't have to because Quentin's eyes shone with understanding. He let go of Augustus. "Make me yours," he said.

He already was. Didn't he realize? He was Quentin's, and Quentin was his. Still, he brought his lips to Quentin's throat and kissed him there. He licked that slight saltiness away, then hummed in pleasure.

"Give me a hickey," Quentin said. "Please. I want to see myself in the mirror and see your presence on my body."

Augustus closed his eyes as he pressed his lips against Quentin's neck and increased the suction. Quentin's hips bucked off the couch. He *liked* that. When he was confident Quentin would see that for days, he let go, and Quentin's trembling exhale was such a damn turn-on.

He gently bit his shoulders, licked a hot, wet path down his chest, then played with his nipples until he sucked them hard and made Quentin growl. Mmm, what a perfect sound. His belly button was sensitive too, and he tongued it for a while. Quentin laced his hands through his hair and pulled and pushed alternatively.

He could've skipped his cock and gone to his legs, but he didn't want to. The need inside him was getting hard to ignore, and Quentin had to feel the same. He nuzzled his legs, the crease between his thigh and his balls that always smelled like...like sweat and arousal and *him*. It was Quentin's essence, and he licked it up, breathed it in.

Quentin's wet cock was painting his cheeks and his hair with precum, but he didn't care. He wanted his smell all over him. Hell, if Quentin wanted to take a piss on him right now, he'd take it, and that had never been a kink he'd been fascinated by in the least. He just wanted to be as close to him as possible.

Quentin's cock tasted salty, sweaty. He licked the head, humming in pleasure when he got the first taste. His own cock throbbed. God, he was so excited at the prospect of burying himself inside Quentin. He took Quentin's length into his mouth as far as he could, and Quentin let out a low rumble of approval. Augustus's hands cradled Quentin's balls, gently rolling them in the same way he'd loved to play with his own. Before Quentin had shown him real pleasure.

He licked a stripe up his cock, then nuzzled his balls. They fit perfectly into his mouth, he'd already discovered, and Quentin loved it when he sucked on them. Especially when he fingered him at the same time.

Lube, he needed lube.

As if Quentin could read his mind, he stretched out and grabbed the lube from the side table, then threw it next to Augustus onto the couch. "You're gonna need that, baby."

Yes, he would. He took a moment to slick up his fingers. Quentin could multitask like a pro, and Augustus would barely even notice when he lubed up, but he wasn't quite that handy yet. When his fingers were nice and slick, he got back to Quentin. He held him with his left hand now, moving with slow, steady strokes at the top of his dick. Meanwhile, his right hand was fumbling to get access.

Quentin pulled up his legs, and there it was, that pretty pink hole. Everything on him was smooth and gorgeous, and so was his hole. Delicate, almost like a flower, and Augustus approached it with care. He was gentle when he pushed, but Quentin let him in with ease.

God, he was tight. Warm and velvety soft. Augustus swallowed, and his cock twitched in anticipation. Quentin's moan as he sank his middle finger deep inside him spurred him on. He thrust it a few times, then switched it for his thumb. That, too, slid in easily, and the sight of Quentin's greedy hole swallowing his digit whole was so arousing he had to let go of Quentin's cock and grab his own. He squeezed firmly until his balls stopped throbbing.

Two fingers were no problem either, and Quentin rocked against his hand. "Curl your middle finger a little... God, yes, *there*. Oh, *fuck*..."

He pumped him deep, finding that spot inside that made

Quentin push back his ass, then jerk away as if hit by a jolt of electricity. "Ugh," he moaned. "I need your cock..."

It was too soon. He hadn't loosened him up properly. "It w-w-will h-hurt."

"Augustus."

He looked up and met Quentin's eyes, full of love and heat. "I *like* that pain. I trust you."

Oh, the weight of that statement. The gravitas of the situation was staggering, and he was soaring. Quentin *trusted* him.

He squeezed out some extra lube and coated his cock. His first time with a man. No matter what would happen, he would never forget that his first time hadn't been sex. It was making love to the man he loved.

He clumsily found a position that would work. Quentin waited for him with patient eyes, his legs pulled up, that pink star beckoning Augustus. He held his own cock and pushed in, first gently, then harder when it wasn't enough.

"Oh!" He slipped in, then almost automatically stopped.

But Quentin wrapped his legs around him. "Don't stop. Fill me, baby. All the way."

Augustus obeyed, sweat pearling on his forehead as he sank inside him. God, he was so fucking *tight*. So perfect and warm and snug. Quentin's face showed a flash of pain, and his eyes widened as Augustus sank in deeper, harder until he couldn't go any farther.

Quentin's mouth had dropped open in a wordless O, a place where pain and pleasure were indistinguishable. Augustus knew that place well, and his belly went weak as Quentin breathed through it, then met Augustus's eyes, and whispered, "Fuck me hard. *Hard*, baby, you hear me?"

He looked like an elf, but he was anything but fragile. The first few thrusts were awkward as Augustus tried to find the right rhythm, but then he had it, and he snapped his hips and drove inside him. Something else took over from his rational mind, something primitive and wild. It wanted Quentin, and it yearned to obey the command to take him hard.

He plunged in, withdrew, and slammed back in. Quentin's fingers bruised his hips, his ass, his shoulders, but Augustus didn't care. His ears roared, his vision became hazy, and all he knew was the reality of him and Quentin, the two of them, one flesh.

Quentin cried out, wailing and moaning and making sounds Augustus had never heard from him, but none of them said no. None of them said stop or red or anything like it. And so he plowed on, but he had to grab his base when he came too close, and he waited a few seconds. Quentin looked at him impatiently, then in understanding, and he smiled.

"You're perfect, baby," he said, and the words flooded Augustus.

He'd never been this in tune with someone else, this close. He was so aware of Quentin, of his smooth, sweaty body underneath his, of his frantic heartbeat that he could feel thud against his fingers, of his green eyes, which saw inside him. He was perfect. They were perfect.

"I love you," he said, the words rolling off his tongue as smooth as they had sounded in his head. Tears welled up in his eyes because for once, his brain and his mouth had gotten the connection right. The one time that it really mattered, he'd been perfect.

Quentin's smile was everything, and when Augustus thrust back inside him, it was slower, softer. He laced their hands together, then lowered his mouth in an almost kiss. The air grew tender, kind, and with each slide, their breaths mingled. Their bodies connected. Their eyes locked. Their hearts beat in sync.

The violent storm inside him calmed down to one big wave that built and built, rising higher and higher until he couldn't hold back anymore. His body burned, ached, his balls tightening so viciously he struggled for breath. And then he let go. He rode the wave, adrenaline and pleasure keeping him going, thrusting, shoving, squeezing every last drop out until he crashed and drowned.

Something hot and wet splashed against his stomach, and Quentin's grunt mixed with his own desperate moan. Their exhausted bodies melted against each other, boneless and satisfied.

Quentin *loved* him.

Augustus fell asleep with a smile on his face and Quentin's cum all over him.

28

The next morning, Quentin helped Augustus in the junkyard. Not so much because Augustus needed the help, but the thought of not being with him these last days they were together was just unbearable. Augustus seemed to either understand or feel the same because he kept giving Quentin things to do. Small things, meaningless things, but tasks that kept Quentin near him.

Not that Quentin had any doubt left about Augustus's feelings for him. For a while now, he'd known Augustus loved him, even if he'd never admitted it to himself or had brought it up. But the tender way they had made love the night before, how Augustus had looked as he took him, had been everything.

Quentin had debated whether or not he wanted to bottom for Augustus, but then he'd reminded himself that not all his experiences with bottoming had been bad. He could take pleasure from it if it was done right. And with the right person. It had been magical to share himself with Augustus, and he'd always treasure the memory.

A pang of pain stabbed his heart. That was all they would have left. Memories. Two more days and he'd have to leave to make it back to California on time. Two more days and after that, only memories. There had to be a solution to their problem, but if there was, he didn't see it. And neither did Augustus, or he would've said something.

"W-would you still w-w-want to find your f-father? F-f-find out if he's still al-l-live?" Augustus asked. Quentin hadn't seen that one coming.

He rubbed his hands, which were turning into icicles again, even though the temperature was slightly above freezing point. That damn wind here made it so freaking cold.

"I hadn't thought of it to be honest. We know he was guilty, so it's not like it would paint him in a different light. We're way past hope for exoneration."

Augustus dipped his chin. "I unders-stand."

Would he want to see his dad again if the man was alive? "How would we even find him? I'll admit I didn't try very hard from California, but I did spend significant time on Google and couldn't find out anything."

"P-p-pI."

A private detective. Of course. Quentin had actually considered that years ago, and he'd even discussed it with his mom, but they'd both agreed it wasn't worth the money. Clearly, his dad hadn't wanted to stay in their lives. Of course, now that he knew the truth, he understood why. Granted, the man could've still tried to contact them after his release from prison, but Quentin couldn't fault him for not expecting a warm welcome as a convicted felon.

"They cost a lot of money."

"I know."

Quentin frowned. "I thought you never tried to find your father?"

"It wasn't f-for that. I hired one to f-f-find out the names of my f-father's v-victims and how m-m-much he had t-taken from them."

Quentin studied him for a few seconds. "So you have someone local?"

"G-good guy. He was n-n-nice to me."

The fact that Augustus counted him as a good man just because he'd been nice to him said everything about how people treated him in general, didn't it? Sadness seeped into his bones. If Quentin thought too long about it, he would get angry all over again, so he pushed it down.

What had seemed abstract before became much more concrete now. Did he want to hire a PI to find his father? God, it was such a loaded question. He had no way of knowing how it would turn out. Maybe his father would be happy to see him, but it wasn't outside the realm of possibilities that he'd reject him all over again. And why, for fuck's sake, had he started thinking of Leonard again as his *father*? There was that stubborn hope again.

"Can we call him? Your guy, I mean? Just to get an idea of his price?"

Augustus dipped his chin, and they went back to work.

They took their lunch break at twelve thirty, and after he had locked the junkyard up, Augustus gave Quentin the phone number. He stared at it while Augustus made sandwiches, then finally decided to take the plunge.

The man picked up quickly, and Quentin took a deep breath. "Mr. Hartford, this is Quentin Frost. You don't know me, but I'm a friend of Augustus McCain. Mac. You did some work for him—"

"I remember him," Hartford said. It sounded friendly. Businesslike, but not unkind. "What can I help you with?"

Quentin's stomach rolled. "How much would you charge to find someone?"

"What kind of person are we talking about? Male or female and what age? And how long has this person been missing?"

"Male, and he's been missing for ten years, I guess. He was in prison, and I'd like to know what happened to him after that."

"Frost," Hartford said slowly. "Are you related to Leonard Frost?"

Of course he'd make the connection. If Augustus had hired him to trace the victims, Hartford knew what had happened. He would recognize the names. But did it really matter? In fact, it might even make things easier because the man knew where to start.

"I'm his son."

"Gotcha," Hartford said, and Quentin loved the casualness of that acceptance. "Well, the good news is that I already have quite a bit of information on him. The bad news is that it has been a while, and the likelihood of him having moved out of state is big, considering the tight-knit community he was from. He would not have returned there."

Quentin thought of the women in Northern Lake and how they had reacted to the mere mention of his father's name. "No, he wouldn't."

"It's hard for me to give you an accurate estimate because I can't know how long it'll take me to find him. If he merely moved states but kept his name, not long. But if he went through a lot of trouble trying to leave the past behind him, things could be more difficult. My rough estimate is anywhere between a thousand and three thousand dollars, depending on whether or not I have to travel somewhere and verify information in person."

Quentin's stomach dropped. Aside from the fact that he didn't have that kind of money lying around, did he even want to spend it on finding Leonard? "Thank you for the information, Mr. Hartford. I'll have to think about this, and I'll get back to you."

"Sure thing." Hartford was quiet for a few beats. "Can I ask how Mac is doing?"

"He's..." Quentin watched Augustus, who was just putting the sandwiches out on the kitchen table. "He's doing well. Better, anyway. And he goes by Augustus now."

"I'm glad to hear that. That was a raw deal he got, being set up like that by his father. I hoped he'd find a way to leave the past behind him."

The concern and care in Hartford's voice warmed Quentin's heart. Augustus might not have known it, but not everyone was his enemy. "He's working on it. On leaving the past behind him. But I'll tell him you asked about him. I'm sure he'll appreciate that."

He ended the call, and Augustus looked at him expectantly. "One to three k," Quentin said. "Depending on whether or not he's easy to find and if he has to travel."

Augustus nodded. "What I exp-p-pected."

They sat down at the kitchen table, and Quentin attacked the egg salad sandwich in front of him. Out of all the sandwiches Augustus made for him, that was still his favorite. "It's a lot of money," he said after finishing off half the sandwich in a few bites.

Augustus didn't say anything, just smiled at him. For some reason, the man never ceased to be amused by

Quentin's appetite. Not that Quentin minded. More importantly, he didn't think Augustus cared either.

"I'm not sure he's worth it. Spending that much money on a man who stole so much from others and who ran out on his girlfriend and child doesn't sound like a smart investment."

"F-f-for cl-closure?" Augustus asked

Quentin shrugged. "Closure to the tune of three thousand dollars? Maybe closure is overrated. I don't have that money, and even if I did, I'd rather spend it on the future than the past, you know?"

The look Augustus gave him was pure love. That settled it. No PI, then. He would do what he'd told Augustus: focus on the future and leave the past behind him. But would he and Augustus have a future together? That still remained to be seen, but for now, he would focus on the practical things.

"I have to sell my car and buy another one to drive back to California."

The word hung heavy in the air between them. *California.* Quentin swallowed back the tightness in his throat. He had to go. There was no other way. So he would suck it up, and he would go.

Augustus's mouth had set in a stubborn line. Uh-oh. Quentin knew what that meant, knew what Augustus was going to say even before he opened his mouth.

"I want you to k-k-keep the c-car." Augustus held up his hand as if he expected Quentin to start protesting right away, and if not for the gesture, he probably would have. "You need a g-g-good car to drive that f-f-far, and I w-won't let you dr-dr-drive in some p-piece of j-j-junk and risk you g-getting stranded ag-gain. It is my g-gift. My..."

His voice sounded choked. "My g-good-bye gift."

And then he cried. That big, strong mountain of a man cried, dropping to his knees in front of Quentin and putting his head in his lap. And Quentin held him, tears streaming down his cheeks as he pulled him close and held on tight.

They sat like that for a long time. Quentin never finished his sandwich. He wasn't hungry anymore.

29

Quentin: Just hit the 81. I'm about an hour away from Syracuse. It's going smoothly so far. Roads are clear.

Augustus: Okay. Just be careful near Cleveland. There's snow expected there.

Quentin: I know, baby. You told me. I'll be careful.

Augustus: Be safe

Quentin: Made it to Erie. Snow is coming down hard, so I stopped. Spending the night here. Barely any cell service, so I can't call you.

Augustus: Glad you stopped. That storm looks bad. Be safe.

Quentin: I will, baby. I promise. Going to bed now.

Augustus: Sleep well. I miss you.

Quentin: God, I miss you, baby.

Augustus: Are you driving again?

Augustus: Quentin, are you safe? Saw the news about whiteout conditions and pileups on the 90. Please tell me you're okay?

Quentin: I am. Sorry, I couldn't even use voice to text. Needed my full attention on the road. It was crazy here. I couldn't see a damn thing with the snow that kept blowing up. Made it past Cleveland now. Much better here.

Augustus: Thank god. I was so worried.

Quentin: I'm sorry. I would've texted you if I could, but I was too scared to get distracted for even a second.

Augustus: [picture of bowl of soup and turkey cheese sandwich]

Augustus: Lunch is very lonely without you. Though it's much faster, since I only have to make a third of what I made when you were here :)

Quentin: [picture of Big Mac meal with milkshake]

Quentin: This doesn't taste anywhere near as good as your food. I miss your cooking. And you.

Augustus: In that order?

Quentin: Well, you know how I feel about food...

Augustus: I love you

Quentin: I love you too, baby

Quentin: It was so good to hear your voice. Thanks for calling and keeping me company for an hour this morning as I drove through Ohio. God, this state is motherfucking boring. Why do people want to live here?

Augustus: I Googled. It does look boring.

Quentin: You've never been?

Augustus: I've never been outside of New York. Oh, once

when we went to Niagara Falls and spent half an hour on the Canadian side.

Quentin: I have so many beautiful places to show you...

Augustus: One day

Quentin: Yes. One day.

Augustus: Where are you now? Can I call?

Quentin: Please call. I'm two hours out of St. Louis and about to fall asleep.

Augustus: That was my first time ever phone sex.

Quentin: Aw, a phone sex virgin. I'm honored to be your first.

Augustus: I feel like you're my first in everything. Everything that matters anyway.

Quentin: Thank you. That means a lot. Was it good? It sounded like you had...fun. Judging by your noises...

Augustus: You're making me blush. Don't ask me how that is possible, but you are.

Quentin: I can picture you now, baby. Watching me with those big puppy eyes. Begging me to touch you. You make such beautiful sounds when you get needy and desperate.

Augustus: I'm not... Okay, I am needy for you. I miss you. My right hand was a poor substitute, even if it was at your sweet commands.

Quentin: I'll think of you when I jack off in my motel tonight...

Quentin: There's a reason why the expression is Bumfuck, Kansas. There's literally nothing here. Nothing. I've been driving for two hours now, and there's nothing. This has got to be the most boring stretch of road in the entire US.

Augustus: How much longer until Colorado? I looked it up, and that seems like a beautiful bit of scenery.

Quentin: It is. It was the best part of the drive on the way in.

Quentin: How was work today, baby?

Augustus: Some tourists who totaled their car. Brand-new Jeep Cherokee. Rental company won't be happy about that. But it was a great deal for me, since I got it cheap. Those parts will sell.

Quentin: Good. Don't work too hard, baby. Take care of yourself.

Augustus: If I keep working, I don't miss you as much.

Quentin: I know, baby. I know.

Augustus: You should be almost home by now, right?

Quentin: Yup. Four more hours.

Augustus: How are you holding up?

Quentin: I'm exhausted. Everything hurts. But I'll make it.

Augustus: Text me when you get there.

Quentin: I will. Don't wait up for me, baby.

Quentin: Never mind. I know you will anyway.

Augustus: Yup.

Quentin: Made it. Exhausted. Going to bed now. Love you.

Augustus: Thank god you made it safely. Sleep well. Love you too.

Quentin: Thank you for staying up for me, baby.

Augustus: Anytime

30

Lucy barked in alarm, bumping his leg with her nose, before he had even heard or seen them. Augustus snapped his fingers and rolled from underneath the Jeep he'd been stripping. Lucy went quiet but kept bouncing at his side. A car stopped in front of the junkyard, a car he recognized all too well. He took a step back, his stomach recoiling.

The Roof brothers. All his life, these two had been his tormentors. They had never ceased to make fun of him, unrelenting in their vicious attacks. Greg, the younger brother, had been in his class, and he had been one of Augustus's most cruel bullies. Warren, the older of the two, had contributed with his friends as well to Augustus's hellish time in school.

They got out of their car and slammed the doors shut.

He balled his hands in tight fists. Thank god Quentin wasn't here. He would've faced them, would've stood up to them, and it might've cost him. Because these two were bad news. Bad, bad news.

He didn't say a word as they walked up to him and

stopped a few feet before him, their arms crossed. Augustus held on to Lucy, who was more than ready to chase them away.

"Our truck keeps stalling. You need to fix it."

That was Warren, his voice cold enough to stab someone with. Augustus wanted to reply, but as always, it took him a second or two to push through his initial fear and reluctance. And with these two, maybe even twice as long as usual.

"It's f-f-fifteen y-years o-old. It's g-g-gonna k-keep st-st-stalling." God, he hated that he stumbled over every first letter. His stutter got so much worse under stress, which frustrated him, which in turn only exacerbated it. And when these two showed up, the stress was sky-high.

Warren's eyes narrowed. "Then you need to do a better job of fixing it."

Augustus almost rolled his eyes at him. What did the guy think he was, some kind of magician? That truck had over three hundred thousand miles on it, and moreover, those two drove it like it was a fucking freight train, always gunning it. The poor thing was held together by duct tape, one hard bump in the road from falling apart altogether.

"I c-can't f-f-fix it anym-m-more. You need t-to rep-p-lace it."

"If you can't fix it, you gonna have to give us another car. And when I say give, I mean *give*. We can't afford to buy another one, thanks to you and your father."

That was what it always came down to with these two. They hadn't lost a damn penny themselves, since they had been far too young, but their father had invested heavily in the resort scheme. He had lost everything, and as a consequence, the bank had repossessed their farm and everything they owned. He had died shortly after of a heart attack, brought on by the stress and shame, as everyone kept repeating.

Augustus forced himself to stay calm. Getting short with these two wouldn't solve anything. "I c-can't g-g-give you an-nother c-car."

Warren took a step closer, and Lucy growled, making him retreat again. It was a public secret that Warren was terrified of dogs, and Augustus had no qualms whatsoever about using that against him.

"Of course you can. And you will. You fucking *owe* us."

Augustus shook his head. "Only eight-t-teen hundred m-more for y-you. That d-d-doesn't get you a c-car."

The two brothers shared a look, as if they were surprised. Hadn't they kept track of the amount? Or did they think Augustus wouldn't keep score?

"That can't be right," Warren said.

Augustus lifted his chin. "I can s-s-show you the rec-c-ceipts. You have s-signed for every one of th-th-them."

Another look between the brothers. Then Greg spoke up, "Well, what about interest? We would've earned a lot of interest over the years from that money."

Augustus stepped back intuitively, blinking fast. Interest? He wanted interest over the original amount? His head spun. Greg was *crazy*. Augustus couldn't be expected to pay interest over all the amounts. That was twenty years of compound interest, and that would easily add another five years to his punishment, to his payment plan. He couldn't. He couldn't do this for seven more years. It was insane. Inhuman. Completely and utterly unreasonable.

"No." The word flew out of his mouth before he realized it, but it felt good, so he said it again. "N-n-o."

Warren came closer again, apparently forgetting about

Lucy for a while. She barked in warning and pulled against Augustus's hold on her collar.

"Don't c-come c-c-closer. I'll l-l-let her l-loose."

Warren hastily walked backward, fury firing up in his eyes. "You will pay, or else..."

"Or else w-w-what?"

It struck him even as he asked it. What could these two do to him? Threaten to sue him? He was under no legal obligation to even pay them off. That had been his own sense of honor, not any legal order to do so.

They could threaten him with physical harm, but where would that get them? At some point, even Sheriff McCauley would have to act. He might've turned a blind eye toward bullying, but even he would not tolerate outright violence. Sure, McAuley had all but ignored some vandalism on Augustus's property, as well as a few break-ins. But Augustus had ramped up his security, and those were a thing of the past now.

No, they had nothing to threaten him with. Nothing else than what they'd tried for years already, which was to make him feel small. Make him feel less, an outsider, a *criminal*. A felon, that was what he was in their eyes and always would be. And for years, he'd accepted that was how people saw him. Maybe he'd even felt he couldn't expect more.

But he was done. He had paid his dues. He had borne the weight of his sentence, of the consequences of the sins of his father. And he was done.

These people didn't deserve his honor. They didn't deserve his attempts at making things right. They had done *nothing*, nothing at all, to ever show him a shred of mercy, of forgiveness.

He laughed, and Warren and Greg looked at him as if he was crazy. God, he *had* been. He had been batshit crazy, completely deluded to think that if he worked hard enough, if he showed them what kind of man he was, they would accept him.

"Get the f-f-fuck off my prop-p-perty," he said. "And d-don't ever c-c-come back."

"You'll regret this," Warren shouted at him.

"I'm d-done," Augustus told him. "Now l-l-leave before I l-let Lucy have h-her way."

In seconds they pulled off his lot, the pickup shaking and rambling and the wheels creaking with the force of their exit.

He was *free*.

Three days later, he'd sold the junkyard and his house. It turned out that Bill, the man who had worked for his grandfather, had a son, Jeremy, who had been looking for a business opportunity like this. Jeremy was a truck driver who had recently married and wanted to stop being on the road so much and grow roots somewhere. When they met, he told Augustus he could fix anything, and Bill's proud look said he wasn't lying.

Once Jeremy had seen Augustus's numbers, he didn't need much convincing, especially considering the price Augustus asked. He knew it was well below market value, but he didn't care. He wanted it gone. He wanted to be free.

He told Bill and Jeremy to set up the sale and arrange for all the paperwork, and he would sign whatever he had to. In the meantime, Jeremy could take over the junkyard. It was a gentlemen's agreement, but he trusted Bill to keep his word. If his grandfather had trusted him, that was good enough for Augustus.

Jeremy made a down payment in cash, and Augustus used it to trade his pickup in for a newer, stronger model. Then he rented the largest trailer he could find and packed up everything he wanted to keep. His books, some furniture he was attached to, keepsakes of his mom, the board games. Everything else, he left for Jeremy. He could keep it, sell it, donate it, whatever. Bill wanted the chickens, so they were taken care of as well.

In the space he had left in the trailer, he packed up the metal sculptures he'd made that he loved the most, carefully wrapped in bubble wrap and blankets. Leaving the others behind hurt, but he would make new ones.

He had everything stowed into the trailer on day five, and he did a final walk-through of the house to make sure he hadn't forgotten anything important. His body buzzed with energy, with adrenaline. He would be on the road for days, but he'd count down every mile. He was on his way to Quentin, and that thought was enough to make him giddy.

Sheriff McCauley turned into his lot just as Augustus put Lucy on the passenger's seat, giving her a blanket on the floor and a toy to keep her happy. Augustus bit back a curse. What did he want now?

"I heard rumors you were leaving," McAuley said.

Augustus closed the passenger door and crossed his arms, not saying anything. He didn't owe him an explanation. The funny thing was that a few months ago, he *would* have explained himself. He would've felt like he had to, to avoid trouble. But Quentin had changed that. He had made Augustus see he was worth more.

"Do you have permission from your parole officer to leave the state?"

Augustus scoffed. "Haven't had a p-p-parole officer in f-fifteen years. I can g-go wherever the h-h-hell I w-want. There ain't a d-d-damn thing you can do to st-st-stop me."

"You still owe people money."

Augustus balled his fists, and maybe the sheriff noticed

because he retreated a few steps. "No, I d-don't. I never owed them m-m-money. From the d-day of the s-sentencing, it was cl-cl-clear that my f-f-father had st-stolen the money, not m-m-me. Even the judge ackn-n-nowledged it. You all kn-knew. You knew it wasn't m-m-me. You knew he had t-t-taken the money and had g-gambled it all away. And still you let me p-p-pay all those years. You made me f-feel like I o-owed you, like I was in your d-d-debt. But I w-wasn't."

He couldn't believe the words coming out of his mouth. He was still stuttering, and yet it felt different. He'd been silent for so long it was a relief to finally speak the truth.

"And you should be ash-sh-shamed of yourself. You were sh-sheriff when I got conv-v-victed, and you never did a d-damn thing to st-st-stand up for me. Hell, even b-back in high sch-sch-school, you knew I was b-being b-b-bullied. You knew all th-these years how p-people tr-tr-treated me, and you a-also knew I hadn't done a d-d-damn thing to dess-s-serve it. Shame on you, Sh-sh-sheriff. Shame on you for ch-choosing the side of the b-bullies, of the b-b-bad guys. You were supp-p-posed to stand up for m-me."

McCauley had paled under his verbal attack, and Augustus wasn't sure if it was because of the content of his words or because he even said them in the first place. No matter how haltingly they came out, it was the longest speech he'd ever given in his life, and every word slashed like a knife.

Augustus took a deep breath. "So yes, I am l-l-leaving. And you can all go f-f-fuck yours-s-self."

He nodded, more than satisfied with his parting words. His hand was on the doorknob when Macauley spoke up.

"Mac... I'm..." He took off his hat, scratched his head, then put it back on. "Drive safely," he finally said, his voice softer and kinder than Augustus had ever heard him. "It's a long drive to California."

Augustus considered thanking him, if only out of politeness, then decided that he really didn't feel like being polite. So he merely nodded and said, "My name is Aug-g-gustus, not M-mac."

He drove off, never looking back, and with every mile he drove, his heart grew lighter.

I'm on my way, baby. I'm on my way.

But first, he had a little detour to make.

31

Quentin had just gotten back from a meeting with his professor and plopped down in front of the TV to relax a bit. He'd worked hard the last week to come up with a different research project proposal, and today, Professor Danson had given his approval. Now all he had to do was wait if the committee would reward him a grant a second time.

God, he was tired. It had been long days filled with frantic research, then writing and revising his proposal, only to revise it ten more times so Professor Danson was satisfied. The man was ten steps beyond being a perfectionist, but at least his anal attention to detail guaranteed it was the best proposal possible on such short notice.

He checked his watch, then calculated the time difference with New York. It was four o'clock there. One more hour and he could call Augustus. Hearing his voice was such a double-edged sword. He missed him so much it physically hurt, and talking to him helped, especially when they did a video call. But those had only happened the first few days after he'd arrived in California, including one incredibly hot session where they had spent a good two hours edging themselves before they'd both come.

Augustus had said he had Internet issues, however, and that his cell signal wasn't strong enough to do video calls. So they'd talked every day, and Quentin always felt better when he heard his voice, but then felt like utter crap afterward. Two more years of this? He wasn't sure if he was strong enough for it.

As much as he loved being back in California because of the weather—and hanging out with Noel again, who had found himself a boyfriend through some kind of dating app called valentine's Inc—it wasn't the same as before. Leaving Mac had left a hole, and it hurt.

He was mindlessly flipping through the channels when there was a loud knock on the door. God, he hoped it wasn't one of the neighbors again. As much as he appreciated how tight-knit the trailer park was he had grown up in, it was a little bothersome to have neighbors asking for help all the time. And since his mom was still at work, he'd have to handle it.

Then again, he couldn't really complain, considering his mother had taken him back in. He'd expected to be in New York a few months longer and hadn't arranged for alternative housing. The drive to the university was longer than he would've liked, but he'd take it. She hadn't even wanted him to pay rent. And he had to be honest, with how crappy he felt, being with her helped. She hadn't said much, but she understood.

With a tired sigh, he opened the door. It was the kid from next door who was nine but sounded like he was an adult. "What's up, Cody?" Quentin said.

"Quentin, I think you had better come outside," Cody said in his adorable adult-like tone.

Quentin frowned. "Is something wrong?"

Cody shook his head. "No, but there's a man here, and he's asking for you."

Quentin put on his flip-flops. God bless California in the winter. "A man? What man?"

Cody leaned in a little. "I've never seen him before, but he looks mean. He has tattoos and piercings."

The door closed behind them with a louder smack than Quentin had intended. His heart skipped a beat. It couldn't be. It was impossible, wasn't it? He had talked to him yesterday.

"Where is he?"

Cody pointed toward the entrance of the park, and Quentin could just make out the shape of a big pickup truck and gigantic U-Haul trailer. "And, Quentin, I don't mean to be rude, but he stutters really bad."

Quentin had started running before Cody had even finished his sentence. His heart leaped with joy, beating as fast as his feet slapped the ground. Augustus stood next to his truck, head bowed, his hands jammed into his pockets, and he looked all kinds of menacing. Funny how Quentin now recognized it as nerves, whereas before, he would've said he was angry, aloof, maybe even arrogant.

Then Augustus raised his head, and his expression changed completely, the biggest smile he'd ever seen crossing over his face. All Quentin saw was Augustus. He was *here*. How was that even possible?

Quentin didn't care who was watching and launched himself at Augustus. His man caught him effortlessly in his strong arms, holding him so tight against his chest that he could barely breathe. Quentin's feet dangled an inch above the ground, and he wrapped his arms around Augustus's neck, taking in his smell.

They didn't even kiss, just hung on to each other as if they never wanted to let go. Quentin didn't know about Augustus, but he couldn't even speak. He needed to feel him first, to reconnect with his other half. Because god, he had missed him. He had been absolutely miserable without him.

"What are you doing here?" he finally asked once Augustus had put him back on his feet. He cupped his cheeks, pressed a kiss on his mouth before the man could answer, then decided that wouldn't do and kissed him for real.

Minutes later, Augustus chuckled into his mouth. "Are you ever g-g-gonna let m-me answer?"

Quentin looked him deep in his eyes. "Are you here to stay?"

Augustus nodded, his face beaming like a lit-up Christmas tree.

"Then that's all I need to know for now."

They stood like that for a long time until the catcalls from some of the other residents became too hard to ignore. "Quentin, aren't you going to introduce us to your boyfriend?" Marianne, Cody's mom, called out. Quentin let go of Augustus. They'd drawn quite the crowd.

"Oh, hush, that's not his boyfriend. That's his sugar daddy," Breanna, another longtime neighbor of his mom's, teased.

"Nope," Quentin said, then gave Augustus a last smacking kiss on his lips. "I'm not gonna tell you a damn thing. I'm going to keep this one all to myself. Let's go, baby. We have some catching up to do."

He looked at Augustus, and when he saw nothing but joy and acceptance on the man's face, he slapped his ass for good measure as they walked back to his truck. That, of course, earned him another round of whistles and catcalls, but he didn't care at all.

"Pull your truck up in the guest parking lot. It's got cameras, and Brian, the park owner, won't mind if he knows you're with me," Quentin told Augustus. He pointed toward the sign that showed the way.

Augustus jumped into his truck, and two minutes later, he came back, holding Lucy on a leash. Quentin kneeled in the dusty grass. "Hi, Lucy, did you miss me?"

Augustus let go of the leash, and Lucy came running toward him, barking a few times in happiness, then allowed Quentin to hug her. "You're such a good girl," he praised her. "I missed you too, but not as much as your daddy."

He took Augustus's hand and led him toward his mom's trailer. He'd never expected Augustus to show up here, and for a moment, he looked at the trailer and how it must appear to him. It was his normal, but what would Augustus think?

"This is where I grew up," he said. "The trailer has been replaced a few years ago, but it's the same park. I know it's not much, but—"

Augustus pulled on his hand and made him stop. "No ap-p-pologies."

Quentin smiled at him, the rush of shame over his background forgotten. Augustus was right. They each had their skeletons, their baggage, but it was nothing to be ashamed of.

They went inside, where he gave Lucy some water and a few strips of turkey deli. She settled down right next to the couch, where he found a spot on Augustus's lap. He breathed him in, rubbing his cheek against the man's beard. He felt like home.

"How?" Quentin asked, and it was all he could think of.

How was it possible that Augustus was here, with what looked like everything he owned?

"You ch-ch-anged me," Augustus said softly. "You made me s-s-see I was worthy of m-more, that I des-s-served better. You made me f-f-feel accepted and l-loved. When you l-left, the d-d-darkness came back, and I c-couldn't st-st-stand it anymore. You're my s-sunshine, Q-q-quentin. I m-m-miss you too much to n-not be with you."

They were the most beautiful words Quentin had ever heard, a declaration of love he'd never expected to receive from another man. "But, baby, how did you leave? You had two more years."

Augustus shook his head. "It would n-not have been enough. They still w-w-wanted more from m-me. They w-w-would've always wanted m-more. No m-matter what I had d-d-done, it would've n-never been en-nough. I rel-leased myself of my p-p-promise because I d-deserve better than to be ch-ch-chained to a town that h-hates me. For years, I didn't s-s-see a way out, but y-you showed me fr-fr-freedom. And I just w-want to be with you. Wherever you are, that's where I want to b-b-be."

What a journey this man had made to find freedom, literally and figuratively. "I'm proud of you. And you're right. You do deserve better." Quentin grinned. "You deserve to be with me."

Augustus chuckled. "C-c-cocky much?"

Quentin slipped his hand into Augustus's underwear and grabbed his cock. "You like it when I'm cocky."

He squeezed, and Augustus's eyes all but rolled back. "Ungh," he grunted. "I d-d-do...S-sir."

Quentin stilled. How he had missed him, missed being with him, missed hearing that word. "Move in with me," he said, releasing Augustus.

As much as he wanted to play with him, it was not the right time, if only because his mom would be home soon. Encountering her future son-in-law naked on his knees was maybe not the best way to introduce her to Augustus.

"We can get a place together. I'm hoping to hear from the committee soon, and I'm sure you could find a job, what with your skills."

"I h-have a j-j-job interview on F-f-friday," Augustus said, the biggest smile ever blooming on his face. "Already m-m-made some c-calls."

"You've come to stay," Quentin said. "You've really come to stay."

Augustus nodded. "For as l-l-long as you w-want m-m-me."

Quentin kissed him. "That would be forever, baby. I will want you with me forever."

When his mom came home, he introduced her to Augustus, and it was mutual love at first sight, even though they were closer in age than he and Augustus were. That was a little detail Quentin hadn't even realized, but it didn't matter. Not to him, and it looked like neither Augustus nor his mom cared.

Later that night, as the two of them lay in Quentin's double-sized bed with not a breath of space between them, Augustus said, "I st-stopped by N-northern L-l-lake when I l-left."

Quentin forced himself to exhale. "Why?"

"N-not to t-talk about you," Augustus said, and boy, that was a relief. As much as he would've appreciated the grand gesture behind it, he wouldn't have wanted Augustus to stand up for him to people who weren't worth their energy.

"Then why?"

"The g-g-guys from the g-gas station."

"You went to the gas station?"

"W-wanted to s-s-see if I c-could figure out the t-truth for you. Because I know y-you're st-st-still c-curious."

Well, there was his grand gesture. Quentin couldn't believe Augustus had done that for him. "And? Did you find out anything?"

Augustus nodded. "L-langley is in l-love with Al-l-lexander. Has b-been for years. The g-gas station is g-going b-b-bankrupt, and Al-lexander r-refuses help from L-langley."

Quentin's eyes widened. Oh, this was even better than he'd imagined. "Why? Just because he's stubborn?"

"Langl-l-ley is s-s-seventeen y-years y-y-younger, and app-perently, Alex-x-xander has a p-problem with that."

"How did you even find out about this?"

"I st-stopped by, and I g-got l-l-lucky. L-langley was there, and they h-had an arg-g-gument. I overheard. They st-st-stopped when they sp-spotted me, but I h-had heard en-nough."

"What did you say? And, baby, I can't believe you went back just for me. It means a lot to me that you understood how curious I was about them..."

Augustus beamed. "I t-told Al-l-lex-xander—g-g-od that name is imp-possible f-for me—that my b-boyfriend w-was fift-t-teen years younger b-but that he was in ch-charge."

"You told them that? Baby, you keep surprising me..."

"You sh-should have s-s-seen their f-faces. I t-t-told them that I w-w-was ab-bout to drive c-c-cross-country to b-b-be with you and that if s-s-someone l-loves you, you n-need to hold on t-t-to that p-person and not b-be a stubborn assh-h-hole. I th-think they g-got the m-m-message."

Quentin kissed him hard, then again because he hadn't kissed him in too long and then again because once he started, it was impossible to stop. Minutes later, he was balls deep inside him, putting his hand on Augustus's mouth to keep him quiet as he fucked him. Not that he had any illusion he could keep their activities hidden from his mom. The rhythmic squeaking of his bed was a dead giveaway. But he could at least keep her from hearing them, even if it meant silencing those beautiful sounds Augustus always made for him.

"Hush now. Be quiet," he whispered in his ear. "Can you do that for me, baby? Can you not make a sound while I take you hard?"

"Yes, S-s-sir."

He was right. It cost him, but Augustus didn't give a peep as Quentin fucked him mercilessly. He came before Quentin, his body going rigid as he spurted out rope after rope of cum. It looked like he hadn't come in days, and Quentin liked that idea. He gave a few more thrusts, then came himself.

"You came without my permission," he said softly as his spent, wet cock slipped out of Augustus.

"Oh." Augustus clearly hadn't realized it or hadn't thought about the ramifications. "S-s-sorry."

Quentin tilted his chin up and kissed him. "Maybe I should lock your cock up so that it won't happen again."

Augustus's eyes widened, then grew darker. As if that wasn't a telltale sign of his appreciation for that idea, his cock twitched and hardened back to half mast. Quentin chuckled. "I'll take that as a yes."

"Y-yes, Sir. Anything you w-w-want."

God, he loved him.

And they really needed to find their own place. Fast.

EPILOGUE

SIX MONTHS LATER

"Baby, I'm home!" Quentin called out as he stepped into their trailer. He'd spotted Augustus's truck in the parking lot, so his man was home.

Lucy greeted him with a happy bark, and he gave her a quick head scratch. Satisfied that she'd gotten attention, she trotted back to her favorite spot in the trailer: her blanket in the kitchen.

Augustus came stumbling in from the bedroom, with just a towel wrapped around his waist, his body still wet from the shower he'd clearly taken. Now see, that wasn't fair. How was Quentin supposed to talk and share his good news when Augustus looked like *that*?

He was a walking wet dream, all those muscles that were now tanned from the California sun on display. His nipple piercings still shone with newness, though he'd had them for four months now. They both loved them, and they had been exactly as perfect to torment Augustus as Quentin had imagined.

"Mmm," Quentin said, dropping his backpack and locking the door behind him. They were only three trailers down from his mom, and she stopped by unannounced regularly, although she'd learned to knock first after a few *incidents*. "You look good enough to eat."

Augustus smiled at him, and as always, that smile had a little shyness, a hint of incredulity as if he still couldn't believe Quentin meant it. He would simply have to keep repeating it until he did.

He kicked off his flip-flops, breathing in the cool air with relief. It was a fucking ninety-six degrees out there. Air conditioning was not a luxury right now.

"Lose the towel," he said casually.

Augustus bit his lip, then did as Quentin asked.

"Mmm." Quentin licked his lips. Damn, this man was beautiful. Every fucking inch of him was perfect.

He took off his shirt as he closed the distance between them, dropping it on the floor. His shorts and underwear came next until he was just as naked as Augustus, whose eyes had grown dark with want.

"It's been a long week, baby," Quentin said. "We've both worked hard, and I feel like I've barely seen you."

"We f-f-fucked on T-tuesday," Augustus said.

Quentin gave a dismissive shrug. "Not our best work, wouldn't you agree? That was more of a quickie to take the edge off."

"Yes, S-sir."

It still sent a thrill through him to hear that word falling from Augustus's lips. "I'm in the mood to play."

Augustus raised his chin and tapped his thigh once. Quentin's expression softened. "Do you need it, baby? Do you need to go silent for a bit? Let me take charge?"

Augustus had scored the job he'd applied for from New York. He'd started out as a mechanic for a car shop specialized in classic cars, but within four months had made it to head mechanic. The customer-service part of his job was still a challenge, but his boss and coworkers had shown a lot of patience and understanding, which in return had helped his stutter become manageable. But he still hated talking to strangers, and at the end of the week, he was tired and wanted to retreat.

Augustus tapped once again, and Quentin stepped in for a kiss on his lips. "I've got you, baby. I bought some new *toys* this week that looked like fun to play with."

"Th-thank you."

The relief was thick in Augustus's voice. "Plus, it's time to see how your dick feels inside me." Oh, *that* got Augustus's attention. His cock jumped up at the mention, and Quentin grinned. "It's been two months, baby. Time to put that gorgeous piercing of yours into action."

Augustus's cock had always been nice, but the Prince Albert piercing he had now made it look stunning, especially when he was hard, like he was now. It stood so proudly, displaying that metal ring, and Quentin couldn't wait to feel it inside him.

But first he had to share his news. Otherwise, he'd forget all about it. "I got the job," he said. "I'm starting my PhD research next month."

"Q-quentin!" Augustus had the biggest smile on his face. "You d-did it!"

He stepped into his hug and held him tight. "I couldn't have done it without your support, baby."

"You're w-w-welcome. I'm p-proud of you."

Quentin kissed him, then leaned back. "You know what one of the perks is about working for the university? They are affiliated with two of the biggest community colleges in California, and family members of employees get a massive discount on courses. You can start on your college degree, baby."

Augustus had brought it up himself that he'd love to take college courses in engineering, even if he never managed to get a degree. It was for him, he'd explained, to prove to himself he could do it. So far, money had been too tight, but now that had changed. Quentin had job security for a while, Augustus had gotten a raise with his promotion, and they had that discount. They could swing it.

Augustus leaned his forehead against Quentin's. "Th-thank you."

"No, baby, that's not something you should thank me for."

Quentin waited. He'd figure it out at some point, right?

Augustus jerked his head up, his eyes going wide. Ah, there it was. "F-f-family m-members? I'm n-not your f-f-family."

And this wasn't how he had planned it. He had a ring, and he had prepared this whole speech that explained how much Augustus meant to him and that he would take care of him and about ten minutes more of that, but fuck it. Their moment was now, and so Quentin dropped to his knees, Augustus's cock almost in his face, and looked up. "Marry me, baby. Become my family, my husband."

The expression on Augustus's face said enough, but he still gave his formal answer. "Yes. Yes, I w-w-will m-marry you."

Quentin rose to his feet and kissed him. "I love you, baby. I love you so freaking much. My car breaking down was the best thing that ever happened to me."

"You are the b-b-best thing that e-e-ever happened to m-me."

He hugged him again, and his heart filled with peace.

"Let's move on to the next item on the agenda. What do you say?"

Augustus let go of him, then sank to his knees, folding his hands behind his ass and taking up a perfect position, his cock proudly jutting forward. "Yes, S-sir."

The End

~

IF YOU LIKED the age gap and the kink between August and Quentin, try *Firm Hand* next. How can Cornell want to call his best friend's son Sir? Or even worse...Daddy?

FREEBIES

If you love FREE novellas and bonus chapters, head on over to my website where I offer bonus scenes for several of my books, as well as as two free novellas. Grab them here: http://www.noraphoenix.com/free-bonus-scenes-novellas/

BOOKS BY NORA PHOENIX

🎧 indicates book is also available as audio book

Perfect Hands Series

Raw, emotional, both sweet and sexy, with a solid dash of kink, that's the Perfect Hands series. All books can be read as standalones.

- **Firm Hand** (daddy care with a younger daddy and an older boy) 🎧
- **Gentle Hand** (sweet daddy care with age play) 🎧
- **Naughty Hand** (a holiday novella to read after Firm Hand and Gentle Hand)
- **Slow Hand** (a Dom who never wanted to be a Daddy takes in two abused boys)
- **Healing Hand** (a broken boy finds the perfect Daddy)

No Shame Series

If you love steamy MM romance with a little twist, you'll love the No Shame series. Sexy, emotional, with a bit of suspense and all the feels. Make sure to read in order, as this is a series with a continuing storyline.

- **No Filter** 🎧
- **No Limits** 🎧
- **No Fear** 🎧
- **No Shame** 🎧
- **No Angel** 🎧

And for all the fun, grab the **No Shame box set** 🎧 which includes all five books plus exclusive bonus chapters and deleted scenes.

Irresistible Omegas Series

An mpreg series with all the heat, epic world building, poly romances (the first two books are MMMM and the rest of the series is MMM), a bit of suspense, and characters that will stay with you for a long time. This is a continuing series, so read in order.

- **Alpha's Sacrifice**
- **Alpha's Submission**
- **Beta's Surrender**
- **Alpha's Pride**
- **Beta's Strength**
- **Omega's Protector**
- **Alpha's Obedience**
- **Omega's Power**
- **Beta's Love**
- **Omega's Truth**

Or grab *the first box set*, which contains books 1-3 plus exclusive bonus material!

Ballsy Boys Series

Sexy porn stars looking for real love! Expect plenty of steam, but all the feels as well. They can be read as stand-alones, but are more fun when read in order.

- **Ballsy** (free prequel)
- **Rebel** 🎧
- **Tank** 🎧
- **Heart** 🎧
- **Campy** 🎧
- **Pixie** 🎧

Kinky Boys Series

Super sexy, slightly kinky, with all the feels.

- **Daddy** 🎧
- **Ziggy** 🎧

Ignite Series

An epic dystopian sci-fi trilogy (one book out, two more to follow) where three men have to not only escape a government that wants to jail them for being gay but aliens as well. Slow burn MMM romance.

- **Ignite** 🎧
- **Smolder** 🎧
- **Burn** 🎧

Stand Alones

I also have a few stand alones, so check these out!

- **Professor Daddy** (sexy daddy kink between a college prof and his student. Age gap, no ABDL)

🎧
- **Out to Win** (two men meet at a TV singing contest)
- **Captain Silver Fox** (falling for the boss on a cruise ship)
- **Coming Out on Top** (snowed in, age gap, size difference, and a bossy twink) 🎧

MORE ABOUT NORA PHOENIX

Would you like the long or the short version of my bio?

The short? You got it.

I write steamy gay romance books and I love it. I also love reading books. Books are everything.

How was that?

A little more detail? Gotcha.

I started writing my first stories when I was a teen...on a freaking typewriter. I still have these, and they're adorably romantic. And bad, haha. Fear of failing kept me from following my dream to become a romance author, so you can imagine how proud and ecstatic I am that I finally overcame my fears and self doubt and did it. I adore my genre because I love writing and reading about flawed, strong men who are just a tad broken..but find their happy ever after anyway.

My favorite books to read are pretty much all MM/gay romances as long as it has a happy end. Kink is a plus... Aside from that, I also read a lot of nonfiction and not just books on writing. Popular psychology is a favorite topic of mine and so are self help and sociology.

Hobbies? Ain't nobody got time for that. Just kidding. I love traveling, spending time near the ocean, and hiking. But I love books more.

Come hang out with me in my Facebook Group Nora's Nook where I share previews, sneak peeks, freebies, fun stuff, and much more: https://www.facebook.com/groups/norasnook/

My weekly newsletter not only gives you updates, exclusive content, and all the inside news on what I'm working on, but also lists the best new releases, 99c deals, and freebies in gay romance for that weekend. Load up your Kindle for less money! Sign up here: http://www.noraphoenix.com/newsletter/

You can also stalk me on Twitter: @NoraFromBHR

On Instagram:
https://www.instagram.com/nora.phoenix/

On Bookbub:
https://www.bookbub.com/profile/nora-phoenix

Printed in Great Britain
by Amazon